Enjoy the moments !

Art James

Dee   2018

Titles by Arthur James

Long Islanders (2016)
Modern Romance

The Adams Sisters (2015)
African American Romance

Hants (2014)
Retro New England

Jason and the Kodikats (2013)
Children

Boston Relic

A Novel

By

Arthur James

Blackstone Books

New York, NY

2018

ISBN –13 : 978-0-9904488-6-0
ISBN - 10 : 0-9904488-6-x

Boston Relic

Publisher Blackstone Books LLC

New York, NY

info@blackstone-books.com

To Betty & Jim

Chapter 1

Nantasket

The word "Nantasket" was derived from the Wampanoag Native American language and means "low-tide place". Nantasket was settled not long after the Pilgrim's Plymouth Colony and before Massachusetts Bay. English settlers referred to the whole area as the "Nantasket Peninsula".

The Nantasket Beach shore has fine, light gray sand and is one of the busiest beaches in Greater Boston. At low tide, there are acres of tide pools, some sheltering star fish and crabs, extending far out into the Atlantic Ocean.

It was a sizzling hot Fourth of July along the Nantasket Beach Strip in Hull, Massachusetts. The soft sand was almost fully covered by multi-colored blankets, towels, and people. Traffic crawled along Shore Drive. An endless flow of suntanned, bikini-clad women walked on the sidewalks and spilled over into the street. The odor of tanning lotion was more pungent than the charcoal smoke rising from the roll-up window take-outs serving up a never-ending stream of pizza, fried dough, grilled hot dogs, hamburgers, and deep fried clams.

Arthur O'Sullivan's parents had brought their family out from Boston to Nantasket Beach regularly during the summer when their children were young. It was only a half hour drive. After his multiple business pursuits prospered, Art decided to build a summer place on a point of land jutting out into Hingham Bay, on the sheltered side of the Nantasket peninsula. Behind a seven-foot high, vertical, stained-board fence enclosing two lots, he erected a traditional, two level Cape Cod colonial house with wide verandas on the front and back. The place became known as the O'Sullivan Compound.

On Saturday of the long weekend, the Compound was brimming over with family and friends. Counting Art and his wife Louise, there were forty people both inside and outside the house, who had come for the family's annual baked lobster, steamed clam, and boiled corn-on-the-cob feed. The O'Sullivan couple were Catholic and had five sons. Louise hoped one of her sons would take Holy Orders; however, they all followed after their father and took wives. The four older boys had several children each. Now she was resting her sights on one of her grandsons for the priesthood.

Carney, the youngest son had been married but was now a widower. His wife Jenna had been involved in a fifteen car pile-up, in the fog, on Interstate 93 in New Hampshire, two years ago. He was considered highly eligible. The sisters-in-law thought it was only a question of time before some enterprising young woman got their brother-in-law into her crosshairs.

He met Jenna Cosgrove in Boston, at a yacht club social, where he gave an after dinner presentation about the Figawi Race Weekend, an annual charity event and regatta from Hyannis, Cape Cod to Nantucket Island on the Memorial Day weekend. She was a petite, energetic blond who worked as a Planner for Massport, which owned, operated and leased approximately 500 acres of property in Charlestown, East Boston, and South Boston. After a long courtship, the couple surprised everyone and said, "I do!" Three years later a daughter was born who they named Dakota.

Mrs. O'Sullivan waved to catch her son Carney's attention and motioned for him to come. He and his seven-year-old daughter were busy telling her cousins, about the Red Sox game they had been to see at Fenway Park, in Boston, the previous evening. A clean cut athletic young man wearing light blue cotton pants, an off white short-sleeve flax shirt, and bare feet stuck into deck shoes ambled up to her.

"Carney, I don't think we're going to have enough ice," his mother complained.

"Want me to go fetch a few more bags?" he drawled in his deep Boston accent.

"Yes Sir, Yes Sir, Three Bags Full," she laughed.

"No problem ma'am!" She liked it when her boys called her ma'am.

Sixty-five-year-old Art was flipping burgers at one of the barbecues dressed in a tie-dye tank top, shorts and sandals when he overheard them talking and interjected, "Hey buddy, here take my keys. I parked behind your car when I came in."

The young man scooped up the keys, dangling from his father's outstretched finger. At this moment Dakota came running dressed in white pedal-pushers, a black and white plaid sun top and a Red Sox ball cap.

"Where are you going daddy?"

"I'm off to get a few bags of ice for your grandmother," he explained.

"Can Bo and I come?" she pleaded holding up her fluffy, Angora cat.

"You stay here and finish telling your cousins about last evening's game. I'll be back in fifteen minutes, okay Miss Muffett." he teased.

"Okay, but hurry, I can't remember everything the way you do," his daughter protested.

"I will," he assured her heading towards the front of the house.

It had been a while since he had been behind the wheel of his father's Jaguar. After buckling up, he worked the shift through its slots, before stopping in Reverse, to back the sleek black car out onto Clifton Ave. What amazed him the most was the incomparable agility and handling of the vehicle as he cruised down the street.

There were stop signs on both sides of Clifton at the intersection with Nantasket Rd. Carney pulled up at the Stop on his side. He noticed a light gray sedan on the other side of the crossing.

"That's a Jag over there," the driver of the sedan said to the passenger beside him. "They said the wise guy lived on Clifton Ave. Here's the plate number," he added, passing the other man a folded piece of paper from his shirt pocket. "Take the glasses and check it out."

From his position, Carney noted the person in the passenger seat looking in his direction with a pair of binoculars. They must be lost he thought and inched forward.

The man with the glasses exclaimed, "It's his car!"

The driver of the gray sedan began to turn into the thoroughfare. Carney gave the larger vehicle the right of way. As it moved past him, the person in the passenger seat lowered his window. The barrel of an automatic machine gun appeared where the glass had been. A quick burst of bullets seared into the driver's side of the Jag as the sedan sped past.

Carney felt something sharp penetrate his lower back and then he passed out, slumping forward on the steering wheel. The vehicle's horn began blaring. Several minutes passed before people from nearby houses came to investigate the sound. As soon as he saw what had happened, one man pulled out his cell and called the Police.

The ambulance and Police arrived at the same time with their colored lights flashing. Two paramedics in yellow vests found a pulse and quickly strapped the unconscious man to a gurney, attached an intravenous feed to his arm and rolled victim and stretcher into the back of their van. Dispatch advised the paramedics the Quincy Medical Center, which was the closest hospital to them, was reporting up to an hour wait time at Emergency Admittance. The nearest alternative was the Medical Center in South Boston.

"That will take too long," ambulance driver Ted Rogers objected. "This is the holiday weekend. I know it's only 35 miles, but traffic into the City is creeping. The trip could take us more than an hour."

"There's always Medi-Vac," dispatch suggested. "We have a chopper on 24-hour emergency at the Point Allerton Coast Guard Station all weekend. Where can they land near to you?"

"Memorial Square playing field is on the corner of Nantasket Avenue and Nantasket Road," the other paramedic offered then flicked her pony tail.

"I have it!" the woman at the ambulance Central responded. "Go there! I'll arrange for a pickup."

The Police examined the bullet-ridden car and called their station to see who the registered owner was. The officer in charge at the scene spoke to the tow truck driver who had now arrived, "take the Jag to our impound yard. We'll need to inspect it."

Police dispatch crackled above the noise of bystanders talking, "The vehicle belongs to Arthur O'Sullivan. He lives on Harbor Point, in South Boston.

One of the officers suggested, "Perhaps someone had seen the car visiting in the neighborhood." He began questioning the spectators. An elderly gentleman replied, "Oh yes, it's a regular in and out of the Compound up the street, all summer long." When the tow truck left, the officers went to visit the O'Sullivan's.

Louise broke when she heard the news and grabbed at her husband, "Why Carney, he's such a good boy. He doesn't have an enemy."

"I'll never forgive myself," her husband exclaimed. "He was driving my car. They must have thought it was me. Where is he being taken to, Officer?"

"I'm not sure just yet. We can find out at the station," he replied. "I'd like you to come in and make a statement. Dispatch can contact the ambulance from there."

"I'm coming with you Dear," his wife insisted frantically. "I'll tell the boys they're in charge here now and we won't be back until very late this evening. I'll ask Naomi to take Dakota back to their place in Boston for the night. " Naomi was the wife of her eldest son, David.

"Tell them to make sure the house and gate are all locked, before they leave," Art advised, then added, "Don't mention the shooting for now. Just say he's had an accident."

Arthur O'Sullivan had been involved with business in and around the Greater Boston Bay area, all his life. There had been a few rough spots over the years, especially where construction projects were involved. It was because of a threat on his life while assembling land for a strip mall that he had left construction and moved into other activities.

At the police station, he explained, "About four months ago I leased a one hundred ATM machines and placed them in locations from Boston out to Hull. Most of the contracts were with independent gas stations or mini-marts. It had taken me about a year to source out, meet with and sign lease agreements with owners of all the locations."

"About a month after installation, someone started sabotaging the machines by squirting liquid plastic into the card slots. I activated the built-in Webcam on each machine and subsequently, several arrests were made."

"The Massachusetts State Police found no link between those arrested. Two of the apprehended were transferred to juvenile court. The other three were charged with public mischief and released with a fine to pay. Afterward, the liquid plastic prank stopped."

"About a month ago I received an anonymous letter at my office, which contained a threat. 'Take your ATM's out or else! It's our territory now.' I turned the note over to the same Police Unit that carried out the first investigation. Whoever was responsible hadn't left any fingerprints on the note or envelope in which the letter arrived."

"As a precaution, I hired a private security company to shadow me and watch my office and the condo my wife and I had moved into on Harbor Point, after selling our family home. I called the security company on the way here. They were on duty this afternoon, in the back of a van parked across from the Compound. They saw Carney getting into the Jag, but didn't follow. He was not the subject of their contract."

In less than half an hour Carney O'Sullivan was being wheeled into the Emergency at Boston Medical Center and then on to the Trauma Unit. He had lost a lot of blood in the Jaguar, but the ambulance paramedics had hooked him up to a drip of universal recipient plasma and placed frozen packs around the wound in his lower back. The hemorrhage hadn't stopped, but his body wasn't bleeding out.

Dr. Lorne Tucker, a forty-five-year-old trauma specialist was on duty with his assistant Dr. Leona Webber. They had worked as a team at BMC for over three years. Both knew their jobs well. It was they who performed the initial examination of the unconscious shooting victim. They knew nothing about him. His clothing gave them no hints. He could be a gangster or an undercover police officer.

"Leona, we need to perform an MRI scan on his lower back," Dr. Tucker advised.

"Yes Doctor," she agreed turning towards the orderly standing off to the side. "Tom would you and Eddy please lift the patient onto the MRI's patient table?"

"Right away, Doctor," the tall, muscular man acknowledged.

When the magnetic resonance images were processed the doctors could see what lay beyond the surface wound, "There Lorne," Leona indicated with her finger. "It's a piece of metal lodged between his second lumbar vertebrae and the disc."

"Doesn't look like a bullet fragment," her teammate commented. "It's probably a piece of the vehicle."

"Could be," she agreed. "Regardless; it's going to have to come out. There also appears to be damage to the vertebrae, the disc above where it's lodged and the spinal and sciatic nerves."

"We're going to need a signed and witnessed Consent to Operate completed by an authorized person." Doctor Tucker told her.

"I'm already on it," she assured him. "The Head Nurse is contacting the Police to see if we can get through to a wife or family member. Orderly, would you please check to see if she's made any progress?"

Tom returned with the Head Nurse who informed them the man's parents were on their way into the Hospital.

"Where are they coming from?" Dr. Tucker asked with concern.

"Hull Doctor, it's about a thirty-five minute drive."

"This is the Fourth, Nurse! With the holiday traffic, it could be two hours before they're standing where you are. This man's system is going into shock. We must operate immediately, or we could lose him."

"I have his father's cell phone number," the nurse informed them holding out a piece of paper which Leona accepted and then said, "I'll call his father to see where they are."

"That's correct Doctor," Art replied as he sat in a long line of cars inching their way along towards the on-ramp of Interstate 93 south of Boston. "I haven't even got onto the freeway yet, but I can see it in the distance. There doesn't seem to be any movement in the lanes headed into the City."

Lorne motioned for her to pass him her cell phone. "Mr. O'Sullivan, this is Doctor Tucker speaking. Your son has an extremely serious injury in his lower back, and his body is going deeper into shock. We must operate as soon as possible, to remove a foreign object from his spine. Can you possibly get to a location where there's a fax machine or is there someone else who can sign the Consent Form?"

Louise O'Sullivan had been listening to the Doctor's voice as it came through the hands-free device clipped to the sun visor of her crossover and burst out immediately, "There's a fax machine at our Compound in Nantasket. His brothers are there. Give the Doctor the number for the fax machine Art. Doctor, we'll phone the boys to tell them what's happening."

Dr. Tucker's voice came through the small speaker of the hands-free relay. "Do I understand correctly? The victim's brothers have access to a fax machine?"

"That's right Doctor," Carney's mother replied with distraught showing in her voice. "I'll give you the number and then we'll phone them to sign the Form and fax it directly back to you."

"Thank you, Mrs. O'Sullivan!"

**

At 3 pm on a Friday afternoon, in the middle of July, Ella Bowdine pulled into the Albany St. Parkade across from the Menino Pavilion, at the Boston Medical Center. She locked her silver Mercedes convertible, after removing a small nylon athletic bag from the trunk. It contained her green BMC Volunteer smock and a pair of flat sole, white canvas shoes. About nine months ago she had started volunteering at the Trauma Unit.

She was of medium height and build with elegant movements. Her style was classic, artisanal, and all about the details. Today she was dressed in a print dress with a scoop neck and a drop hem. On her feet were a pair of sling back sandals, with a peephole and stacked heel.

Two years prior she had been through a messy divorce, after several years of an unhappy marriage. Volunteering was a way to get by the divorce. A way to mingle with people again, without becoming involved. To the staff and patients, she was known as Mrs. Ella Brown.

For the past three months, Ella had been visiting Lieutenant Andrew Beattie who had been assigned to the 1st Calvary Division at Fort Hood, Texas. A grenade launcher malfunctioned during a training exercise. Two other soldiers near him were killed and he was severely wounded. Massachusetts was his home state. He had been evacuated to BMC for advanced surgery on his brain to remove a piece of shrapnel. As his recovery progressed, he had agreed to receive a weekly visit from a hospital volunteer.

Ella was the fourth generation of a French Huguenot family who fled France during a political persecution and became architects in Boston. She wasn't a boy, but she followed in her father's footsteps anyway. After a practicum at a rival firm; she accepted a junior position in the family office.

As fate would have it, she fell madly in love with one of her clients. They were married, without actually knowing much about each other. The union lasted two years, and then it took a year for the divorce. A little over a year ago she finally fell out of love with her former husband and decided it was time to get along with life.

The first project was to move out of her family's house on Pond Street, in Boston's Jamaica Plain neighborhood. She had taken refuge there during the divorce. Her coming out choice fell on a $900,000 condo, at Number One Louisburg Square, in Boston's Beacon Hill district, one of the city's oldest communities.

Beacon Hill gets its name from a beacon that once stood atop its hill to warn locals about foreign invasion. It is home to the Massachusetts State House. The neighborhood's architecture and layout are reflective of colonial Boston, consisting of red brick row houses with beautiful doors, decorative iron work, brick sidewalks, narrow streets, and electrified gas lamps.

Number One Louisburg Square was a three level red brick building sitting on a light gray concrete foundation, protruding above ground on the front. The window frames, wrought iron French balconies, and wooden shutters were all painted black. A refurbished, gas lamp was set into the red brick sidewalk at the corner. Across the street was a small boulevard park enclosed by a black wrought iron fence.

When she stepped off the elevator at the Trauma Unit, she went straight to the Nursing Station to sign in. The Duty Nurse greeted her with a broad smile. "Mrs. Brown, don't you have anything else better to do on such a beautiful afternoon?"

"I do, but I promised Andy I'd stop to see him for fifteen minutes, before taking off for the weekend."

"Andy, you mean Andy Beattie?"

"Yes," she replied, signing the register.

"Didn't anyone phone you, Mrs. Brown?"

"Phone me about what," she asked apprehensively, silently fearing the worst.

"Mr. Beattie was transferred this week to the Veterans Clinic in Quincy. The request came from his family. The clinic provides a transition to outpatient care."

"Oh well," Ella exclaimed with surprise. "I'm sure his family will be happy having him closer to home. He must be on the mend. I'll have to make arrangements to go to visit him there."

"He is on the mend, and it's a shame you came all the way here because nobody notified you. I feel responsible."

"It's nothing," Ella assured her, beginning to turn back towards the elevator.

"Wait a minute Mrs. Brown; we have a new patient who is recovering from a spinal cord operation. He hasn't requested any volunteer visits, but I could just pop in and suggest it to him.

Ella looked at her watch. It was still three hours before her flight from Logan Airport to Martha's Vineyard. What was she going to do to fill the time? Her weekend bag was in the trunk of her car. She thought for a moment and replied, "Okay, see what he says!"

Several minutes later she walked into the intensive care room. There was a bed with low sides at the far end. The last third of it was tilted upward slightly. There were monitors and gages on both sides of the bed. A man with black hair lay on his back with an intravenous tube leading down from a clear plastic bag on a hook was attached to his left fore arm. She began by introducing herself. "How do you do, Mr. O'Sullivan? I'm Ella Brown. How are you making out today?"

The man in the bed tried to smile and then replied, "I've been better!"

"Have you been receiving a lot of visitors?" the volunteer asked politely

"Quite a few, I have a daughter, parents, four brothers and their families. They take turns so I don't get stressed out."

"How long have you been here?" The woman in the green smock continued, pulling a chair up to his bedside and then sitting in it.

"It's been two weeks this weekend," replied the patient who also had a two-week growth of whiskers on his face.

"Does it bother you to talk about why you're here?" She pried ever so carefully.

He thought for a moment. He didn't want to mention drive by shootings and mistaken identity. "I'm okay to talk about it. I had an operation on the Fourth of July to remove a chunk of metal from my spine. The doctors said it looked like a piece of spring from an automobile seat."

His visitor supposed he must have had a car accident and didn't press further.

Then it was his turn. "The nurse said you came to visit another patient and the hospital forgot to notify you he's no longer here."

"Correct," she replied with a tight smile.

"Did he or she pass on?" Carney tested.

"Actually quite the opposite, it was a young serviceman who was injured in a training exercise, in Texas. He was transferred to the Veterans' Clinic in Quincy this week and will start to have outpatient privileges with his family."

"I'm to be transferred out of the Trauma Unit soon myself. They're going to move me to General Care. I guess space is limited here and it's a busy unit."

"Maybe you'll be getting outpatient privileges soon too," she encouraged.

"Maybe," he laughed and then added, "It would be good, but there's a little hitch."

"Would you like to talk about it?" she asked sympathetically flicking her long dark hair back with a quick movement of her neck and shoulders.

He knew he had to talk about it and not just with his family. He felt water coming up in his eyes and blinked to take it away. "They got the piece of metal out of me, but couldn't repair all the damage. For now, at least, I can't feel my legs or wiggle my toes."

She saw the water in his eyes and knew it had been difficult to say. "Thank you for sharing," she replied with a supportive tone. "Like you said, I'm sure it's only for now."

"The doctor says my therapy begins with me accepting there might be a permanent change in my life."

She smiled and consoled him. "Many people with the same type of injury get by it and lead full and at times, remarkable lives."

"I know," he laughed. "I've seen them playing basketball in wheelchairs on TV."

"Sports are a great outlet," she agreed, "but never-say-never. There have been some miraculous cases of recovery.

"Thanks for saying so. How long have you been a Volunteer?" he inquired casually, not wanting to dwell on self-pity.

"About nine months now, I believe. Yes, I started last October. It's been quite an eye opener. I've had four regular patients during that time. Mostly they wanted me to talk to them, read to them or fetch things from the Tuck Shop for them."

"Things," he queried with a puzzled look.

"Sweets and gum mostly," she clarified with a smile before continuing. "I also assisted with the Christmas party. We had a Santa move from room to room. At Easter, I took three geriatric patients outside on the patio and sat with them until it was time to come back in."

"They have a patio here?"

"Yes and an extremely pleasant garden with walking paths. The flowers weren't blooming at Easter, but they are now. If you're transferred to general care, you'll have access to both areas, as long as you are attended at all times."

"Does the Hospital supply attendants?"

"No, it would be one of your visitors or a volunteer like me."

"I see!" he answered without showing any disappointment

"What did you order for dinner this evening?" she enquired.

"I'm not on solids yet. The sutures come out tomorrow."

"Then you're getting one of those milkshake thingies," Ella joked, looking at her watch.

"I am, and actually they're not unpleasant. Do you have to go soon?"

"Not just yet, but I do have an appointment later on," she admitted readily.

They chatted together easily until she had to go. "Well," he sighed, "You know where I live. Anytime you're in the neighborhood, pop in for a quick hello. The invitation also applies to the General Care area too, if I'm transferred there."

"I'll take you out into the garden next time," she encouraged, standing up and then pulled the chair back to where it had been.

"It's a deal. Thanks for the visit."

**

The following week Carney O'Sullivan was transferred out of the Intensive Care Unit. He still had a private room, but there was more exposure to general hospital life. Staff who worked in this area drifted into his room during the first day to introduce themselves and informed the new patient how things worked in their sector. Doctors Tucker and Webber were replaced by Dr. Norm Murray, a sandy hair six-foot tall man who bicycled to work and avoided the hospital elevators if he could.

"Dr. Murray makes his rounds in the morning," a nurse whose name tag indicated, Jennifer White, informed him. "He's a stickler for therapy with accident patients. He will want you to get used to movement again. At first, it usually means sitting in a wheelchair and having someone gently walk with you."

She pushed the curtains back and continued, "There are two cardinal rules with wheelchairs. First, a patient must never attempt to get into a chair alone. They should be assisted by an orderly. Number two rule you can't leave your room in the chair unless you're accompanied. The seat will be fitted with a rubber air cushion shaped like a C so your buttocks take the weight, leaving the operation area suspended in an opening at the back of the cushion."

Sunday visiting hours were 2 to 5 pm. Dakota's grandmother drove her into Boston from Nantasket Beach, where she had been staying since her father's mishap. The girl hadn't been told it was a shooting. Mrs. O'Sullivan told her granddaughter she was running a few errands and would pick her up in her dad's room at 3 pm after the visit. The first few minutes between father and daughter were emotional. When he saw her eyes beginning to get moist, he consoled her,

"Now Dakota, you're a big girl. Pull that chair here beside my bed," he urged, patting the blankets beside him.

"Okay Daddy, I'll sit in the chair!" the deeply tanned little girl who had her mother's looks and blond hair murmured and pulled it over closer to the bedside..

"What have you been doing today?" her father asked.

"I woke up early. I was excited because of coming here. We went to Mass before we ate breakfast. The Priest prayed for your speedy recovery at Church. I asked God to make you better soon. On the way home, Grandpa stopped and bought fresh donuts to eat with our breakfast. Then

I just had to wait until Grandma said it was time to go, so I played with my dolls and Bo."

"And how are your dolls and Bo doing these days?"

"They're well, but I don't play with them as much as before. I'm seven now you know dad. In a few weeks, I'll be starting Grade 2. Bo really likes it at Grandma's place. He has explored the whole of their condo. Grandpa set him up a litter box in the kitchen. I take him out for walks on a long leash at least twice a day. He likes doing his do-do in the sand better than in the kitchen litter box. "

"Grade 2, wow, I still remember your first day of kindergarten," he kidded.

"I don't remember kindergarten anymore," she confessed. "I had such a good time in grade one that it washed kindergarten away."

You'll have to start a diary to help you remember," he suggested.

"What's a diary?"

"A book where you write things that happen during the day that you don't want to forget."

"I can't write very well yet, but I'll think about getting a diary anyway."

"I see you brought your school lunch box with you today, anything in it?" her dad pried.

"I brought a picnic for us. Grandma told me you aren't eating solid food yet, so I brought something that's very soft, something you like."

"Let's see, something soft that I like. Is it lemon meringue without the lemon?"

"No, it's cherry jelly with a dab of whipped cream on top. Aunt Joy came over to visit Grandma yesterday and made them a bowl of jelly with fruit. I had her pour some into two, paper cupcake molds. When it set, I added a dab of whipped cream from a spray can. There's one for you and one for me."

"You're getting to be quite the cook," he joked.

"I like cooking," his daughter assured him. "Would you like to see your jelly cupcake?"

"Sure and why don't we eat them too?" he replied licking his lips.

His daughter spread out a paper napkin beside him on the bed and set the desert on top of it. "There you go," she indicated. "Take little bites."

"Aren't we going to say grace, before we eat?" her dad asked.

"I think we should," she replied. "Let's say it together."

They made the sign of the cross and began, "Bless us oh Lord for these thy gifts which we are about to receive from thy bounty through Christ our Lord, Amen."

An hour passed fast. A few minutes before three o'clock her father inquired, "Have you been saying your prayers, while I'm gone?"

"Every night, before I go to bed to either Grandpa or Grandma," she assured him.

"Why don't you say your prayers to me now and give your grandparents a day off," he suggested.

"Okay, that's a good idea," she agreed.

Dakota was just finishing when Louise entered her son's hospital room, followed by his eldest brother David.

"I was going to stay for a visit too," his mother explained, "but I met your brother downstairs and he wants to talk a little business with you."

"It's fine mom," he reassured her. "Maybe you can pop in sometime during the week."

"I will, promise. Come along now Dakota, your daddy and uncle have some business to discuss, about the boat shop."

His daughter looked at him as if to say, can't I stay longer, but he knew his mother and said, "Come say goodbye, Honey!"

She climbed up onto the bed beside him, wrapped her arms around his shoulders and sobbed, "I love you, daddy."

"I love you too kitten. If you come next weekend, maybe you'll be able to take me for a ride in the wheelchair. My Doctor said he's starting me in it this week."

"Bye daddy!"

"Bye kitten!"

When the brothers found themselves alone, there wasn't any awkwardness.

"Hey, little brother, what's new?" David exclaimed.

"You'd be surprised!" Carney assured him with a wink.

"Surprise me."

He thought for a moment, to bring order to his ideas and then declared, "As you can see, I'm out of the ICU. Life's more normal here if being in a hospital can ever be called normal. Also, I'm going to start my apprenticeship with that roadster," he laughed, pointing at the wheelchair.

"It's the first step, man!"

"I know, and the new Doc is a good head. He showed me the piece of steel they removed from my spine. I get to keep it as a souvenir."

His brother couldn't resist, "That's mighty generous of him. You could put it on a gold chain and wear it around your neck." They both laughed.

"He also showed me two sets of X-rays, before and after the operation. It's only a tiny piece of metal, but it did some major damage in an extremely delicate area. You can actually see how the vertebrae and discs are crushed."

"What did he say about your recovery?" his older brother asked seriously.

"He didn't beat around the bush or try to put me on. The prognosis is that wheelchair and I are going to make a very serious commitment to each other."

"Is it really so bad?"

"You're the first I've told. I'd like to keep it between you and me for now, but at this point, they think it's going to be permanent paralysis from the waist down."

"You're tougher than me to sit here and say it. I'd cry or just want to get drunk."

"I felt the same when he first told me, but then we talked about therapy. It's two parts. They get me up to speed in the chair and then there's life counseling."

"I'll give you as much help as I can little brother. You can count on it," David assured him.

"What's the news from my boat shop?"

"I went by like you asked the last time I was here. Your manager, Casey, is extremely competent, and the guys all know their job. Your lawyer gave me a copy of the Power of Attorney he had on file, and I gave it to your account manager at the bank. The accountant is preparing the cheques as usual, and I'm signing them."

"Where are they in the production schedule?"

"There's still a lot of work to do on the schooner and nothing has been done on the two yacht orders. The office manager said someone new has called about having a schooner built."

"I didn't get any details," he added. "She told them you would call when you got back."

"I've got to see if I can use a cell phone, for business calls, now that I'm in general care."

"Keep talking like that and you'll be out of here in no time."

"How's your business?" Carney asked his older brother.

David O'Sullivan worked around several hotels in Boston during the summer while in high school. After graduation he enrolled in a two year certificate program at a Massachusetts Community College studying Hospitality and then went to work on cruise ships. At first the runs were short and mostly to the Caribbean; however, before moving on he had sailed to Russia, knew all the ports in the Mediterranean and was more than familiar with South East Asia. When the thrill of travel wore off, he came ashore and enrolled in Hotel Management.

He and two friends from growing up days bought their first hotel with borrowed money. Recently they had added a new spot to their expanding group. It was near Logan Airport.

"We've had a less than 5% vacancy rate since the beginning of summer. I inked a contract with a new trans-Atlantic airline called Atlantic Express. We're going to provide accommodation for all their in and outbound cabin crews at Logan.

"Bet there's good coin in it?"

"Comme ci, comme ca! They're a budget outfit and couldn't afford the rates at the airport hotels. I trimmed our margin some to get them in, but now we can count on a guaranteed minimum of forty room nights a week, for three years as long as they don't go banco. But anyway, I'm here about your business."

"I had Casey go over the materials lists for those two yachts and break out what should be ordered to start up. I'll leave this list of keel items with you to check over. If you're okay with them, simply sign off. I'll pick it up later in the week and fax it back to him."

Carney was feeling good about his brother and wanted to show him. "I'll have a few sips out of your coffee too Bro if you don't mind. Dakota brought me a jelly thing and it seems to be sticking part way down."

David stood up, placed a sheet of lined paper on the bed and steadied the paper coffee cup, while his brother took a gulp. As he was leaving his brother smiled and declared, "Don't worry man, we're going to beat this. We're family!"

The younger O'Sullivan called after him, "Say hello to Naomi and the kids!" David waved in acknowledgment as he opened the door.

Carney owned a small company called Seahorse Marine Inc. It was located in East Boston, on Marginal St., not far from Logan Airport. Most of the contracts were for yachts without sails, but there were occasional requests for sails. Minimum yacht lengths started at 100 feet. With motor installed they were $5 million and up, depending on how they were finished. The company had twenty full-time people on the payroll. Carney handled all the design work, as well as management and marketing. An expansion was planned that would give the firm both motor yacht and sail yacht divisions.

The injured man felt much better after Dakota's and David's visits. He was confident the future would somehow resolve itself. Dr. Murray coming through the door the following morning didn't raise any apprehension in him. He was the first to say, "Good morning Doctor!"

"So, Mr. O'Sullivan, I see you are making progress." His patient only smiled. "I have news for you. By my calculations, we should be releasing you to go home about mid-September."

Carney knew he wasn't going to be walking. "Do you really think we're not rushing things a little?"

"Oh, don't worry, that's not the last you'll be seeing of me," Doctor Norm smiled. "We're still going to be having you back for physical therapy sessions. I'm going to ask the orderly to get you started in the wheelchair as of today."

"The wheelchair today," he stammered, with a bit if panic noticing a tall muscular orderly enter the room.

"You got it, buddy, now Tom is going to help you roll over so I can get a look at the incision on your back"

The assistant's large arms went under the injured man like the tines of a fork-lift. He felt his whole body move until he was lying solidly on his left side. The Doctor pulled up his gown and made a low murmuring noise.

"You're a tough man Mr. O'Sullivan. Your system has come back on-line and is working overtime around the wound area. The bruise is still large, but there is no puss, and the swelling has gone down considerably." Tom helped him roll onto his back again when the examination was over. "I'm going to leave you two gents now, but I'd like you to do about half an hour in the chair this morning."

Dr. Murray looked directly at Tom who replied with a one finger salute.

Orderly Tom was strong. He could have picked Carney up and set him down in the chair without a word, but he didn't. "You're about to start living in the fast lane again buddy. Has anyone told you the two cardinal rules about wheelchairs around here?"

"Yes, Nurse Jennifer – no getting in alone and no roaming around unattended."

"Good, your mind is as clear as it was before the accident. Apart from those two guidelines, there's one more thing, no matter where you may be. Have you any idea what that might be?"

Carney lay quiet for a moment, looked at Tom, at the chair and thought about what common sense would say in the situation. He grinned and replied, "The brakes!"

"You have it. Now I'm going to put on the brakes and then lift you up and set you down in the chair with one movement. Your behind and lower back could find it quite disagreeable. Grit your teeth and hold on. It will pass."

As soon as Tom's arms were gone, and the chair began to support his weight, the patient could feel the agony coming. Where the paralysis began, he was numb. Above that point, there was a flash of pain. Beads of sweat formed instantly on his forehead and the hair at the nape of his neck became drenched. His hands and arms were shaking. He grabbed for the sheet on the bed, stuffed a corner of it into his mouth and bit down hard until his face was covered with tears. He felt like he was going to be sick, but couldn't even ask for the bed pan.

Tom dried off his face and waited until he stopped shaking. "So, are you're going to live?" he joked.

"Oh, my God, what a whack," he murmured. "Thought I was going to pass out!"

"It was nothing compared to what your spine went through when the chunk of metal sliced into it. I've seen the x-rays. Parts of three vertebrae are crushed. There's a groove across them like a skid mark on the highway made with studded snow tires."

Carney straightened up and smiled, "Thank you for helping me into the chair, Tom. So, what's next?"

"I'm supposed to walk you in it for half an hour. Those are the doc's orders. If you don't feel like meeting the world outside your door just yet, we can stay in your room for today."

"Let's warm up in here first then do about the last ten minutes in the corridors," Carney responded wiping new perspiration from his brow with the back of his forearm.

Outside his room, it was a completely different world. Staff was coming and going. There were other patients in wheelchairs. Tom knew everybody.

The floors in the hallways were finished with large diamond shaped tiles. There seemed to be three lanes – two for traffic and the third was a parking area for everything from beds to food carts. He was glad when the thirty minutes were up. It seemed like one of the longest half hours he had ever lived. It was such a relief to have the weight taken off the bottom of his spine and to lay out full length on the bed again.

That afternoon, Carney had a visit from the Massachusetts State Police. The two officers were in charge of investigating his shooting. They hadn't laid any charges, and they still didn't have any leads.

"What can you tell us about the time immediately preceding your shooting?" the first officer asked.

"It all happened so fast. There's not much to tell and my mind has difficulty focusing on the whole incident."

"Take your time and retrace your steps. You left your father's Compound and drove towards Nantasket Rd."

"Yes, I remember driving."

"Did you see anything unusual when you got to the corner?"

 "There was nothing unusual, but a car was pulled up at the Stop sign, on the other side of the intersection."

"What kind of car?"

"I don't know. There are so many of them."

"What color was it?"

"Gray, light gray, and it was a sedan," O'Sullivan stammered.

"Did you notice the driver?" the other officer asked.

"No, but the passenger was looking around through a pair of field glasses. I figured they might be lost."

"What about the front of the car? Was there any grill work?"

"Yes, now I remember, it did have a lot of grills. As I started to turn right, they turned left into my path, so I gave way to them. It was then I felt the sharp pain in my lower back and passed out. Do you think it was someone in the car who shot me?"

"It's highly possible, Mr. O'Sullivan. Thanks to your memory, we now have something to look for."

"What's that?"

"A light, gray Chrysler sedan," the officer replied.

"Chrysler?"

"They're the manufacturer of the most grills on the market today."

When the Police had cleared the patient's room, the officer in charge commented, "We'll have to come back to visit him with photos of vehicles, to see if we can narrow it down."

His partner agreed and added, "The passenger in the sedan looking at the Jag through binoculars confirms the father's suspicions of mistaken identity."

"Good point, if the son can identify a model, we'll see if the father has ever seen anything like it following him."

**

Ella Bowdine had come to Carney's room several times since he had been transferred out of the ICU. Earlier that morning, she popped in for a moment to say she would be free in an hour and if he would like her to take him out into the hospital garden, he should arrange to have an orderly lift him into his chair. Her long brown hair was a mass of tangles and covered one eye. He didn't resist her offer.

She came back to his room at 2 pm and brought the wheelchair over beside the bed. Once the brake was set, she left for a moment and returned with a male orderly. The new man was just as efficient as Tom. He hoisted him up before being brought down gently on the inflatable rubber cushion.

Soon they were making their way towards the electronic glass doors at the back of the patient's lounge. When they arrived on the patio, she found a bench set off by itself, in the shade. It was a lucky find as there were many patients out in the garden, given the sun and the temperature that afternoon.

"This is the first time I've been out here," he beamed as she set the brake.

"Really!" she exclaimed. "That's those orderlies. They stay on the beaten path, up and down the corridors. So how have you been doing?" she asked sitting down on the wood bench.

"There are big changes coming for me!" her excited charge exclaimed.

"How so," she wanted to know?

"I'm to be released to outpatients shortly after Labor Day Weekend."

"Wow, that is big time! Do you feel ready? "

"No, absolutely not," he replied seriously. "In fact, I feel quite apprehensive about it. I haven't felt like this since I was a kid. In those days, I'd go to church alone and pray. It inspired me with confidence."

"There's a chapel here in the hospital. I could take you there if you like."

"I've been there for Sunday mass," he explained calmly, "but it doesn't produce the same effect in me."

"Was the church in which you received your inspiration in the Boston area?"

"Yes, it was Gate of Heaven in South Boston."

"Oh, I know the area," she confided. "My dad took us out to Castle Island a number of times for Sunday drives."

"My brothers and I played cowboys and Indians on Castle Island with other boys from the neighborhood," he informed her.

"You were raised in South Boston?" she asked assumingly.

"Yes, my dad owned a five-bedroom, three-level house on Columbia Road."

"There were a lot of Irish living around there," she commented.

"We were as thick as potato soup," he laughed. "My parents sold the house, but still live nearby in a condo."

"I've purchased a condo too recently," she informed him. "It's on Beacon Hill."

"A pleasant area," he commented. "My daughter and I live in Jamaica Plain."

"Oh really, I grew up in that neighborhood," she informed him. "My father still lives there. We went skating on Jamaica Pond in the winter; however, it seems global warming has put an end to skating. The ice is too thin now, even in the dead of winter."

"Dakota and I have lived across from Jamaica Pond for eight years and have yet to see anyone skating on it in the winter."

"Is Dakota your wife's name?" Ella inquired.

"I'm a widower," he explained. "My wife died in a highway accident about two years ago up in New Hampshire. It was a multi car pileup in the early morning fog. Dakota is my seven-year-old daughter."

"I think I saw her pushing you along the corridor in your wheelchair, petite, blond and with a skip in her step."

"Yes, it would have been her. We went for a roll several times. She hasn't really accepted the wheelchair yet. She's convinced it's only a temporary measure."

"You're raising her alone?"

"Not exactly alone, we're a big extended family. I have four brothers and each has started tribes of their own. Dakota has four aunts, a grandmother and a grandfather on my side, who compete with my wife's brother and two sisters, to include her in anything and everything they can which involves her cousins."

"Well if you're going to become an outpatient soon, we should do something special. Do you have any ideas?"

"They have great ice cream in the hospital's Tuck Shop," he suggested.

"You can have ice cream anytime," she bantered. "I was thinking of something more personal, like a short visit to Gate of Heaven."

"Would it be allowed?" he asked with astonishment.

"I'm not sure," she admitted. "I'd have to talk to your Doctor. However, if you are being released soon, maybe he would agree with you going out for a couple of hours. South Boston isn't far from here."

"How would we get there?" the stricken man asked in earnest. "I haven't really visualized how I'm going to move around when I'm released.

"We'll get a wheelchair taxi. It'll be a good introduction to them, for you. The fare will be a present from me."

"You're really serious about this," he laughed, smiling at her.

"Everything is tentative until I get the okay from your doctor, but if he authorizes it, when would you like to go?"

"You only visit on weekends, don't you?"

"That's right," she replied with a sigh. "The week is too hectic!"

"Next weekend is Labor Day long weekend," he reminded her. "My family told me they would come in shifts on Saturday and Sunday, but nobody will be visiting on Monday as everybody is at my parent's compound on Nantasket Beach for a family barbecue."

"I'll be over on Martha's Vineyard myself next Saturday and Sunday, but I'm returning to the city late Sunday as I have a critical meeting Tuesday morning and want to be prepared. I'll call your doctor tomorrow."

"It's very kind of you Ella," he assured her. "I'll give you the number to my smartphone. I keep it beside the bed."

"It's a deal," she laughed, clapping her hands together.

"I just noticed when you clapped that you're not wearing your wedding band today."

"My, but aren't you the observant one," she smirked, flashing her eyes at him. "I must have left it in the car." She kept her old wedding ring in the parking meter change dish in the Mercedes and usually slipped it on before going into the Hospital.

"So which high school did you attend?" he asked to draw her out a little.

"I'm a Mount St. Joe's girl," she replied. "We called ourselves Mounties'."

"St. Joe's in Newton?" he guessed.

"Correct and yes, it's private."

"I wasn't going to ask you but now that it's out in the open, did your father's chauffeur take you there in the morning?" he joked.

"Actually I bused it," she replied without pretension.

"Are you Catholic," he enquired.

"No, it was my mother's idea to send me to Mount St. Joe. There were quite a few girls who weren't Catholic. We had Library while the other girls had Religion. We had to turn in a book report to the Librarian. It all worked out quite well, and I still have friends I made there." They continued to chat for about a half an hour. When he started to tire, she took him back inside.

Dr. Murray did give Ella permission to take Carney out for two hours the following Monday afternoon.

She called the Church to make sure it was open. The doors were not locked, before five o'clock. She arrived at the hospital in a Taxi Van about 1:45 pm. By two o'clock his chair had been pushed up the side door ramp, strapped into place so it wouldn't move and the sliding side panel door snapped shut. It was a short trip. The driver said he would return in exactly one hour to take them back to the hospital.

The original Gate of Heaven was completed in 1864. It was a brick structure, with a pleasing exterior and could comfortably seat 1,500 parishioners. Tragically, in 1894, the old church suffered a devastating fire. Much of it was destroyed; however, some statues and other religious artifacts were saved. The cornerstone of the new Church was laid as soon as possible, and the first service was held in 1900. Construction was finally finished in 1912.

The parish always had a strong Irish American component in its congregation. In the 1860's, some priests came out straight from Ireland. Later, others like Father Murphy were American born.

There was a wheelchair ramp to enter the Church. The ceiling was exceptionally high and the upper Church held aloft by massive white columns running up to the altar. Between the pillars, there were double banks of pews separated by a central aisle and outside the pillars, single banks of pews running the full length of the nave. Gate of Heaven is unquestionably about its stained glass windows. Each tells a unique story. Each flooded a different color of light down over the seats.

The interior of the church was much darker than outside. It was cool too and sounds were muffled. The air had a clean, fresh smell. A small bird flew out from somewhere, swooped down over the center isle and then flew up and perched on the ledge of one of the columns.

Ella felt a bit odd about being there. She was a Mason. She knew that Catholics were not allowed to become Freemasons. Catholics and their churches were always a mystery. Even during her time at St. Joe's she had never ventured into the school chapel or told anyone she was a Mason.

"I'll take you to a spot and then leave you there," she told her charge. "I'll wait in the last row near the center aisle. When you're ready to go, just signal me. I'll come to get you."

"Thank you!"

"Where would you like to go?"

"At the very front, on the right-hand side, there's a small nave built in the wall at pew level. A statue of Our Lady is there. It was brought over from Ireland when the Church was rebuilt after the fire. I liked that spot when I was a kid."

She left him at the exact spot he requested and went to wait at the back of the Church. As soon as he couldn't hear her foots steps anymore, he began to pray silently. First, he prayed for Dakota, his mother and then his father. Secretly he feared another attempt would be made on his father's life. He prayed for himself and the men at his shop. Once all personal intentions were fulfilled, he turned his attention to the statue in front of him.

It hadn't changed much. It didn't get exposed to the sun inside the nave. The paint hadn't faded. The same cast iron straps held the statute in place on a granite block. The enamel paint on the bolts was not cracked, testifying that they had never been removed. He inched the chair as close as possible by putting his arm inside the nave to hold onto the base of the figure. Like the little boy of yesteryears, he began to whisper softly to the plaster woman, asking her to make him strong and to help guide him in the challenges he would meet soon.

He had just started to say the 'Hail Mary, full of grace' when the chair moved. His hand reached further behind the statute to renew his grip. All of a sudden he felt odd. It seemed almost as if electricity was running through him. The statute's face became flesh like. It began to glow. He saw her lips move.

Inside his head, a woman's voice spoke from far away. She was telling him not to have fear. He must have faith in her son.

As suddenly as it started, the experience ended. He slumped back exhausted. At the rear of the Church, Ella checked her watch. The taxi would be back for them in seven minutes. It was time for her to go fetch him.

Carney didn't hear her approach. When she was close, she called his name softly, so as not to startle him. He didn't appear to hear her call. She came up and looked at his face. He seemed to be sleeping with a broad smile on his lips. It was the first time she really noticed the squareness of his jaw. Volunteer Bowdine shook his shoulder gently, and he opened his blue eyes.

"Time to go, Carney," she advised him in a low voice, noticing he would soon be needing a shave.

"Already, it seems as if we have just arrived," he complained earnestly.

"No, it's been an hour."

"We better not keep the driver waiting," he agreed. For the first time, he put his hands on the wheels and helped her move the chair towards the Church entrance. As they were walking towards the vehicle, Ella advised, "If anybody asks, say we went to watch sailboats out on Boston Harbor this afternoon."

"We did, what's up?" he asked seeming confused.

"Dr. Murray is a sailing enthusiast," she explained. "I knew he'd understand a boat builder wanting to watch sailboats in the wind, easier than he would you wanting to go to church."

"You told him we were going to watch sailboats?" Carney chuckled.

"I suggested it. He jumped to conclusions. I didn't want to spoil his high opinion of you."

"Am I ever going to see you again after I leave this place, Mrs. Brown?"

She looked at him seriously, smiled and showed him her wedding band before answering, "We shall see, shan't we Mr. O'Sullivan, but I must warn you, one of the conditions of my volunteer agreement with the hospital is that I will report any and all stalking."

"I won't stalk," he assured her.

"I hope you don't. If you try to contact me, I'm supposed to report it."

During the night, Carney woke with a dull pain in his groin. He knew he drank too much ice water during the evening. Without any thought, he flipped back the covers and swung his feet out onto the floor. The tiles felt cold, as he walked over to the bathroom and urinated for two solid minutes.

When it was finished, Carney turned and looked in the mirror. He was conscious of himself, but it seemed he was dreaming. He reached out and touched the mirror with his hand. It was real. The astonished man walked back to his bed, without turning on the light, and climbed in. He didn't sleep another wink for the rest of the night.

**

After the meal cart girl had taken the breakfast dishes away, orderly Tom came in to ask Carney if he would like to sit in his chair for a while. Tom was a big man with very muscular limbs. Before coming to work at the hospital he had been a stevedore on the Boston Docks.

"Tom, I have a surprise for you."

"What's up buddy?"

"I can get into it by myself."

"You know the rules, Mr. O'Sullivan. The first one is, we don't get into the chair unassisted. Just because, you're getting close to release, doesn't mean they don't still apply. As a matter of fact, they're just as indispensable when you go home as they are in here."

"I'm not trying to break the rules, Tom. Push the door closed for a moment. I've something to show you." Tom knew the rules. He liked his job but decided to humor Carney. The patient flipped the covers back. First, he raised one leg and then the other straight up into the air.

"You're not supposed to be able to do that," the orderly objected seriously.

"There's more," the patient replied, swinging both legs out over the side of the bed before standing up, without any support.

"I think you better get back into bed now Mr. O'Sullivan. I must go find Doctor Murray and report this."

Ten minutes later Carney gave the same demonstration for Dr. Murray. He too excused himself to look for the radiologist, Doctor Roger Samuelson who made a space in his schedule to come and witness.

The patient was brought to the Radiology Department for a lower back x-ray. When the image had been digitalized, the two physicians came to Carney's room with a tablet, closed the door and stood on either side of the bed. The Radiologist held the tablet out so that Carney could see the screen.

"As you can see," he said, pointing at a spot on the image, "this is the date we took this first x-ray, and there's your name. Here's the film we took fifteen minutes ago. It too bears your name."

"I understand. It's a permanent ID for that image. It can't be tampered with."

"Exactly, we also have the images taken of your lower back with the MRI. Each one of them identifies the patient in a similar way."

"I understand Doctor, but what's the point you're trying to make?"

"Look at this first image taken a month and a half ago. You can see the lower discs are crushed and scored. The nerves are no longer attached to them, as they are attached to the discs higher up the spine, outside of the injury area."

"You showed me this before Doctor," Carney objected

"But you haven't seen the images we took today," the Radiologist replied. "Look here at this one. There is your name and today's date. Now, look at the lower spine. All the discs appear normal. There's no score mark caused by the piece of spring as it moved along your lower spine and the nerves are attached to the lower discs again, just the same as the ones along the upper spine. How do you explain this, Mister O'Sullivan?"

"I don't know Doctor," the patient admitted with confusion. "It looks like a miracle."

"Both physicians looked at each other, smiled and then Dr. Murray said rather presumptuously, "Carney, here at BMC we don't believe in miracles. We would like to put you through another MRI."

He looked at the two men hovering over his bed. He had shown them he could raise his legs and stand free of the bed. Now they wanted to prove it wasn't so. Better still, they wanted him to prove some kind of a hoax wasn't being played on them. He felt a little angry, but complied, "Sure Doctors, go for it. Give me another scan."

The MRI results confirmed the x-rays. Carney O'Sullivan had made a complete recovery. Before he left for the day Dr. Murray stopped by his patient's room.

"How was your day Carney?"

"Restful!"

"Been doing some hard thinking?" the physician prompted.

"Doctor, how does something like that happen?"

"A religious person might call it a miracle," the medical man replied raising his eyebrows

"What would you call it?" Carney asked sincerely.

"I had a long conversation with Dr. Samuelson this afternoon about you," Dr. Murray answered. "He has a theory he calls post-traumatic-release or PTR. Basically, he thinks, at the time of some accidents, the whole body, nervous system and mind go into a traumatic lock down. He has a number of compelling cases to support his theory. They have helped him build his thought around the subject. However, none of his cases are as dramatic as yours."

"PTR, I don't get it, Doctor."

"You're familiar with changes along the coastline. One storm will wash a sand bar away, and another will build it back up.

"It has something to do with changing currents and the tide," the boat builder assured him.

"Well, Doctor Samuelsson thinks similar processes occur in the body and damage can be reversed, when PTR occurs."

"What do you think?" O'Sullivan coaxed.

"I'm a doctor, a man of science. I accept certain things can occur that as yet, we don't know how to explain. Take a false pregnancy for instance. I've treated women who went the full nine months, with all the body changes of a pregnant woman and then went into labor and even started to lactate afterward; however, there never was a baby."

"Wow, talk about unusual!" his patient exclaimed.

Dr. Murray laughed, "You're one to talk about unusual."

"So, what happens to me now?"

"I'm releasing you to outpatients tomorrow. They'll set up two weekly, therapy sessions for you. Some general muscle toning is required. When they release you, you're a free man and you can go back to building boats and raising your daughter."

"It's almost like a happy ending to a novel."

"Talking about writing, Carney, I've given Doctor Samuelsson permission to use all the materials in your case history for a write-up. He has published several articles on PTR and thinks your case merits being known by the medical community. When he's finished, he'll put a brief up on BMC's research Web site, and if it gets enough thumbs up, it might be selected to be published in a hard copy quarterly journal. Don't worry, your name and identity will never be known."

"I don't mind Doctor. I mean it's a contribution to medical science."

Carney was released the following day and about a month later his case was the subject of a well written article on Boston Medical Center's Research Web site. Dr. Samuelsson sent him an email with a link so he could take a look at it.

***

Chapter 2

The Crucifixion Relic

Doctor Samuelson's study on PTR did produce a flurry of comments and other academic discussions on the pros and cons of his theory: however, all were agreed, short of being a miracle, this latest restoration of an injured spinal cord added much credence to what he had been saying for several years. The research published on BMC Quarterly Journal of Radiology's Web site at mid-September was noted by more than the international medical community.

The Governor's Palace is a five level low rise building located in the Vatican Gardens behind St. Peter's Basilica in Rome. In an out of the way office, a priest worked alone and tirelessly on three computers with specialized analytics software. He was tri-lingual and followed anything trending on the Internet in English, French and Italian. He was a special advisor to the Pope.

He first noticed the chatter coming in the English speaking blogs then it spread into other languages. Something had happened in America. It took him some time to follow all the threads. From the letters after their names, he knew they were qualified medical people. They were talking about a miracle. He decided this must be reported, so left his chair, straightened his clothing and left his office being careful to lock the door behind himself and headed off to the Apostolic Palace.

The Apostolic Palace is a series of self-contained buildings arranged around the Courtyard of Sixtus V. It is located northeast of St Peter's Basilica. The Palace houses both residential and support offices of various functions as well as administrative offices not focused on the life and functions of the Pope himself.

Father Henry Beal had been waiting two hours for an audition with the Pope. The Vatican was in an unusually busy period. Preparation had begun for the Christmas season. Discussions were under way with higher Moslem clergy concerning a meeting to be held in February. A request for a sitting of the Roman Curia in Lima, Peru had been received. Some priests there were ignoring their vows of celibacy and had started taking wives. The Pope had to be kept appraised of all. Finally, Father Beal's turn did come. With great care, he revealed to the old Patriarch of the Church, the whole subject of an article a radiologist at Boston Medical Center had published on the Internet.

"So, what are you trying to say, Father?" the Pope asked with impatience.

"It's not medical science Your Grace!"

"What is it then," the Pontiff demanded, drumming his fingers?

"It's a miracle!" The roly-poly cleric burst out.

"Come, come Father we both know miracles don't just happen. The Church has documented every miracle occurring for the past two thousand years. With the exception of very few, they all fall into a precise pattern. What makes you think this is a miracle?"

"It's the perfect restoration to normal the patient experienced. We've contacted the Board charged with reviewing all supporting documents and materials before they accept any research for publication. A team of six specialists examined the original x-rays and MIR scans and certified they had not been tampered with."

"So, what do you think it is Father Beal?" The Pope asked as he toyed with the Fisherman's Ring on the third finger of his right hand.

The ring was part of the Pope's regalia. The Pope was the successor of Saint Peter who was a fisherman before he became Christ's disciple. According to the tradition of the Catholic Church, Saint Peter later became a "Fisher of Men" bringing the word of Christ to all people.

"I think it's a relic, Your Grace. I believe a relic has found its way into that city in America. Someone has discovered a way to use it."

"You understand what you're saying, Father? There's only one relic having the power to mend an injury like this.

"I know Your Holiness!"

"What you're saying Father Beal is the Crucifixion Relic has surfaced again after 150 years."

"It does sound preposterous Holy Father, but that's what it must be."

"Did you ever hear about what they did with the relic 150 years ago in Ireland?"

"Begging your pardon Your Grace, but I'm not a specialist in relics."

"The relic had lay in peace and quiet at an Irish monastery for 500 years. We in the Church didn't know where it was. Then the Irish used it to bring a man back to life, so he could testify against his murderer. Of course, the accused could no longer be hanged for murder, but he did get 20 years of hard labor because of the dead man's testimony."

"Why did they do a thing like that, Holiness? It's almost like a carnival act."

"The dead man was a hero on the Catholic side and the accused was a Protestant," the Pope explained. "But you're right; it did almost become a carnival. Overnight thousands of people were booking passage to Ireland. There would have been a tragedy if one monk hadn't taken the Crucifixion Relic and simply disappeared off the face of the earth with it."

"What are we going to do Your Grace?"

"You might not be a specialist on relics, Father Beal," the Pope replied, "but we do have several in the Church who are professionals. In fact, we have a priest who has devoted a substantial part of his life to the study of the Crucifixion Relic. He's a Spaniard. His vocation has led him to become the pastor at the Cathedral of Amalfi. I would like you to contact Father Rafael Torres. Arrange for him to come to see me. And Father, this is absolutely confidential."

"I understand Holy Father!"

"You don't fully understand Father Beal but then how could you. That's confidential too."

"What "that" are you referring to, Holy Father?"

"My health Father, last week my physician advised me I should seriously think of retiring."

"Oh, I see!"

"There are so many things going on here at the Vatican. It's not the season for retiring. The moment I retire, procedures to elect a new Pope would begin almost immediately."

"Your Grace, it saddens me that your health is not holding up. You can rely on me to say nothing to anyone about it."

**

Amalfi is an extremely old city on the southwest coast of Italy. First references to the Cathedral at Amalfi were found in Papal writings of 596 AD. The Cathedral of St Andrew Amalfi is a complex made of two communicating churches, a crypt, a stair, an atrium, a church tower and a cloister. In the early 13th century, the Church became a final resting place for the relics of St. Andrew the Apostle.

Saint Andrew is the patron saint of Amalfi as well as Scotland and Russia. Andrew spread the gospel in Greece until he was executed by crucifixion on a diagonal cross at Patras. Andrew's remains were transferred from Patras to Constantinople around 357 AD to be placed in Constantine's new Church of the Holy Apostles. Numerous miracles have been attributed to St. Andrew's intercession over the centuries.

In the early part of the last century, Amalfi was a popular holiday destination for the British upper class and aristocracy. The City is still a Mecca for tourists and the wealthy. Private yachts anchor in the Bay and several cruise ships stop for a day or so. Three traditional events draw numerous visitors to Amalfi.

First are the feast days of Saint Andrew, celebrating the city's patron saint. Then there is "Byzantine New Year's Eve" celebrating the beginning of the New Year according to the old civil calendar of the Byzantine Empire. The third event is the Historical Regatta, rowing competition among the four main Italian maritime republics: Amalfi, Genoa, Pisa, and Venice. This event is hosted by a different city every year, so it comes to Amalfi once every four years.

Father Rafael Torres had been brought up in an orphanage by nuns. After seven years of study culminating in his ordination as a Jesuit, he had returned to his native village of Avila in Spain to take up pastoral duties at the side of an old priest who was preparing to retire. He might have lived a quiet and uneventful life and finished up the same as the man whom he replaced, had it not been for his hobby, which was a keen interest in relics. As a boy, he had been fascinated by St. Teresa of Avila and the stories linked to her relics. In his spare time, he studied other Saints and relics located in Spain such as Venerable Mary of Agreda, St. James the Greater of Compostela, St. and Sudarium of Oviedo.

He had not been content to simply study relics and lead his flock. With the consent of his Bishop, he began to participate in Roman Catholic online discussion groups where he met Catholic minds from all over South America and former Spanish possessions in Africa, Asia, and Oceania. Later he started his own Blog and spent hours at his computer in the evening. Eventually, the Blog had 120,000 members. His knowledge, understanding, and insight evolved so much through online discussions with Relicologists that he aspired to become one himself.

One of his new cyber acquaintances was a professor at the Roman Catholic University in Rome. All professors and students at the school were priests who were active in the Church all over the planet. The professor encouraged Rafa, as he was commonly called, to apply to study at the Department of Relicology.

Since completing a Masters and Ph.D., he had been attached to the Cathedral at Amalfi as an assistant. Regularly the authorities at the Vatican sent him to explore issues concerning relics. When he wasn't on assignment or assisting with the Mass schedule at St Andrew's, Father Torres worked on a book about the miracles at Medjugorje, in the Federation of Bosnia and Herzegovina.

During the summer of 1981, six Catholic children reported receiving visions and messages from the Blessed Virgin Mary at Medjugorje. The village became a popular site of Christian pilgrimage, with an estimated one million pilgrims annually, surmounting to about thirty million in total. The visionaries claimed God sent his Holy Mother to affirm his existence and to lead people back to Him.

In the rough draft of his book submitted to the Jesuits, Father Torres was skeptical. He argued the "Bureau of Verification of Extraordinary Healings," did not come under ecclesiastical authority. The claimed healings need to be submitted to the proper judgment of the Church. Until this was done, the claims had no validity.

The request from the Vatican didn't come as a surprise. He made arrangements to travel to Rome.

**

Father Beal wasn't the only person in the Church who had noted the published research on the Quarterly Journal of Radiology's Web site. Far to the north, in the city of Edinburgh Scotland, a nun had printed off the article from the Internet and after much analysis, thought and prayer had decided to show it to her Mother Superior. Sister Angela Stuart belonged to the Society of the Sacred Heart, which ran schools for girls from higher income families in Scotland, France, and the USA.

At the Sacred Heart day school for girls in Edinburgh, she taught grammar, composition, and history. There were many well-qualified nuns at the Mother House. They were obliged to rotate by term so everyone had a chance to teach. Some terms Sister Angela didn't get a course and devoted her time to study and prayer. As well, she volunteered among the city's poor. Currently, she devoted four hours a day to a community kitchen in Niddrie Mains, a deprived area of Edinburgh.

Niddrie Mains is an area of east Edinburgh. The name referred to the farm of Niddrie which occupied the land on which the social housing estate for southeast Edinburgh was built in the 1920s. Until recently, Niddrie was one of the most drug-riddled communities in Scotland. Antisocial behavior, gang fights and knife crime were fairly common.

For reasons now lost in time, Acca, Bishop of Hexham in Northumberland in England, withdrew, or was driven from, his diocese in 732 AD. Some sources say he became bishop of Whithorn in Galway, Ireland while others claim he founded a 'See' on the site of St. Andrews in Scotland. In any case, he brought with him relics collected on his Roman tour.

Sister Angela had a theory. She believed Acca's relics were split. Part of the collection went to Galloway in Ireland while part went to St. Andrews. She believed a monk devoted to Acca went to Ireland and the Crucifixion Relic ended up in a monastery in Galloway. In spite of her best efforts, she had not been able to trace this relic since its disappearance from Ireland, after a murdered man had been brought back to life to testify against his murderer in Court.

Mother Superior Shelia Kirk sat behind her desk listening to Sister Angela explain what was in the printout she held in her hands. The Reverend Mother wore a traditional habit and white wimple covering her neck and a black veil attached to the top of her head cascaded down over her shoulders. A silver cross hung around her neck on a chain. She tried to digest the thread the young woman had traced. It linked this recent incident in America to Ireland and Scotland.

"Then you think the Crucifixion Relic has resurfaced again, in America this time?" Sister Kirk ventured.

"I do Mother!" the subordinate replied with deference. She wore a black dress and white bib instead of a wimple and a black veil partially covering her brunette hair. A natural wooden cross hung from her neck on a leather thong.

"Are you currently teaching Sister?" Mother Superior questioned.

"No, I have this term off. It was one of the other nun's turn to teach."

"Have you ever visited Boston?"

"I saw it once, before I took my vows."

"Would you like to go to Boston to pursue your theory further?"

"I hadn't really thought of it," she replied hesitantly. "Would such a thing be possible?"

"Sister, you are the only member of our Society here in Edinburgh who takes an interest in relics. I would have to clear it with the Committee, but yes, it would be possible."

**

After the Crucifixion of Jesus Christ, his body was laid out in a new tomb, which had been hewn from solid stone. It belonged to a man named, Joseph of Arimathea. The body was wrapped in a clean linen cloth. A huge stone was rolled into the entrance of the tomb.

Joseph was a wealthy Israelite, a virtuous and just man, looking for the kingdom of God. He was a disciple of Christ, perhaps since his preaching in Judea; however, he didn't declare himself openly for fear of reprisal from the Sanhedrin. Unmindful of the personal danger, he asked Pilot for Christ's body. Together with Nicodemus, he wrapped the body of Jesus in fine linen and laid it in the new tomb made for him. This fulfilled Isaiah's prophecy. The grave of the Messiah would be with a rich man.

Very early on the Monday following the crucifixion, while it was still dark, Mary Magdalene went to the tomb. The woman saw the stone had been moved away from the opening. She ran to Simon Peter and the other disciples telling them what she had seen. Peter came immediately. Strips of linen cloth were scattered around inside the tomb. The face cloth was rolled up in a place by itself.

The torn linen and cloth were gathered up and taken away by the women who accompanied Simon Peter. The tomb was given back to Joseph. He sealed it again with the same boulder Mary found rolled away from the entrance. The tomb was not reopened until it was needed for its owner from Arimathea.

At this time, there was less confusion than there had been on the occasion of the burial of Jesus. An old woman was sent in to sweep up any accumulated dust and to freshen up the vault. While she was sweeping she found a small piece of linen cloth with what looked like a splinter of bone stuck to it. She knew the history of the tomb and hid the object in the folds of her clothing. Her name was Joanna, and she had faith.

Many years prior, Joanna had tripped and fallen on a rocky path leading down into a small ravine where a well was located. She was carrying a large earthen jug on her shoulder. Its shifting weight caused her to roll off a ledge and land on her back. Her husband had come looking for her and carried her to where they lived. When her spine healed, Joanna walked with a permanent stoop.

Not long after the burial of Joseph of Arimathea, the woman awoke one morning to find she no longer walked with a stoop. Her daughter was the first to notice her mother stood straight It didn't take the two women long to figure out the cause of this transformation. They used the object to heal others in their group. Thus began the legend of the Crucifixion Relic

The small splinter of bone was actually a chip off one of Jesus' ribs where the soldier had pierced him in the side with his lance. It became attached to the linen cloth the body was wrapped in and had fallen into a crevice in the rock inside the tomb when the linen was torn into strips.

It didn't take long for news to spread. Soon after her miraculous recovery, the restored woman received a visit from Nicodemus. He was a friend of Joseph and also a prominent member of the Sanhedrin. Nicodemus warned Joanna. News of her cure and of what she possessed had spread far across the land. He told her she was in grave danger and offered to help her escape into anonymity.

Joanna remembered Nicodemus. He had questioned his fellow Pharisees about the legality of the method by which they proposed to deal with Jesus. He said the accused had to be given a chance to speak in His own defense. He had also helped bring the body to the tomb after it was taken down from the cross. For these reasons, she trusted him. Joanna was never heard from again, but the Crucifixion Relic did resurface long after the natural death of Nicodemus.

In 155 A.D., Justin Martyr mentioned a baptism in one of his writings on practices of the early Christian Church. It seemed one of the faithful suffered a heart attack while he was being baptized and drowned in the arms of his brother. The man was laid out on the ground and covered with a blanket while the event continued. As night began to fall, an *episkopos* or early bishop arrived to give the drowned man the last rite of Unction. As he anointed the man's forehead, the overseer touched him with something concealed between two fingers and the dead man rose and went home with his brother.

Saint Andrew was the brother of Simon Peter. He was born in Bethsaida on the Sea of Galilee and became a follower of John the Baptist. Andrew is said to have been martyred by crucifixion on an X-shaped cross at the city of Patras in Greece. Around 357 AD the relics of Saint Andrew were taken from Patras and deposited at the Church of the Holy Apostles in Constantinople. Many rumors circulated through Christendom as to the where abouts of the Crucifixion Relic, but its exact location remained a secret. Finally, a persistent story put it to be encased in a statue of the Blessed Mary, Mother of Jesus and hidden in the Church of the Holy Apostles in Constantinople.

Around 1129, the Knights Templar claimed to be in possession of, and guardians of the Crucifixion Relic. Then in 1208, following the sack of Constantinople, those relics of St Andrew which remained in the imperial city were taken to Amalfi, Italy, by Cardinal Peter of Capua, a native of Amalfi. It was believed the statue of the Blessed Virgin was transferred along with St. Andrew's relics to Amalfi. The Knights Templar was dissolved in 1312, and much of their property was given to the Hospitallers who later became known as the Knights of Malta. One of the Maltese main claims to fame was being the guardians of the Crucifixion Relic, in spite of the belief that it was at Amalfi.

When the relic turned up in Ireland, not long before the great famine and migration to America, the Church was caught off guard. Clergy stopped talking about it even though every Pope was under sworn obligation to find the relic and bring it back into the Church. The Knights of Malta were disgraced and made a public apology. Henceforth every strange happening whether claimed to be a miracle or not was investigated by the Holy See.

**

Vatican City is a landlocked sovereign city-state whose territory consists of a walled enclave within the city of Rome, Italy. It encloses an area of approximately 110 acres and a population of just over 800. It has the world's lowest crime rate. Yet within the walls of this ancient city, on rare occasions, even espionage has occurred.

There was not sufficient space within the walled City for all the buildings attached to Church administration. Certain properties of the Holy See were located on Italian territory, most notably in Castel Gandolfo and the major basilicas. The basilicas were patrolled internally by police agents of Vatican City State and not by Italian police.

The Holy See acts and speaks for the whole Roman Catholic Church. It is recognized by other countries as a sovereign entity, headed by the Pope. Diplomatic relations are maintained. The Pope governs the Catholic Church through the Roman Curia. The Cardinal Secretary of State is the See's equivalent of a prime minister. The Secretariat of State is the only body of the Curia situated within Vatican City.

Among the most active of the Curial institutions is the Congregation for the Doctrine of the Faith, which oversees the Catholic Church's doctrine. Once it was known as the Holy Inquisition. In the 16th century, it conducted tribunals against witchcraft and heresy. Its offices are housed at the Palace of the Holy Office in the Vatican. The head of this Congregation bears the title Prefect.

**

Father Rafael Torres had taken the bus from Amalfi to Salerno, the main Italian town on the Amalfi Coast. The bus dropped him at the train station where he purchased a ticket on the private Circumvesuviana train to *Napoli Centrale*, Naples' main train station. There, he required a second ticket for a train to *Roma Termini*, Rome's central train station. The total time from Salerno to Rome was about two and a half hours. Between Naples and Rome, he took the communication from his breast pocket he had received from the Vatican and read it over.

His appointment was with the Cardinal Secretary of State at 3 pm. He should be at Roma Termini shortly after noon. He decided to walk from the station up through the City to the Vatican and stop at his favorite café for lunch.

Romans like their coffee, strong and burning hot. It was part of their lifestyle, a persistent aroma enveloping them from morning till after dinner. Cafes were like temples. Rafa liked the environment. His spot was also a chic trattoria, where he could eat local.

When the visitor from Amalfi arrived at the Apostolic Palace five clergies sat in the high-backed, carved armchairs outside the Cardinal's office. He registered with the Secretary's Assistant at the desk near the door leading to the inside chambers. To his surprise, his name was called before two of those who had been there when he arrived.

The Secretary was an intense, thin man who spoke with a Greek accent. He was brief.

"Father Rafael Torres I received a request from one of His Holiness's close advisors. I was to require your presence here in Rome and make an appointment for you to meet with the Prefect," the Church official said dryly. Then realizing the priest might not be familiar with the Prefect he added, "Who is the head of the Congregation for the Doctrine of the Faith."

Rafa Torres felt his stomach muscles tighten. He hoped he had done nothing wrong. He trusted he hadn't written anything inappropriate online.

"I prepared a brief biography about you Father Torres and forwarded it to the Congregation," the Secretary explained. "The Prefect has set up an audition for you at 10 am tomorrow morning."

"Thank you, Cardinali," the younger priest replied.

"Not at all my son," the senior clergy countered cheerfully and extended his hand holding out a piece of paper. "This is your letter of introduction to the Prefect as well as a two-day pass for the visiting clergy residence."

"Thank you Eminence," Rafa responded while accepting the documents from the ecclesiastic who was wearing red Episcopal vestments.

"I still have more business to attend to this afternoon," the older man said, "but I do have time for a question if you have any."

Rafa cleared his throat and spoke, "Cardinal do you know what this is about? Am I to be reprimanded?"

"I'm sorry my son, I have no idea what the Prefect will discuss with you."

Rafa checked in at the visiting clergy's residence and after receiving his key, dropped off his travel bag. The receptionist said supper would be served in the lower floor cafeteria between 5 and 6 pm. He decided to wait and take his evening meal there.

It was a warm evening and the visiting Priest didn't feel like staying cooped up in the residence. Outside the streets were full of tourists. He decided to go for a walk through the Palatine, one of ancient Rome's seven hills. Legend says the twins Romulus and Remus were taken to Palatine Hill by a she-wolf who raised them. It became one of the most affluent areas in the ancient City. The following morning he rose early, went to a vacant altar where he performed Mass in private and after breakfast went back out into the City and walked to the Apostolic Palace.

The duty of the Congregation for the Doctrine of the Faith is to promote and safeguard the doctrine, on faith and morals, throughout the Catholic world. Everything which in any way touches such matters falls within its competence. This duty extends to investigations of threats and crimes against doctrine and faith. Miracles fall under its power of investigation since they are often based on faith and since they have the power to disrupt normal order. The current Prefect of the Congregation was Cardinal Fathi Abbas, an Iraqi.

Father Rafael Torres was shown into Cardinal Abbas's office at exactly 10 am the following day by his assistant, Cardinal Priest Dakila Moreno of the Philippines. Cardinal Abbas was clothed in red, just as the Cardinal Secretary of State had been. He liked to keep his hair in a close-cropped buzz cut and balanced this with a salt and pepper goatee. His Eminence waited until his guest was seated and his assistant had retired, before speaking, "I trust you had a pleasant trip and were welcomed at the Residence, Father Torres?"

"Everything was perfect Cardinal," the invitee replied respectfully

"I suppose you are wondering why we've summoned you here, Father."

"I must admit, I am a little curious."

"Are you familiar with the work of the Congregation?"

"I remember studying about the Congregation in a Church History course when I was in the seminary, but my vocation has led me into other areas."

"Let me refresh your memory a little. One could compare us to the Interpol of the Catholic Church. We investigate, sanction and try heresy and crime within the Church and investigate and inform the Church about threats from the outside."

"Am I being investigated?" Father Torres asked quietly.

"No, we would like you to help with an investigation."

"Help, I don't understand."

"I have read your file, Father. You are considered to be a first rate Relicoligists."

"It has been my hobby, since before I entered the seminary."

"In addition, I understand you are a specialist on the Crucifixion Relic."

"I do know everything written or rumored about the relic up to its disappearance in Ireland about 150 years ago."

"That is why you have been invited here to help us. We believe there is a possibility the artifact has surfaced recently in America. Every Pope is sworn to recover the relic for the Church. His Holiness has asked us to investigate this possibility and if it should prove to be true, to do our utmost to recover this property."

"How can I help Cardinal?"

"Father Torres, there are mentions in your file of travels you made on behalf of the Church to attest to the authenticity of relics the Church was in the process of acquiring before they ended up in antique auctions."

"I did travel in Russia for almost six months and identified eight genuine artifacts. One of these was recently returned to the Orthodox Church in Istanbul by his Holiness as a gesture of good will between them and us."

"Exactly Father, which brings us to the point of this meeting. We would like you to go to America for us. Be our eyes and ears surrounding the possibility the Crucifixion Relic has resurfaced. Let me go even further. If you find reasonable evidence of a genuine artifact, we would like you to do your utmost to reclaim the object for the Church, even if it must be purchased."

"Where in America is it believed to have surfaced?"

"In the city of Boston," the Cardinal replied.

"Is there a plan or an agenda I am to follow?"

"Not only is there not a plan or an agenda Father Torres, you going to Boston for the Church doesn't even exist. We would prefer you travel as a lay person. Also, this meeting with me and your mission must never be mentioned to anyone."

"Is there a reason for the secrecy Cardinal?" Rafa asked curiously.

"You know what happened in Ireland Father. It was 150 years ago, but given the nature of American society, they might start performing miracles before huge numbers of people, in sold out football stadiums and televise it to the whole planet. Who knows, they might even try to bring President Kennedy back to life in front of a television audience, especially if it's the Irish or their descendants who are in possession of the relic."

"I understand Cardinali. How will I survive there?"

"We have arranged for you to represent an antique dealer in Madrid. Money will be transferred to a bank account in New York. When you land in New York, you will go to the bank and request a credit card and debit card be issued on the account. Use them for all your needs. Don't be hard on yourself Father. The few dollars you might economize could very well put in jeopardy your real mission."

"When am I to leave?" the Jesuit inquired, beginning to warm to this new project.

"Return to Amalfi. Put your affairs in order. In about a week you will receive a one-way ticket from Leonardo da Vinci International Airport to JFK International Airport along with bank information."

"Will I have a contact here in Rome?"

"You will have a contact in Madrid. His name, telephone number and e-mail address will be given to you with the airline ticket."

"How will I find this possibility in Boston?"

Cardinal Abbas extended a thin file folder. "All we know is what's in this folder. You can read it before leaving my office and make notes. Then you're on your own."

"May I take a computer?"

"Yes, take one, but clean it. We don't want the Church's business plastered all over the world, should it go astray."

"I have a Notebook for traveling. It hasn't been used for much besides Internet browsing and email."

"It will be fine. There's one last thing Father."

"Yes?"

"If you do happen to come in possession of the Relic, we don't want you to bring it back to Rome immediately."

"What am I to do?" the Spaniard pressed.

"There's a Benedictine Abbey a bit south of Boston. It specializes in retreats. Go there and check in for a retreat. We will contact the head Benedictine with instructions for you." Cardinal Abbas replied and continued. "Things are not always what they appear to be in Rome. We must take precautions, in case there is a struggle between factions, each trying to gain control of the Relic. We already suspect the Illuminati have picked up the scent and are being extra vigilant everywhere."

"I understand Cardinali. Do you know the name of the place where the Abbey is located?"

"The town is called Hingham!"

Certain conspiracy theories propose that world events were being controlled and manipulated by a secret society calling itself the Illuminati. It was claimed notable people were members of the Illuminati. Even some offices of the Holy See in Rome were suspected of been infiltrated.

When Father Torres had gone, the Prefect of the Congregation for the Doctrine of the Faith put his desk in order, made a few phone calls and then went out for lunch. After he left, his assistant Cardinal Priest Dakila Moreno went in to empty his superior's Out-Basket and to add to his In-Basket. He noticed the Cardinal's agenda lay open on the blotter and casually read the only entry for the day.

Father Moreno was from the Philippines where his father had been an undertaker. He hadn't fancied himself entering the family business, even though he spent many hours working there when not in school. After high school, he expressed an interest for the Seminary as a way to continue his education. At the Seminary, the undertaker's son excelled and won a scholarship to go and study in Rome. When he returned to Manila, it took several years of maneuvering, but he did manage to get back to Rome. Now only his family remembered him back on the Islands.

In the 10 am slot was written *Father Rafael Torres* and under his name, *Crucifixion Relic*. There was also a file labeled, Father Rafael Torres. The Prefect's Assistant opened it briefly. It contained clippings from a medical journal summarizing the facts of a patient's case in Boston, in

America. The assistant left his superior's office and shut the door behind him.

There are three orders of Cardinals in the Roman Catholic Church – Cardinal Bishops, Cardinal Priests and Cardinal Deacons. It is the first who collectively elect the Pope and handle the day-to-day governance of the Church in Rome. The Cardinal Priests, on the other hand, are attached to dioceses throughout the world or hold positions in the Roman Curia in Rome. The Deacons are priests who have distinguished themselves but are over eighty, so no regular duties fall to them.

Father Moreno was happy to be a Cardinal Priest and to live in Rome. He liked the duties assigned to him and performed them diligently. In all bureaucracies, there are always those who envy others. In the Order of Cardinals, certain members did not agree with the elevation of Bishop Abbas to the rank of Cardinal.

Some didn't think it was appropriate that a man who had been born and raised a Moslem should be a Cardinal in the Church of Rome. The common reply to these detractors was to remind them of the English Bishop Newman, who as an evangelical Calvinist held the belief that the Pope was the antichrist then later converted and was elevated to the rank of Cardinal within the Catholic Church. In spite of this, Cardinal Abbas had some silent critics who were always vigilant in case he went astray.

When he became Cardinal Abbas's assistant, Father Moreno became aware of the current of thought against his superior. He had not gone in with it. The pessimists soon let him be. They did, however, continue to filter every word of the unsuspecting assistant.

One of the silent detractors was a man named Father Tony Alfonso who performed functions at the Vatican Press and was a secret member of the Illuminati. Father Moreno regularity took reports and briefings prepared by Cardinal Abbas to the Press to have multiple, bound copies prepared for distribution to the College of Cardinals. He became acquainted with Father Alfonso in the course of these duties. Sometime the two men met by chance outside of work in the City. A number of times they had stopped to take coffee together. The day after Father Torres meeting with Cardinal Abbas one of these seemingly chance meetings occurred. The two priests stopped at a nearby café for a friendly chat.

"So, Dakila how goes the battle," Father Alfonso inquired?

The Pressman was a husky man with large shoulders. He had been born and raised on a farm in Tuscany and as a youth used every muscle in his body for heavy manual labor. After courting a local girl for seven years he finally had saved enough to ask for her hand. They were both very happy and wanted a family, even if it was small. A year and a half later his beloved and their child died in childbirth. Tony was devastated. His religion saved him and he decided to go into the Church. The Illuminati was like his family.

Father Moreno didn't know many people on a personal level in Rome. He liked the way the Italian called him Dakila when they met. "Oh you know, Cardinal Abbas is very busy and as a consequence, I am too," the Cardinal Priest replied.

"I haven't seen you around at the Print Shop lately."

"There haven't been any reports or briefings to prepare for distribution."

"But you said you were busy," Father Alfonso rebutted.

"My work doesn't only concern the College of Cardinals," the Filipino defended himself. "There are investigations too."

"You're involved in investigations Dakila," Tony exclaimed.

"Why sure, like Bishop Abbas often says, we are the Interpol of the Catholic Church."

"Oh yes I remember, you people found that pedophile in the Diocese of Johannesburg."

"Yes, there was that case. He was excommunicated. Lots of change has come to the Church as a result of his trial."

"What sort of change," the pressman laughed, taking a sip from his cup?

"The Congregation for the Doctrine of the Faith established a new program called, "The Review Committee". It sponsors and assists any parish, anywhere on the planet, to set up a Review Committee."

"What's a Review Committee?" the Tuscan asked.

"A Review Committee is a parish group that examines all clergy and lay people who come in contact with youth, in the church, school or at parish activities," Father Moreno answered. "They examine complaints, no matter how minor and keep files and records of all their undertakings and findings."

"I totally approve Dakila. We must put an end to this issue in the Church."

Cardinal Priest Moreno was pleased by this affirmation from his friend. It made him feel important. Then rather casually his friend asked, "What sort of investigations are you and Cardinal Abbas involved in now?"

Father Moreno forgot himself for a moment. "Well, there is the Crucifixion Relic investigation. A Father Torres was here yesterday and Cardinal showed him some clippings from a medical journal."

"What sort of clippings?"

"I don't know, they were in English," he replied.

"I've never heard of the Crucifixion Relic," Father Alfonso admitted, "but I'll look it up when I get back to my computer."

"I'm the same. There seem to be so many relics."

"That's good work the Congregation does Father Moreno. Someone must attest to the authenticity of these artifacts for the rest of us in the Church."

By the end of the following day, a small group of select clergy in Rome was aware of Cardinal Abbas's new investigation. They were in possession of detailed research on the Crucifixion Relic and had a biography of Father Rafael Torres. They also knew he had told his associates in Amalfi he would be leaving for America in about a week on Church business. They were all secret members of the Illuminati.

It was only a rumor, but rumor had it the Illuminati had made inroads into the Church, especially among the higher clergy in Rome. It was also rumored sympathizers would try to favor a select candidate for the office of Pope when next one was elected.

One member of this select clergy, Father Nigel from Estonia, had many contacts in Rome. Some of them lived on the criminal fringe. On a number of occasions, he had sold information to a low life named Lorenzo Caballero. The Crucifixion Relic investigation wasn't considered high priority by anyone, but perhaps Caballero would be interested. I will only divulge Father Rafael Torres name if I'm paid, Father Nigel thought.

It was almost midnight in a walled compound in Hammana Lebanon when the phone rang. The Director was working late as he had been communicating on a short wave receiver-transmitter with one of his members in a time zone located on the other side of the world in China. When he picked up the telephone a voice said, "This Lorenzo Caballero speaking."

"Ah yes Lorenzo," the Director replied, recognizing the name. "How can I help you?"

By the end of the conversation, the Director had decided there might be some value in the Crucifixion Relic. Rich people all over the world seek longevity. Some of them might pay well for such an object, even if it turned out to be bogus. "Okay Lorenzo, get me the name of the priest and the day he leaves Rome and we have a deal."

**

Lebanon is a country in Western Asia, on the eastern shore of the Mediterranean Sea. It is bordered by Syria to the north and east, and Israel to the south. The earliest evidence of civilization in Lebanon dates back more than 7,000 years. Lebanon was the home of the Phoenicians. It is a parliamentary democracy. The National Legislature is divided equally between Christians and Muslims.

Hammana is a village located on the west side of the Mount Lebanon mountain chain, about 30 km east of Beirut. The district is served by a network of secondary roads twisting and turning between cherry orchards and bean fields. The Brotherhood of the Eternal Light or the BEL as locals know it is a monastic community located at the end of a mountain road in the Hammana District. The brothers have been there since 1812. Prior to them, the buildings had been vacant for 100 years after the resident Christian order decided to relocate to America.

Regardless of who they were, all members of Brotherhood were expected to contribute to the material well-being of the community. Some worked on local farms, others opted for short contracts in Beirut or elsewhere and returned to their new family, when the contract was done. Annual expenses are not inconsequential. The 14th-century monastery was in a continuous state of repair or replacement. The new Director was a modernist and had made the community self-sufficient in many ways.

One of his early projects was the addition of solar panels and banks of hydrogen batteries attached to their energy grid. Today there were no restrictions on the use of electricity. Expenses didn't only originate from the monastery operations; they also came from special projects. The brothers ran a free medical clinic in a remote agricultural district of eastern China, not far from the border with North Korea.

Within twenty-four hours of his first telephone call to the Director of the Brotherhood of Eternal Light, Lorenzo Caballero placed a second call,

"His name is Father Rafael Torres."

The Director wanted to know what he looked like. "I don't have a photograph of him, but there are several on the Internet. He's a well-known Relicoligists. He has his own Web site and contributes to a number of Discussion Groups on relics."

"When does he leave Italy?"

"I did a reservations check with Alitalia. He's on flight number 1030 at 2:15 pm next Monday, October 3rd. There are vacant seats on the plane."

"Thank you, Lorenzo. An advance of 5,000 euros will leave here within a day and will be delivered to you by one of the brothers. Can he contact you on this telephone number when he arrives in Rome?"

"No problem, it's a good number. How about the other half of the money," the small time crook pushed?

"You'll have it when I have the relic in my hands, whether it proves to be genuine or fake."

"The Church wouldn't be sending a specialist after the thing if there wasn't a good chance it was genuine," the caller rebutted.

"Exactly," the Director agreed. "So there's an excellent chance you will be collecting the other half."

There were almost 300 men living under the Director's guidance. He prided himself on knowing something about each one of them. When he hung up, the community's leader went off on foot to look for Brother Mustafa Hadad who was devoted to physical fitness. He started his search in the exercise room beside the gym. The Brother was there in shorts and running shoes skipping with a rope, very fast. When the door opened, the skipping stopped.

"Pardon me for interrupting you Brother Mustafa," the Director declared, bowing slightly at the waist and bringing his two palms together.

"Not at all, Brother Director, I was getting ready to stop anyway," the tall, athletic man said with an easy going tone. "Do you need me?"

"I have something to discuss with you. After you get cleaned up, come have tea with me."

"Give me half an hour."

The Director smiled, offering a half salute and left as quickly as he had appeared.

Ivan Gaspirali, the Director was born to a Crimean Tatar father and an Armenian mother. His Crimean Tatar ancestors were forcefully resettled to Simferopol the capital city of Crimea under Joseph Stalin during

World War II, after his peasant father's land was confiscated. He learned to speak Russian and Armenian in youth and later Lebanese Arabic. As a young man, he changed sides too many times and eventually became blacklisted. Like Hadad, he found refuge with the Brotherhood of Eternal Light.

Mustafa Hadad was typical of many men in this part of the world. His early life was a series of catastrophic events, which didn't break him but marked him. He was a loner. Fifty-three years ago he was born on a caravan route to a Lebanese mother and a Syrian father. When the family's three camels all caught the same disease and died under load, his father made a deal with another camel master to take his wife and son to Damascus. The young father stayed behind hoping to buy beasts from someone in the next caravan in exchange for part of his load. He told his wife he would search for her in Damascus.

The young woman found a room for herself and the boy in the strange city, up a narrow alley, which was only a footpath between the buildings. The father never showed up. Perhaps he met with foul play or perhaps simply decided to move on. When the other kids in the alley started to go to school, young Hadad followed them and became a registered person for the first time in his life. It was a hard life for mother and son. Then she became pregnant.

She wanted to get rid of the new life before it could grow, but couldn't afford the price required by the illegal abortionist. The last thing Mustafa remembered about his mother was her dying in childbirth, in their hovel and her telling him to go to Beirut, to see if he could find any of her family. The nine-year-old set off alone to travel from Damascus to Beirut.

He did not find any of his mother's family, but the Police found him and he was turned over to the Lebanese Child and Family Services. They located an old Druze woman who would keep him and send him to school for a modest sum every month. Her name was Sarah. They grew to like each other.

She taught him Lebanese Arabic. He went to the shops for her, faithfully bringing back all she needed to feed them both. He always handed her the correct change from the money she had given him. It was through her he made contact with religion for the first time in his life. When Mustafa was sixteen and a half, Sarah had a heart attack. The money from the government stopped coming. He was evicted and started to survive in the streets.

The teenager became a member of a youth gang for his own protection. As part of the initiation ritual, he had to kill someone. It had to be witnessed by a gang member. He chose an old seaman sleeping outside, down near the docks. It was quick. The man didn't even wake up. As a result of the experience, he found his life's calling and became a professional assassin.

At forty, Mustafa Hadad felt an overpowering desire to be a part of something. He wanted a family. First, he made up stories about make believe relatives who lived far off. Then when he would go off to kill someone for pay, he told his crowd in Beirut he was going to visit Uncle Ali or Aunt Sarah. Everyone knew he was just another stray. There were no aunts or uncles.

One of the older men told him about the Brotherhood of Eternal Light. Mustafa felt comfortable with the Brotherhood. It was the closest thing to family he had ever known. Thirteen years passed since he had become a Brother. It was a good life. He liked living in the community.

As Brother Mustafa left the athletic complex and headed towards the old monastery he thought to himself, the Director had probably been offered a contract to have someone killed. Now he wanted to ask Mustafa if he would take the job. He was still an assassin and all the money from his contracts went to the Brotherhood. It was his contribution to community life. The other Brothers thought he was a specialist in artificial insemination. When he periodically disappeared; he was off on a job inseminating cattle or camels.

The Director's office was in a very large room with tall windows along one wall. It was set up and furnished like a Bedouin's tent. There were multiple layers of thick, hand-woven, wool carpets and an abundance of cushions. His desk was at the very back under the windows. When Mustafa entered the Head Brother got up from his desk and came to meet him. They sat on the carpet and the host poured two cups of strong tea. There was also a snack made of herbs of *habuck* and *marmaraya*. First, they talked about the Brotherhood and their community and then the guest's health. When the tea was near done, an *Arguileh* was lit and the men passed the tube between them savoring the cherry flavored *shisha* tobacco.

"Do you have a computer, Mustafa?" His host asked in a casual manner.

"Yes, I have a very good notebook. I don't use it much here as we don't have an Internet connection, but I use the free Wi-Fi in the airports and hotels when I travel."

"Have I ever showed you my tech shop?"

"No, I didn't know you had one."

"Come," the leader invited, beginning to stand up. "I will show you," and he walked back towards the desk.

The room was concealed behind a bookcase set on a track on the floor, so it could be easily slid out of the way. The space wasn't large, but it contained several servers and routers as well as a short wave radio and a workbench upon which were the dismembered remains of a number of computers. When the visitor finished his look, both men went to sit at the desk. It was then the Director began to explain about the Crucifixion Relic.

"And so you see, there are people who would pay well for such an item. The Brotherhood could do many things with the money obtained from the sale of the relic, but I do have a special project in mind."

"What type of a project?" the assassin inquired curiously.

"There are several phases, but it would start with building a communications tower here at the monastery equipped with a dish to beam in and out, a T1 Internet connection from Beirut. Afterward, we would create a Wi-Fi environment everywhere inside the compound. The third phase would involve equipping every Brother with the latest Notebook technology and teach them all to use a computer and the Internet."

"It's is a very ambitious and expensive project Brother Director," the subordinate member of BEL declared.

"You are correct. I have never mentioned this project to anyone before today. I must ask you to keep it confidential."

"My lips are sealed," Hadad promised leaning forward to touch the desk. "But why do you want to undertake such a large and complicated task?"

"It will be my legacy to our family. You may not realize it, but I'm twenty years your senior and in a year or two, I will be stepping down. The realization of this project would move the Brotherhood forward. It would help us attract new recruits going into the future."

"If you are showing me all this, I imagine you would like my assistance in some way?"

"Mustafa, I realize you are an assassin and not a thief. The two callings require very different temperaments and skill sets; however, we are not the only ones interested in this relic. I don't think a plain thief would be successful because he would very likely be killed by other forces seeking the relic for their own ends."

"But you think an assassin would survive and bring back the relic?" The tall muscular man concluded.

"I do, but let me explain. An unusual opportunity has come our way. One of my sources in Rome has informed me that the Catholic Church thinks a relic may have surfaced after being out of circulation for one hundred and fifty years. It has very strong powers associated with it when used in the proper circumstances by a person of knowledge. In fact, before it disappeared, it is rumored to have brought someone back from death. Now it has come to light again in Boston in the United States."

Mustafa stood up and walked over to the window. Out in the compound, he saw a Brother patching a crack in the outer wall. After watching for several minutes, the lean man with a close-trimmed salt and pepper beard turned back towards the desk.

"So do I Brother Director, but it will not be easy. The United States can be a hidden minefield."

"As always, you are not obliged to accept," the Director reminded him. "However, if you think it is something that would please you, a Priest flies from Rome next Monday, October 3rd at 2:15 pm on Alitalia flight

1030. His mission is to recover the relic. You will need a reservation on the same flight if you hope to connect with and follow him. Also, before boarding the plane; I would like you to deliver 5,000 euro to the friend in Rome who has informed us of this opportunity."

Mustafa smiled, gave a half salute and declared, "Consider it done!"

After his visitor left, the Director sat silent thinking. He never engaged in idle speculation or built castles in the sky. Everything was linked. Mustafa's acceptance had opened another door for him. He updated his plan in his head, looked at his watch, rose from his chair and slid the bookcase back. It took a few minutes, but soon he heard Dr. Ogland's voice coming from the speaker of his short wave receiver-transmitter.

Dr. Ogland was a Norwegian who joined the BEL about the same time as the Director. In fact, they did their initiation together. The former Director started a medical outpost clinic in eastern China, near the North Korean border. When the resident doctor passed on, Dr. Ogland consented to replace him. There was no pay or government support. The Brotherhood supplied everything.

"Hi Dag, it's good to hear your voice," the man in Lebanon commented. "How's life out in the rice paddies?"

"It could be better," the Norwegian sighed. "We experienced heavy rain and flooding several weeks ago. Now the mosquitoes have incubated. I've had a number of new cases of malaria originating from mosquito bites."

"Well, I have news for you. There is a very good chance we will soon be coming into possession of a significant source of funding." He went on to explain the possibilities the crucifixion relic offered to their community without revealing anything that anyone picking up their communication could use detrimentally against the Brotherhood.

The Director spoke directly into the microphone. "When the funding comes in, there are a dozen projects needing watering; however, your little clinic is near the top of the priorities list. No promises, but I'm going to try to get you an auxiliary diesel generator and a fully equipped field operating room."

Dag Ogland knew how the BEL operated and casually inquired, "Which brother is going to facilitate this prospect for us?"

"It's Brother Mustafa Hadad!" the Director replied with excitement. "I spoke with him during the past hour and he has accepted.

"I'll pray for him," Dr. Ogland replied. "We so desperately need an operating room."

**

In North Korea, the Worker's Party emphasizes Juche, a national ideology of self-reliance, as its fundamental ideology. It emerged from the Chairman's leadership. The regime justifies its dictatorship with arguments derived from concepts of collective consciousness, the superiority of the collective over the individual and appeals to nationalism, and citations of "the Juche idea." The core concept is the ability for North Korea to act independently without regard to outside interference.

Originally described as "a creative application of Marxism-Leninism" in the national context, Juche became a malleable philosophy reinterpreted from time to time by the regime as its ideological needs changed. It is used by the North Korean Worker's Party as a "spiritual" underpinning for its rule. All young communists undergo a Juche initiation and indoctrination when they enter the party. With some, it's simply another referential layer helping them relate to the group at large. Others, however, embrace it as a personal religion and seek out practical applications in their own life. Su Nam was one of these latter.

Su Nam was born and raised in Pyongyang, North Korea not long after the end of the previous Supreme Leader's rule. Her father died in a skirmish along the DMZ with South Korea. Her mother placed her in a collective nursery to be raised, while she went to work helping to feed the nation. The two women spent time together during holidays and during the monsoon season. The Chairman occupied a position akin to a spiritual father in Su's life. Her mother approved of this as she understood her daughter needed role models, in order to move up in the Party.

Su had been a member of the Workers' Party's Youth Wing. She studied hard. Because her father had died in the service of the Party, she was given consideration for university studies. Her application was finally approved when her mother fretted out and witnessed against an anti-social manager in her district who had committed crimes of selfishness against the collectivity.

After the establishment of North Korea, an education system modeled largely on that of the Soviet Union was implemented. It included primary and secondary divisions. Su had received a good education. At her mother's insistence, she studied English as her second language requirement in both primary and secondary school. At university, she did four years of Arabic as the language requirement for her degree. Today Su worked for the Party as a Strategic Analyst in the Capital City of Pyongyang. In addition, she had received Foreign Operative training. Some of her projects required her to go outside of North Korean.

One of her projects was the BEL medical clinic in China not far from the border with the North Korean province of North Hamgyong. Her superiors were curious to see if some foreign influence would use the clinic as a springboard to enter their country. She monitored all short wave communications with Lebanon and received 24/7 satellite scans of telecommunications into and out of the Director's office. As not much happened beside the treatment of the sick, clinic communications were mostly restricted to requests for supplies. Then all of a sudden everything changed.

Su picked up the words Crucifixion Relic in a scan of short wave communication from the Director's office and did some independent research. From the moment she understood what it was, she became convinced it was a must have for the Party. With it in their possession, they could keep leaders alive for centuries. She worked hard to prepare a report and recommended she be sent into the field to investigate.

Ms. Nam's superior, General Kam was impressed by her report. He sent for her as soon as he understood the significance for the Party. When this relic wasn't being used to keep their leaders alive, it could be used to extend his life, as well as the lives of other Party elite.

"So, Ms. Nam, how will you find this Mustafa if you were to go to the United States?" General Kam asked.

"I have a picture of the Priest retrieved from the Internet. If he and Mustafa arrive on the same plane, presumably Mustafa will stay close to him with the hope of either beating him to the relic or of stealing it, after the Priest finds it. All I must do is find the priest and Mustafa shouldn't be far behind. Then I'll follow Mustafa."

"How will you find the Priest?"

The only thing he knows is that everything happened at the Boston Medical Center. He has the name of a radiologist who signed off on the published research. If I was this priest, the first thing I would want to do would be to talk to the Doctor. I will ask our consulate to set up a surveillance net and find out whatever they can about Doctor Samuelson."

"This Hadad will quite likely be armed. I had research run a routine check on him. It seems he is wanted by Interpol for questioning in relation to incidents in several countries."

"I have weapons training Sir and I did procure a handgun to carry on a mission in Australia. When I arrive in the US, I will contact our organization to express my need for something small I can carry in a thigh holster."

"America is quite different from Australia. There are a million security cameras watching 24 hours a day. Only a small fraction are operated by the police. The rest are private and they see everything"

"I will be careful and won't take any foolish chances if you authorize the mission."

"I must confer with others higher up. You will have my answer before the end of the day. Do you have anything special to tell them?"

"Tell them the highest good the individual can do is perform the will of the People. I accept that they are best qualified to interpret the People's will."

The Committee approved the Mission. They acknowledged it would be a tall order to tell Su Nam she must return with the relic. They told her if she couldn't secure the object for North Korea, then she should do her utmost to make sure it didn't fall into the hands of BEL. The Committee didn't want them dispensing cures just north of their border in China. They also didn't want them to sell the relic and use the proceeds to reinforce and develop the clinic they were operating.

Within a day, Su Nam boarded a flight in Pyongyang. She was five foot three inches and wearing a mini check overcoat which had a zip in lining. Her dark hair was pulled back into a fold with a part in the center. Under the overcoat, she wore a white blouse which had a collar and a navy blue straight skirt. A black ribbon under the collar finished her neck off with a bow. She looked like a corporate employee on company business. After a complex multi-stop itinerary, she would land at Logan International Airport in Boston. In her purse was contact information for a commercial attaché who worked out of North Korea's office at the UN in New York.

**

Brian Robertson stood at the window of his office in the Berkley Building in Boston, looking out at the distant Charles River Basin. He was a tall, well-built man whose athletic body had not been used up by a life of toil. As the National Executive Director, of a successful not-for-profit, The American Handicap Society, he had a good life and wanted to keep everything as it was. The road to the top had been circuitous. From a humble start as a Special Ed Teacher in St. Paul Minnesota, he went to his first administration job as Program Coordinator for the New York Paraplegic Association and then onward through the Repertory Foundation, the Melanoma Society, and America for War Vets. He always kept his eye on the top and to achieve this end, his CV included a degree in management which had been purchased from an online university in the Midwest.

Lately, the American Handicap Society had run aground on financial shoals and was finding itself in the difficult position of having to function with reserves barely sufficient for six or seven months of operations. During the boom, the Society had expanded to thirty-two states and had a working staff consisting of twenty-five hundred people. The economy hadn't been strong for the last year or two and donations had dried up. Now the organization was faced with the prospect of some downsizing and though he hated to think about it, maybe even closures.

Brian looked at his watch impatiently. The National Director of Fund Development, Sharon Norris and he had a meeting at 2 pm. It was now five minutes to the hour. She was good at what she did and he liked her. They were a similar type of people. She had studied Marketing as an undergrad and then did a Masters in Philanthropy. She had also raised lots of money for a dozen organizations on her way to becoming National Director of the Society. Neither of them had a deep commitment to the handicapped. It was a job. What mattered was it paid well. Both wanted to keep their current positions unless they could serve as a stepping stone to something paying more.

However, they both had to watch out for the volunteer Board of Directors. They were people who came from society, the affluent. Most were what some would readily call, do-gooders. If Brian and Sharon were not able to keep the ship afloat, the Board would replace them, without any qualms of conscience.

At two o'clock sharp, there was a soft knock on the door. He called out, "Come in please!"

Sharon Harris was a tall, slim, good looking woman who had her shoulder-length brown hair streaked blond and dressed stylishly. Both she and the Executive Director were divorcees. Each had secretly flirted a little with, what-if, in their quiet moments; however, the demands of their jobs and their relationship with the Board never seemed to leave any personal time. Both were frequently on the road visiting one of the thirty-two state divisions or welcoming visitors to the Boston Headquarters.

Brian left the window and with an extended arm indicated one of the soft leather easy chairs in front of his desk, "Good to see you, Sharon. How was Denver?"

She smiled tightly and then replied, "It's the same everywhere, there's no money. Everyone is wondering if their job is on the line. I keep telling them Human Resources is not my department, except for regional and state level business development staff."

"I know, I get the same far and wide, but you didn't request to see me to discuss what we both know."

"No I didn't!" she replied quickly and moved forward to sit on the edge of the arm chair. "How much time do we have right now?"

"As much as we need," he replied seriously. "I wasn't exactly sure what you were coming to see me about, but you sounded serious, so I didn't schedule anything else this afternoon."

"Good," she exclaimed drawing in a deep breath, as she booted up her Notebook. "Have you ever heard of a Web site called Charity Chats.com?"

"No I haven't, but should I?" the sleek well-groomed executive inquired.

"It's one of several I try to monitor."

He sat down, put his fingers on the mouse resting on the blotter pad on his desk and said, "Let me bring up Charity Chats to start with. We'll both be on the same page."

"Look for Discussions along the top Menu Bar."

He clicked several times, confirmed he was there and inquired. "Is there anything I should be looking for?"

"Look for a discussion titled Miracles," she advised. "There were 139 entries in the thread the last time I looked."

"It's up to 147 now," he informed her.

"Okay, this discussion is new and for now, it's at the top of the heap. That's to say, this topic has been mentioned in at least five blogs, six other discussion groups, and probably a dozen Chat Places," she explained quickly, unfolding a sheet of paper, before sliding it towards him on the desktop. "These are the addresses to the blogs, discussions, and chats where it has been a topic in some form or another during the last two weeks."

He clicked on Miracles and the topic expanded downward on the screen showing a thread for the other 147 comments. "So what's it all about Sharon?"

"You'll have to read everything for yourself, but I can give you a brief summary."

"Yes please do!"

"To make a long story short, there was some sort of a mishap during the summer and someone suffered a spinal cord injury. It should have paralyzed them for the rest of their life. Then all of a sudden the injured person's spine was restored to normal. A Boston doctor wrote the incident up and it was put online, pending the next published quarterly review."

"At first the doctor's article caught the attention of the medical research community. Some of them commented on the restoration to normal. Some agreed with the doctor who wrote the article. He's in favor of calling this a case of post-traumatic-release or PTR; however, some of the medical scientists said it also looked like a miracle.

The miracle comments came to the attention of the non-medical community and a lot of people have been discussing this case online, all over the world. Lately, the tone of the discussions has changed dramatically. Many commenters' are now talking about a relic, in addition to a miracle. In the latest thread, at least a dozen posters are referring to the Boston Relic."

"What is it they're calling a relic," he asked keenly.

"I'll explain later, but first I want to get you up to speed."

"Okay!"

"All major Christian religions, except the Roman Catholic Church, have issued unofficial denials about having a relic in the Boston area. Now the charities and the not-for-profits have entered the fray. Everybody is hurting financially. They think the person or persons who have control of the Boston Relic should be obliged to turn it over to NPO's to help with fundraising."

"Now I've got it," Brian murmured, peering intensely at the computer monitor on his desk. "Nobody has really seen a relic but the restoration leads one to the conclusion that there must be one. Let's backtrack through some of these screens and those other sites you mentioned, so I can really wrap my mind around this."

He turned the monitor sideways so she could see and said, "Pull your seat up closer or I could get you a chair on this side of the desk."

"This arm chair is quite heavy," she admitted. "Perhaps I should come around to your side."

He rose and got her a chair from near the wall. As they surfed through the computer screens, they printed out anything which seemed like it might be important. It was four thirty when they began to feel satisfied he was in the loop on the Boston Relic. As he was clicking closed the last site on her list the Executive Director said, "I agree, if there is a relic, it should be used to raise money, at least for the American Handicap Society. The Catholics can't hog this all to themselves."

"They will only haul it off to Rome," she offered, feeling satisfied with herself. "Nobody will see or hear it talked about after that."

He stopped looking into the monitor and stared directly at her before saying, "We must get an injunction against the Catholics to stop them from carting the Boston Relic off to Rome."

"Yes, we must do something before it's too late," she agreed. "A relic would breathe new life into our Society. Just think of how much money rich people would donate for simple cures. It wouldn't be necessary to cut any programs. We could stop thinking about closures."

He leaned back in his swivel chair and exclaimed, "The Board would probably authorize raises or at least bonuses for both of us."

"Oh, I could so use a raise," she sighed. "I want to get a bigger place and get away from the southern exposure. The sun is just too strong."

"How would you like to continue this discussion over dinner?"

"Now there's an idea, I didn't take anything out this morning, but I should go home and feed my cat first."

"I feel like a shower too. Why don't I pick you up at six?"

"It's a deal," she accepted and then wrote her address and home telephone number on the sheet of paper with the Web site addresses she had given him. "Call me when you're outside and I'll come down."

Brian was happy that Sharon had accepted. He wasn't cut from the same cloth as her, but he tried hard. She had only been to State, but it was more than he had. Financial problems obliged him to go to a community college. After graduation, he began to work. Later he looked at part-time continuing education. Nobody knew and they wouldn't until he graduated. He was half way through a degree in Operations Management through distant learning. For now he made do with a degree in Management he had bought from a diploma mill in the mid-west.

***

Chapter 3

Boston Relic

Father Rafael Torres's plane came down at Terminal 1 at John F.
Kennedy International Airport on a Monday. Once he retrieved his bag
and cleared customs, he stopped at an Information Booth to ask a few
questions then made his way to the JFK AirTrain. There he boarded the
line going to Jamaica Station and transferred to the regular subway to
Penn Station in midtown Manhattan. Mustafa was inconspicuous but
never far behind. During the ride into the city, Rafa reviewed the
instructions given to him before leaving Rome.

Upon arrival at the commuting hub, he went to the Penn Station Chase
Bank branch, showed his passport and waited while the staff prepared
him credit and ATM cards to access the account the antique dealer in
Madrid had set up for him. When the banking was done, the Relicoligist
from Amalfi bought a ticket to Boston's South Station and went to a
waiting room until his train was announced on the public address system.
Mustafa also bought the same ticket but went to wait in the platform area.

It was a three and a half hour trip up to Boston. The scenery between the
two cities was engaging in places, but gradually the weariness of the
journey began to overwhelm him and he dozed off from time to time.
South Station, New England's second-largest transportation center after

Logan Airport is located at the intersection of Atlantic Avenue and Summer Street in Boston. It's the largest train and intercity bus terminal in Greater Boston. A nearby subway station offers connections to the Red and Silver Lines.

Before leaving the terminal, the incognito priest bought a domestic SIMS card for his smartphone. While he was paying the cashier, Mustafa stepped up behind him and quickly pushed a small object into the slot on the top of his travel case, where the extensible handle drops out of sight. It fell down between the interior and exterior lining of the bag.

Brother Hadad moved back from the kiosk and sat on a bench facing in the opposite direction. He removed his smartphone from his breast pocket and tapped on an app with his index finger. As Rafa began to walk towards the escalators, Mustafa watched the tiny red tracer on his phone screen move in the same direction. The tracking device he had dropped into the slot was working.

Rafa came up from the trains on an escalator into a triangular, glass structure built on the sidewalk. A line of yellow cabs were waiting, so he pulled his roller suitcase in their direction. The first driver came to meet him, and he passed the cabbie a sheet of paper, upon which were written the name and address of a hotel.

Mustafa waited for the cab to pull away and then instructed the next taxi driver to follow. When he judged sufficient time had passed for the Priest to clear the lobby, Brother Hadad left the sidewalk, entered the same hotel and also registered for a room. After leaving his coat, hat and suitcase in the room, he went exploring in the hotel with an app on his smartphone. It didn't take long to locate the room where the travel case and his tracking device were located. Its occupant had attached a Do Not Disturb to the outer knob. He probably won't wake up until the morning the Syrian thought, heading back to his room.

When Torres woke, he was disoriented. What the church wanted him to do was almost impossible. How could he hope to find an individual whose identity had remained hidden and who had probably reintegrated his regular personal life? Also, there was the language problem. He had studied English from tapes. The instructor had a heavy British accent. He felt comfortable in Europe with the accent, but not here.

America was very different from Europe. He was apprehensive. He couldn't understand a lot of what Americans were saying to him. From the look on their faces, he knew they too were wondering what he had said. For a brief moment, he wished he could zip up his things and go straight back to Italy, without even taking a shower. Then he decided to take a shower. Afterward, his frame of mind improved remarkably.

Mustafa had risen early and done his exercises. First came the squats, sit-ups and then leg stretches. These were followed by push-ups until he couldn't do another. The routine finished with ten minutes of running on the spot.

Breakfast service started being available at 6:30 am. He was one of the first to be served. After eating, he picked up a newspaper and found a secluded spot in the lobby, from which all could be seen. He waited for the little holy bunny to leave his burrow. It was almost 8:15 am when the Priest exited the elevator. Clergy are such lazy creatures he thought. They wouldn't have the energy required for the Brotherhood.

Father Torres took double scrambled eggs as they would stay in his stomach the longest. He was a bit late getting started, but he had a plan and knew exactly where he was going and what he was going to do. Before coming down he studied a large map of Boston and the suburbs and installed the new SIMS card. While he ate, he browsed the Maps app on his smartphone, using the hotel Wi-Fi. When his coffee was finished he knew where he was going and felt comfortable, except for one thing. He missed his white clerical collar.

Once on Tremont Street, he tapped the start button on the phone screen and began to listen to directions in Spanish through the bud in his ear. He turned left on Massachusetts Ave, continued as far as Albany Street. The directions in his ear stopped when he stood in front of the Menino Pavilion. Without hesitation, he entered the Emergency door and was intercepted by a security guard, "Would you please go to the Registration Desk, Sir?"

Outside the hospital, there were several short-term parking spots, for trades' people. A white utility van was parked in one of the stalls with its rear doors facing the Emergency Entrance. Greater Boston Steam Fitters was written on the sides with peel off lettering. The top half of each of the rear doors contained a black, one-way window.

Inside the van, two men stared at computer screens of images coming from the two cameras affixed to tripods and aimed out through the back windows. They had been parked only a short time. The men whispered together in low voices then one of them stopped and pointed at his screen. Immediately the other swiveled his camera so it too was focused on the same spot. They stopped the film, extracted several still photos and enlarged them, before comparing them to a photograph they had been given.

One of the men picked up his cell phone and called a speed dial number. Su Nam was drinking a cup of coffee at a nearby breakfast spot. They spoke in Korean, "We have him!"

"Excellent," she replied. "And do you see Mustafa?"

"No sign of him yet, but the Priest has entered the Emergency."

"The little hood will probably hang back somewhere. He wouldn't chance it to go in and then be spotted by the Priest at the same hotel where he is staying. One of you get out and walk around. Look for someone who appears to be passing time."

Sure enough, the Korean agent spotted the Syrian within a few minutes of exiting the vehicle and spoke into the microphone on the cord leading from his cell phone. "There's a fellow in a windbreaker and a peaked cap on the sidewalk, opposite the Ambulance Entrance, who seems to be waiting."

"Don't do anything suspicious," Su warned.

"He hasn't looked my way yet. I'm going to get back in."

"Good idea, I'll finish my coffee and cruise by. We won't know for sure until the Priest comes back out. If it's him, he'll follow."

"Then we'll get a picture of the thief who's following."

"Exactly!" she agreed. "We need a clear shot of him to send to the Mission in New York. They will forward it to Headquarters at home. He might be in our database." She was pleased with herself. She just knew the Priest would try to contact the Doctor who had published the research. It was what she had told General Kam back home, when he asked how she would find the Priest.

Inside the Emergency, Father Torres waited his turn at the Registration Desk.

"Yes Sir, how can I help you?"

"I was wondering if it would be possible to speak with Dr. Roger Samuelson."

"Do you have an appointment with Dr. Samuelson?"

"No, I haven't made one yet."

"I'm sorry Sir if you don't have an appointment, you'll have to make one. What exactly do you want to see the Doctor about?"

"It's about one of his patients."

"What is the patient's name?"

"It's about the patient he wrote up on the Internet, who had the miraculous recovery with his spine."

"I need the patient's name."

Rafa thought quickly and said, "Rafael Torres!"

The woman filled in the card then looked up, "And your name is?"

"Rafael Torres," he replied.

"I see," she affirmed, looking at him suspiciously. "And what was it you wanted to talk to the Doctor about."

"His article on the Internet about the man whose spine was miraculously cured," he repeated.

"I didn't read that one yet," she admitted with a little smile. "There are quite a few Doctors around here who write up their patients on the Internet. We don't have time to read them all. Just a moment while I call his Admin Assistant to see what might be available."

She put her hand over the receiver and declared, "She says normally Dr. Samuelson doesn't see people at the hospital, unless they are a patient, but since you are the gentleman he wrote up on the Internet, she thinks it might be okay. She can only schedule you a fifteen-minute appointment. It would have to be this Thursday at 4:45 pm."

"I'll take it," Rafael blurted out.

When he left the hospital Rafa was walking on air. He couldn't believe what had just happened actually did occur. He walked past Brother Hadad, who had his back turned towards him and didn't notice anything. The Koreans were watching. As soon as they saw Hadad begin to follow; they backed their van out of the parking spot and set off in pursuit. Both cameras were aimed at the sidewalk. They captured Mustafa from various angles as they passed the walking figure..

There are no diplomatic relations between the Democratic People's Republic of North Korea and the United States. In the DPRK, Americans use the Swedish Embassy. In the US, Koreans use their UN Mission in New York. Agent Kang from the Mission called Su within the hour, "I think you are going to need the device you requested, Miss Nam."

"Why, what did you find out?"

"His name is Mustafa Hadad. He's suspected of being an international assassin and is wanted for questioning in multiple jurisdictions for unsolved murders," the agent in NYC replied.

"I see, what is available here?" she pressed, with curiosity showing in her voice.

"We have a model that will be fine for you. It fits on the thigh like a garter belt."

"Sounds good" then after a short pause, "How will I get it?"

"Go to the Boston Common and make your way to the Central Burying Ground tomorrow morning at 10 am. Look for a Korean man wearing a green tie. When he is confident you have seen him, he will sit on a bench. Go sit beside him. When he departs, pick up the paper bag he will leave."

"Thank you," she said feeling homesick.

"I must request you don't contact me again, Miss Nam. Please erase any trace of this call from your cell phone as well as my number. Tourists don't usually have it. The boys in the van will follow the Priest and the other gentleman to their hotel and then text you the address. Once you have copied it, please erase any trace of conversations with them from your phone. Good luck Miss. Nam."

"Thank you, Agent Kang and goodbye!"

**

The Central Intelligence Agency (CIA) is an independent US Government agency responsible for providing national security intelligence to senior US policymakers. At times, it maintains a Boston field office, which is not publicized and is unmarked as with most organizations having no need to interact with the public. It is not uncommon for the Agency to have a close working relationship with local FBI, which also has an intelligence mandate. In Boston, the FBI is located in One Center Plaza, which is part of the massive Government Center complex on Cambridge Street in the Downtown core.

Senior FBI Agent Tom Reardon called the operatives meeting to order, "Alright gents, can we bring this meeting to order. I know you are all busy, and I won't keep you. Everyone has been given a briefing sheet with information on our current priority investigations. Two items aren't on the list. They arrived within the last half hour." He waited for quiet. "It seems two foreign agents came into Boston within the last 24 hours. Their names are Mustafa Hadad and Su Nam."

"Hadad is a Syrian national who works out of Lebanon. Interpol suspects him of being an international assassin. He should be considered dangerous and approached with caution. Nam is a North Korean. The Australians tipped us off when they had her under surveillance last year for low-level spying, while in their country. We don't have any information about why they're in Boston. For now, we're only making you aware of their presence. Here are their pictures."

**

Brian Robertson and Sharon Norris had requested a special meeting of the American Handicap Society's Board of Directors for Wednesday of that week. It was short notice and not all the directors could attend; however, there was a quorum, and so the two administrators had been able to deliver a presentation. Binders were distributed to each Director.

The information package contained copies of Doctor Roger Samuelson's article downloaded from the Internet as well as print outs from Chat sessions and Blogs, which discussed the report. The executives worked their way carefully through the material, explaining the relationship between the sections they had highlighted in yellow. At the end were a Summary and a Conclusion.

The winding up was abundantly clear. Robertson and Norris told the Board in their opinion, this relic would be particularly useful to the Society. It had the potential to solve many of the financial problems currently being experienced if cures could be sold. They urged the Directors to pass a Resolution recommending an Injunction be sought against Dr. Roger Samuelson and others to prevent them from transporting the relic outside of the United States and to initiate legal procedures to have the relic transferred to the Society for safe keeping and service on behalf of the people of the United States.

The Board was impressed by what the two had discovered and commended them for it. They were also interested in the financial possibilities control of the relic would bring. As for the Resolution, it would take the full Board and only after a detailed discussion by all the Directors. The Chairman said they would take the matter under consideration and would get back to them should a majority decide to move forward.

Rafael Torres sat in a lounge area at the Boston Medical Center on Thursday afternoon waiting for his meeting with Dr. Roger Samuelson. The doctor didn't know the name Torres and his assistant hadn't found the name in their records. He decided to speak with the man in the waiting room to see what he wanted.

The waiting area was large with banks of blue, leatherette seats set facing all four directions. A flat panel monitor was attached to each wall on which the News was showing. Instead of sound, a horizontal scrolling marque contained subtitles explaining the broadcast. Rafa didn't have any experience with hospital waiting rooms and was fully engaged in people watching.

At exactly 4:45 pm a tall thin man with thick, long white hair pushed back behind his ears and wearing a white hospital coat over a black shirt, tie and charcoal slacks appeared in the area and called out, "Mr. Torres!"

Rafa stood up declaring, "I am Mr. Torres!"

Doctor Samuelson walked over and sat down beside him. "Good afternoon Mr. Torres, my assistant seems to think you are a former patient, but I don't recognize you."

"She was confused by my English Doctor. I am not a former patient, but I want to talk to you about one of your patients."

"Which patient are you referring to?" the medical man asked seriously, already seeming to appear suspicious.

"The one whom you wrote about recently on the Internet whose spine was miraculously restored after being damaged by the intrusion of the piece of metal."

"What exactly do you want to know about this case?"

"I would like to know the patient's name."

"Why would you want such information?"

"It's a long story, but to make it short, I am a member of the Catholic Church. Some in the Church believe this man came in contact with a relic and this contact restored his spine."

"Are you a Priest?"

"Yes!"

"I don't want to be disrespectful Father, but I don't believe in miracles or relics. In addition, this is not the first time such an option has been suggested to me. As I understand it, the Catholic Church has already long since condemned the use of relics as a means of cure, given the number of scams and abuses that have occurred in the past."

The Priest became serious, "What you say is entirely true Doctor, but in order to prevent these scams and abuses as you say, we must investigate reports of unexplainable happenings such as described in your article."

"I made it exceedingly clear in the write-up. This was a case of a post-traumatic-release or PTR. I supported my hypothesis with at least five arguments. In addition, it is absolutely impossible for me to discuss the identity of the patient involved. First, he could sue me and the hospital for breach of privacy and doctor/hospital confidentiality. In addition, before he would agree to let me use his case for the article, I had to sign a standard medical declaration stating he would remain anonymous. He has a copy of the Form."

"I see Doctor, are there no exceptions?"

"That's your fifteen minutes Father Torres. I must ask you not to try to contact me again on this issue or I will be obliged to report it to the hospital authorities."

When Rafa arrived back at his hotel, he felt depressed. How could he find the individual if the doctor wouldn't give him his name? Quickly he calculated the time he thought it should be in Madrid on his fingers. Madrid was six hours ahead of Boston. It would be midnight. The antique dealer wouldn't be at his shop. He would have to wait until the morning.

Mustafa had seen Torres go back to the hospital. He was starting to have a little more respect for the man because he didn't use a taxi. He also liked to walk. The FBI had seen Hadad and Nam hovering about the BMC during the latter part of Thursday afternoon. What they were up to was still a mystery for the Bureau.

After breakfast on Friday morning, Rafa used his international calling card to contact Madrid. At first, the antique dealer refused to cooperate. He was a Madrilenos and as such spoke a pure form of Castilian Spanish.

The man recognized that Rafa was not from Madrid by his accent. Their accent is one of the clearest and they speak with few idiosyncrasies. One of the most common oddities found in Madrid Spanish was a tendency to pronounce the final 'd' in a word as a Spanish 'z'. He kept putting on airs and talking down to the caller, but the man of God persisted and finally convinced the merchant of his identity. He gave the connection in Madrid a message to pass on, concerning his meeting with Dr. Samuelson. Then it was his turn to be surprised.

"I too have a message for you, Father Torres." The aristocratic voice on the other end of the line declared.

"A message for me," he exclaimed, "from whom?"

"The Vatican!" the antique dealer replied.

"What is it?" Father Torres exclaimed, secretly hoping he was being called back.

The man in Spain whispered, "It seems you are not the only person in Boston who is trying to find the Relic. A sister of the Society of the Sacred Heart in Scotland, who is an amateur Relicoligists and who has also, specialized in the Crucifixion Relic is there. Her Mother Superior notified Rome. The nun has been given permission to transfer to their House in Boston where, in addition to performing duties assigned by the local congregation, she will be able to pursue her theories on the Relic."

"Why are you whispering?" Father Torres demanded.

"My dear fellow," the Castilian laughed. "I'm not whispering. You are imagining things.

"Is that all?" the Priest enquired politely.

"You are authorized to contact her if you think it might help you."

The Society of the Sacred Heart is an international community of women in the Catholic Church, founded by a rich woman. Her desire was to ease the pain and division of this world by helping others to find the love of

God. She chose to do this primarily through education and spirituality. Today there are 2,600 religious, available in 45 countries around the world. Three hundred and thirty-one of them are located in the United States.

Rafa didn't want to annoy the man so drew him out incrementally. "Do you have any idea how I would contact her, should the need arise?"

"I was told she will be teaching at a primary school called Sacred Heart," the Madrilenos replied brusquely then softened. "Her Order must have a mother house of some sort there."

"You have been very helpful Senior Ruiz," Torres said in Spanish, "and I thank you for the message." As he hung up, Rafa began wondering if there was also a Sacred Heart church and thinking about attending Mass there if one existed, on Sunday. He needed to find a listing for the Archdiocese of Boston. There might be more than one Sacred Heart in the city.

An Internet Search on his Notebook returned thirteen Sacred Heart parishes in the Archdioceses of Boston. Four of them were located in the Central District, and only one of them had a primary school attached to the parish. It was located in Roslindale.

Roslindale is a residential neighborhood in Boston's western suburbs, bordered by Jamaica Plain and Hyde Park. Rafa decided to go to the noon Mass on Sunday. During the week, he took a practice run to learn his way around and find the church.

To his surprise, Sunday Mass was in Spanish. Without his collar, Father Rafa looked like everybody else. At the end of the ceremony, the Priest who had performed the Mass, went outside to shake hands with those who had attended.

Torres waited his turn then went over and introduced himself. The Parish Priest, Father Gomez was thrilled someone from so far away was attending his church. He invited Rafa to come to lunch. During the meal, the visitor worked the conversation around to the parish school and its staff. Father Gomez said the nuns who taught in the school lived in a house not far away. He agreed to call the Superior to enquire whether Sister from Scotland was staying there. As luck would have it, there was a Sister Angela Stuart living there who was from Scotland.

At 2 pm, Rafa Torres climbed the six steps up onto the wide veranda of a three level green shingle house in the Village of Roslindale and pressed gently, on the doorbell. The nun who answered was wearing the traditional habit.

"Good afternoon Sister, my name is Rafa Torres. I've come to see Sister Angela Stuart."

"I'm Sister Angela Stuart," the nun declared. "How may I help you?"

"It's rather complicated Sister. Is there some place where we could talk? There's something I'd like to discuss with you."

"Won't you please come in?"

Torres followed her into the living room, where another nun was reading and then on through to the kitchen, where she offered him a chair. Rafa came straight to the point.

"First I should tell you that I'm a Priest. I'm just not wearing my collar today."

"Sometimes I go into the city not wearing my habit," she informed him hoping it would make him feel more comfortable. "Now then there was something you wished to discuss with me?"

"I think you and I are in America on the same mission."

"Mission!" she repeated with puzzlement, "What mission?"

"I have been sent to Boston to look for the Crucifixion Relic. This week my superiors in Rome notified me that the Mother Superior of your Order in Edinburgh had informed them that one of her nuns had transferred to a teaching position in Boston with the hope of finding some clue to the Crucifixion Relic."

At this point, she recognized his name and confessed, "I've read most of the postings on your Blog that were in English."

He laughed and relaxed as did she.

"It's a small world, isn't it Father, and would you like to have a cup of tea and perhaps a snack?"

"I will accept a cup of tea Sister, but I must apologize, I had lunch with Father Gomez at the parish church and am rather full."

They chatted away for half an hour as if they had known each for a long time. The Crucifixion Relic was the main topic of their conversation. Then finally it was time to leave.

"We must communicate and exchange any information which would be mutually beneficial," she prompted as she picked up their cups and placed them on the kitchen counter.

"Yes, yes, I agree," the Priest replied.

"Here is my telephone number here at the house," Sister Angela obliged, passing him a slip of paper.

He responded by asking her to pass him the pad and pencil and after quickly writing on the paper, removed the top sheet and said, "Here is the address and telephone number of the hotel where he was staying. As well, I've added my cell number after the hotel information."

Following this, there wasn't much more for them to say. She walked with him to the door and out onto the veranda, where they shook hands before he turned and left.

Su Nam had followed the priest to the church and then to the parish house, where he had been invited for lunch. Afterward, she found a secluded spot not far up the street and kept a constant watch on the nun's residence. When she saw the two religious shaking hands as the Priest was leaving, the North Korean surmised they were not relatives or they certainly would have given each other a quick hug.

She had a picture of the Nun who shook his hand and would have a better look at her later when the file was transferred from the camera to her Notebook. She hadn't seen Mustafa anywhere today. He must have decided not to follow, supposing the Priest only went out to attend Sunday services some place.

***

Chapter 04

The Albatross

Massachusetts State Police officers didn't waste the information they obtained from Carney O'Sullivan during their hospital visit. The shooting victim recalled a light charcoal colored sedan with ample grill, idling in the intersection opposite him. The troopers had been back to see the young man with pictures from different angles of about a dozen vehicles. Carney didn't make a positive identification, but he did narrow the field to four possibilities.

The Commonwealth of Massachusetts is divided into 11 State Police detective units operating from various district attorneys' offices. Boston, Springfield, and Worcester are the only cities in the Commonwealth having the right to investigate attempted or confirmed homicides. Sargent Gordon Nash and Corporal David Craven were both veterans of the force. They were adept at what they did. Both men were firm believers in the power of investigative procedures.

Nash had gone into the Navy Seals straight out of high school and Craven had been a Marine. Back on Civilian Street, their military service was of particular interest to the State Police who offered a salary while at the Police Academy. Their early careers were spent in the smaller divisions around Massachusetts. Now they were the front line in Boston.

After Carney picked out 4 vehicles from those the troopers showed him on a tablet, while he was still in the hospital bed; they had gone to see the young man's father. The visit confirmed their suspicions. His son had been the victim of an act based on mistaken identity. Nash and Craven were of the opinion a second attempt would be made if the hit men wanted to get paid.

The two policemen didn't hide their suspicions from Arthur. He was going to have to be extra vigilant until they came up with a way to ID the perpetrators. The officers gave Arthur their card. If he or the private security company he employed noticed anything, they were to be advised immediately.

The call came several weeks after Carney was released from the hospital. Arthur had been to see his insurance agent that afternoon. He was driving along State Street, in Downtown Boston watching for Devonshire, where he intended to turn left. The unmarked private security car was visible in his rear view mirror. Art signaled to declare his intention to enter the flow of one-way traffic on Devonshire and made the turn. A quick check in the left side mirror revealed his security vehicle right behind him. While still looking into the mirror, he noticed a car drive through the yellow light and pull in hastily behind the security company vehicle.

Arthur had forgotten nothing the State Police had told him. The car that had run the yellow traffic signal was a light charcoal color. A moment later he caught a better glimpse of it. It was a sedan with lots of grills on the front. Arthur reached for his cell phone, pressed speed dial and then the #1, which was where he had keyed in the State Troopers phone number from the business card they gave him. It rang several times and then a clear, crisp voice answered, "Sargent Nash, may I help you?"

"Sargent, this is Arthur O'Sullivan. It was my boy who was accidentally shot in Nantasket, over the 4th of July long weekend. You were one of the investigating officers, and gave me your card."

"I remember you, Mr. O'Sullivan. How can I be of service this afternoon?"

"I'm not sure. I'm driving in Downtown Boston, heading in the general direction of my home at Harbor Point. I've just noticed a light charcoal colored sedan with a lot of radiator grills run a yellow light, two cars behind me. For some reason, I have a feeling it's following me."

"Is your security with you this afternoon?"

"Yes, the company's car is between me and the light gray sedan."

"Can you patch the driver in on this call?"

"I don't know if I can manage something like that while I'm driving."

"If you can give me his number, I can patch him in from here."

"Wait a sec, I have it written on the sun visor. It's (617) 864-3520."

They could hear the dialing, and then a young man's voice answered, "Hello, who is calling?"

"Mike, it's me, Arthur. I'm just in front of you."

"I know I can see you, Art, what's up?"

"Mike, we're on a conference call with the State Police."

"Hi Mike, I'm Sargent Gordon Nash."

"What's this all about Sargent Nash?"

"Arthur thinks there might be a car tailing him. We advised him to be on the lookout for it."

"Which car are we referring to Sir?"

"The light gray one, directly behind you," Nash declared.

"Okay, I see it now. What are we going to do?"

"We don't want to make them suspicious."

"I understand. I am carrying an arm and I'm authorized to use lethal force to protect Mr. O'Sullivan."

"Let's hope it doesn't come down to that," the Trooper replied. "There are too many non-related third parties in the downtown area. I'm going to see if I can get the Boston Blues to pull over Arthur."

"Arthur, what's your intersection? Which route are you taking home to South Boston?" Nash asked.

"I'm at Devonshire and Water, where the huge US Post Office building is located."

"Ok," the State Policemen affirmed. "I'm going to switch over to another line now and call the Boston Police Department. Don't either of you hang up."

The call took about four minutes and then Nash was back. "Okay, Mr. O'Sullivan, I've talked to the Department. "A regular City Police officer is going to pull you over when you turn left onto Summer Street because you didn't have your turn signal on."

"My turn signal," the old man repeated.

"Yes Arthur, your turn signal," he repeated. "It's a traffic violation, and you're going to be pulled over. Your security car and the light charcoal colored sedan will be waved through. The officers on the street will get the plate number of the suspect vehicle so we can get a better ID. We'd also appreciate it, Mike, if you stay with the sedan as long as possible."

"You can count on me," Mike exclaimed.

"Arthur, two plain clothes detectives in an unmarked car will escort you home, and you won't really be receiving a ticket."

"Thank you, Mr. Nash," Arthur replied.

As Arthur was turning left onto Summer Street, he suddenly switched lanes, without giving any turn signal. Two Boston Policemen stepped onto the roadway from the sidewalk. One motioned for him to pull over while the other kept traffic moving. The occupants of the sedan watched what was happening as they drove past. "Stupid old goof," the passenger commented. "He didn't even use his turn signal. They're always watching on turns like this."

Mike stayed a little under the speed limit and eventually the car behind, pulled out and passed him. He followed from a reasonable distance. Ultimately, it ended up in Chinatown and pulled into an alley between two buildings. Mike didn't stop but noted the address of the buildings on either side of the alley.

Both the City and State Police staked out the back-lane for several days. The driver and his partner came and went, in the vehicle and on foot to connect with others in nearby restaurants. It didn't take long for the Police to determine the layout of the building and the rooms where the pair was lodged. Once they had the apartment number, there was enough detailed information for a Judge to authorize a Search Warrant for the premises.

Nash and Craven waited until they saw the two men leave together in the light gray sedan. Then they entered the three level apartment building and mounted the central staircase to the top floor. They were quite sure no one was in the unit but they knocked anyway. After a short wait, Nash opened the lock with one of the dozen master keys he carried on a ring.

"Hello, anybody home?" Craven called out as they entered with revolvers drawn. Then he opened the hall closet while his partner moved along to the living room. There was nothing there so Nash advanced to the kitchen where he opened a broom closet and found a gym bag. David was just entering the kitchen when Gordon sang out, "Bingo, Bingo Baby!"

"What did you find?" David asked with excitement.

Sargent Nash pulled out a sawed-off shotgun, cocked it and exclaimed, "It's loaded!" Then he removed a machine gun.

"That looks like a Heckler & Koch," Corporal Craven cooed.

"You are correct my man. The Gent knows his machine guns." Nash congratulated and added, "It's loaded too."

When they were finished in the kitchen they moved back to the hall. There were two bedrooms. "David, you take the one on the right and I'll take the left," Gordon declared.

"Will do, Sarg!" the junior trooper replied.

Five minutes later they were back looking at each other in the hallway. Corporal Craven held up an arm and a bundle of $100 bills. "What is it," his superior questioned?

"I would say we have a 9 mm Luger semi-automatic pistol with one round in the chamber and five thousand dollars."

"Where did you find it?"

"Under the bed," Craven replied.

"I looked there but there was nothing."

"Did you check the drawer?"

"What drawer?"

"There's a drawer fitted with the box spring near the head of the bed."

In less than sixty seconds his partner returned smiling. "Now I've got a 9 mm Luger semi-automatic pistol with one round in the chamber and a bundle of $100 bills which I will hazard a guess is also five thousand dollars."

Ballistics matched a bullet from the machine gun to bullets found in Arthur's old Jaguar.

Soon after the pair of illegal Columbian's were arrested, preliminary charges were laid. During the ensuing questioning, it was learned they were only hired hands. They were in it for the money. In exchange for being allowed to plead guilty to a lesser degree of crime, they agreed to cooperate.

Nash walked up to the interrogation table where they were hand cuffed to a metal bar extending the length of the wooden surface. "Okay boys, we have a procedure to take care of here. It protects us and it protects you. I'm going to read this declaration to you. If you agree, say so and sign above your name." The Columbians nodded their heads in the affirmative. "Do you Juan Carlos Lopez and you Andres Felipe Rojas agree the assistance you are about to give the FBI was obtained from you voluntarily and at no time was there a threat of violence or coercion? Please reply out loud."

"Yes, no threat," Juan Carlos and Andres Felipe replied together. "We agree, no violence."

Corporal Craven came forward with a pen and they both signed and then repeated. We don't know the man in the Jaguar. It was only a job."

"Who hired you," David asked immediately.

"We don't know his name," Juan Carlos replied.

"Well, how did you get in touch with him if you didn't know him?" Craven continued.

"We were in a restaurant where guys from Columbia hang out. A guy walked in and asked out loud, 'Anyone here want to make a few bucks roughing a guy up'? I put up my hand. He came over and sat down." Andres Felipe explained.

"He wanted to know if we had wheels," Juan Carlos continued. "Then he said we might need guns and we said we both had a rod. Then came the real clinker!"

"Yeah, the real clinker," Andres Felipe exclaimed. "We had to go down to Atlantic City to meet the Dude.

"Good thing I just had the tires changed on my machine," Juan Carlos declared. "Or we might not have got the deal.

"Okay, let's skip all the small stuff," Sargent Nash suggested. "So you're in Atlantic City, you know how to find Mr. X and obviously you found him cus both of you had a lot of hundred dollar bills at the apartment. Did you get his name?"

"No officer, we didn't get his name. We got O'Sullivan's name, his address, make of car and the plate number along with half the money we were being paid for the hit."

"Do you remember what Mr. X looked like?"

"Oh yeah, we remember what he looked like."

"That's wonderful boys, exactly what I wanted to hear," Gordon laughed. "Juan Carlos you are going to come with me," he said unlocking the man's hand cuffs. "We're going to go to a Police artist down the hall and you're going to help him prepare a sketch of Mr. X. Andres Felipe is going to stay here with Corporal Craven and another artist. If we get close to the same portrait from each of you, we've got a deal."

Individually they did help police portrait artists who prepared two sketches that were quite similar to each other. Arthur was advised of the arrests and the charges. The trial date wouldn't occur for several months. Both he and his son would be called as material witnesses. They would be asked to identify the sedan. They asked the older man to have a chat with his son so he wouldn't be surprised when the Notice to Appear was served.

**

When Art and Louise O'Sullivan sold their family home on Columbia Road near Pleasant Bay in South Boston, they didn't move far. In fact, their new home was only a short hop down the beach at Harbor Point, where the campus of the University of Massachusetts – Boston was located. Two high-end residential complexes were built on the water, between sections of the campus. It was a strategy that helped reduce the cost of the land for the University.

Electronic authorization cards were required to raise barriers giving access to the suburban streets. Private security controlled the entire area 24 hours a day. It was one of the expenses built into the common area condo fees.

The O'Sullivan's lived in a two story residence with all windows giving a view of the seashore and Bay. There were no balconies on their building. Their unit had two bedrooms, a den, and bathroom on the upper floor. There was a normal sized kitchen, dining room, living room, office and bathroom on the main level. It was slightly compressed after living thirty years in a three-story, sprawling, five bedroom house, but the two of them were happy. They spent quite a bit of time at their compound on Nantasket Beach, during the summer.

The O'Sullivan's invited two of their sons and their families for Sunday evening dinner the week after they received the news of the arrests of the Columbian hired killers. Carney sat on one side and his older brother Jonathan and his wife Roberta were seated opposite him. Jonathan was an attorney with the District Attorney's office in Boston and Roberta, who had studied Civil Engineering, bought, renovated and sold houses in and around the city, through her own firm. Their three children Sandy, Paul, and Charlotte sat at the kitchen table with Carney's daughter Dakota.

During the meal, Art told his son's about the incident with the sedan and how the Police had found the machine gun. Jonathan knew right away both his father and brother would have to act as witnesses and told them so. His father thanked him for his knowledge and then asked the youngest boy if he understood what his brother had said. Carney looked towards the kitchen. Dakota wasn't watching, so he asked, "Does it mean I'm going to have to testify in Court?"

"Only to identify the vehicle you saw stopped on the other side of the intersection before the incident," his father declared. "It's the same for me. I'm only there to identify the car I saw bolt through a yellow traffic light and begin to follow me on Devonshire."

"It's standard procedure," Jonathan beamed. "The Police must show everything leading up to the issuance of the Search Warrant so the Judge won't think they went on a fishing trip and just happened to turn up a machine gun that fits a crime."

Carney assured them there wouldn't be any problem. He asked them not to say anything to their children as he hadn't told Dakota what had happened. After her mother's death in the traffic accident, the girl lost her voice for three months and had nightmares for at least six months. She was happy now and had transferred mummy to him. He didn't need any relapse.

**

The Directors of the American Handicap Society held their meeting as requested by Brian Robertson and they were favorable.

I know a gift horse when I see one," Director Dr. Louie Tang declared. "Even if the relic story turns out to be a hoax, trying to save an artifact like that for Americans would be excellent publicity for the Society."

"Hopefully, donors will reward our patriotism and be generous during the upcoming, direct-mail fundraising campaign," Director Cedric Goldberg trumpeted.

"Then it's a unanimous decision," Dr. Tang concluded. "This Board authorizes national executive, Brian Robertson to do whatever is necessary to protect the relic for our Society and the American people."

Director Goldberg added to this. "In addition, let's appoint Sharon Norris as Brian's Special Assistant for the duration of the project." All raised hands meant it was confirmed.

In private Cedric Goldberg assured both executives, "there will be a significant reward for you if the Society's acquiring the Relic proves to have a positive effect on the funding campaign."

The team did not waste any time after receiving approval from the Board. They contacted the Society's attorney who handled the necessary procedures with Civil Court. Within a day, the Trial Court of Massachusetts, Superior Court Department held an ex parte special hearing on the application for an Injunction. Judge Donald Benson declared,

"I'm issuing a Temporary Injunction ordering the "Boston Relic" not be transported outside the Commonwealth of Massachusetts. It is to be brought to the Court Registry as soon as possible." Then he completed his judgment, "Doctor Roger Samuelson is directed to appear in three days' time in Superior Court for the continued hearing on a permanent Injunction concerning the "Boston Relic"."

Doctor Roger Samuelson appeared after receiving the Subpoena. "Your honor, I must beg doctor-patient confidentiality."

Judge Benson was ready and replied, "If I might remind the good Doctor how close to contempt of Court he is". Finally, Samuelson relented and told the Court Officer the name of the patient in the research he had posted on the Internet. The Doctor was asked to appear in three days' time, for a continuance. Then the Judge made it final, "Officer, please also issue a Subpoena for Carney O'Sullivan, ordering him to appear at the same time."

At the continuance both Dr. Samuelson and Carney were present. Under oath they swore, "We have no knowledge of a "Boston Relic" and we have never been party to any miracles."

The Judge issued a Permanent Injunction against Dr. Samuelson and Carney O'Sullivan not to take the "Boston Relic" outside the Commonwealth of Massachusetts and to deposit it with the Court Registry, as soon as possible.

That evening, Sister Angela Stuart, sat at the kitchen table after dinner reading the Boston Globe. It had been her habit to follow the Legal News in Edinburgh. Mention of the Injunction and the parties involved appeared on page fifty-six of the Globe. Two words, "Boston Relic" caught her attention, and she read the Notice.

The following morning before leaving for school, she phoned the hotel number her visitor had given her and asked for room 1900. The Desk asked her the name of the guest in room 1900. The phone rang three times and then was answered.

"Good morning, this is Rafael Torres speaking."

"Good morning Father Torres, I am Sister Angela Stuart," she declared shyly. "You visited me several Sunday's ago."

"Oh yes Sister, I recall. How may I help you?"

"Father I'm phoning to tell you about something I noticed in yesterday's newspaper, the Boston Globe," she explained hesitantly.

"Yes Sister, what did you spot?"

She hoped she was doing the right thing. "Father there was mention of a "Boston Relic".

"A Boston Relic," the voice on the other end of the line repeated.

"Yes Father, and there was also mention of that Dr. Samuelson, who wrote on the Internet."

"On what page did you read this, Sister," the priest asked with excitement?

"It was on page 56, the very last item mentioned in the Legal News, in the Globe."

"Just a moment Sister, I'm writing this down."

"And Father," she continued. "I must hang up now and go to teach the children."

"Thank you, Sister, I'll call you if I learn anything.

"Thank you, Father! I say goodbye for now," she replied with a thick Scots accent.

"Just one second Sister, do you have email?

"Yes, I have an email account. There's a computer here at the house and several at school."

"Send me an email. I wrote my email address on the back of the card I gave you. Then I'll have your email address too," the priest asked.

"I'll do that the first chance I have Father. Have a wonderful day!"

**

Rafa quickly glanced over at the bedside table. It was 7:45 am and he hadn't eaten breakfast yet. The priest pulled on a short sleeve polo shirt, jeans and running shoes then went straight down to the main lobby. There were no newspapers on the tables. Then he spotted Mustafa sitting in a high back armchair in a corner by a pillar. He was reading a paper. The restless Spaniard wondered if it was yesterday's edition.

He approached the man from Lebanon at a brisk trot. Brother Hadad wondered if his game was up. Mentally he prepared himself for the worst, lowered the paper and folded it on his knee.

"Excuse me, Sir," the Relicoligist blurted out across the narrowing space between them.

"Me," the seated man exclaimed pointing at his chest with an index finger.

"Yes," Torres responded and then asked, "Are you reading yesterday's paper?"

"Oh, sorry friend," Mustafa replied, feeling his body's adrenaline seeping back away from his muscles. "This is today's edition. You might try the Registration Desk."

The priest stopped in mid-stride, didn't add another word then turned towards the hotel Registration Desk. When he arrived in front of the large marble topped counter, he quickly asked the clerk who was completing vacancy reports, "May I have a copy of yesterday's Boston Globe, please."

"I'm sorry Sir," the attractive woman replied. "We don't have any available. Your best chance to get a yesterday's anything is to ask one of the cleaning staff. They start their rounds at 8:30 am. They might have a discarded paper on their cart."

He went into the hotel dining room. After filling a paper cup with coffee and putting two Danish on a paper plate at the buffet, he headed back towards his room. While waiting for the elevator, he looked back towards the corner near the pillar. The man with the paper was gone.

At 9:30 there was a light knock on his door. One of the blue smocked maids held out a paper for him.

"Oh Senorita, a thousand thanks!" he said hurriedly pressing a dollar into her hand.

"Not at all, Senor!" the woman replied and then immediately left.

It didn't take long to find the Legal Notice. Then he laughed out loud, "Ah Doctor Samuelson, it is you." He couldn't believe how this man had humiliated him at the hospital. Now he had learned the patient's name anyway. Father Torres stopped, stood still and blessed himself while whispering in Latin, "Deo Gratias!"

There was more. "Who is this American Handicap Society?" the Priest wondered out loud. "Who are Brian Robertson and Sharon Norris?"

Most of all, he wanted to understand what was an Injunction? He turned on his Notebook and went to a Translate site. It didn't take long to discover the legal terminology meant *mandato* in Spanish. Then he understood.

Now he had to find out whom this Carney O'Sullivan was. He remembered how his surprise call on Dr. Samuelson had ended and didn't want a repeat that experience. For the next few minutes, he ran Internet Searches. The name came up several times.

A Carney O'Sullivan had been the victim of a drive-by shooting in July. Another was the President of a company called Seahorse Marine in East Boston and another lived on Jamaicaway, not far from where Sister Angela lived.

Using the Maps app on his smartphone, he quickly located the address in East Boston and then switched back to the computer where he saw that MBTA's Blue Line ran through the neighborhood. There was a Station at Maverick Square, near the street he wanted.

Unbeknown to Rafael Torres, Mustafa Hadad had visited his hotel room while he was out. Mustafa carried a hotel flash card with embedded sensors, which plugged into his smartphone. An app activated a scan of the door lock and synchronized the code on the card so that the door unlocked. The key card device had been purchased at a Spy Shop in Bonn, while on another mission.

All he found were brochures about antiques in the Priest's room. There was nothing on the Notebook but pictures of antiques. While he was there, Hadad installed a small, wireless camera in the room and tested it with his smartphone before leaving. The camera was motion-sensitive, so the battery would last longer. When he returned to his room, the camera also worked with his Notebook.

Mustafa watched Torres talking on the phone. Then the priest looked up something on the computer, before starting to put on his outdoor clothes. Hadad also quickly readied himself and exited his room. That morning he followed his quarry into the underground trains and finally came up in Maverick Square, in East Boston.

It wasn't hard for Rafa to find Marginal St. with Spanish audio instructions coming from the blue tooth bud in his ear. Soon he was standing in Piers Park. Seahorse Marine was located beside the Park. It was a sizable manufacturing company with a dock at the rear and a huge motorized sling to lift boats in and out of the water.

He counted twenty-four cars in the parking lot. Only five spaces had reserved signs stuck into the ground at the grass line. The license plate numbers of the vehicles occupying these spaces were duly keyed into his phone. His Lebanese shadow didn't see him do this, but the North Korean did.

Hadad couldn't figure out what was going on but did try to speculate. This location was close to Logan Airport. Perhaps the airport figures into the plan? Maybe they are going to bring the relic here and ship it out on a plane?

Torres stayed at the boat shop approximately ten minutes and then headed back to the train. Once on the Downtown Boston side of the Harbor, he left the subway and made his way on foot to Faneuil Hall Marketplace. No purchases were made. Both shadows came to the same conclusion independently. This was a tourist stop. When he left the complex, the Relicoligist headed in the direction of the hotel. Mustafa saw him go in and decided to go down the street and have his hair trimmed. Nam also surmised the day was over. She went into the Car Park, across the street, to retrieve her car.

Rafa got as far as the elevator and then looked at the Lobby clock while waiting for the cage to arrive. It was 4:00 pm. There was still some time left in the day, he thought. I might be able to get out to Jamaicaway and take a look around, before dark. The elevator door opened. He turned and walked back towards the hotel entrance. Su Nam was leaving the Parkade when she saw the Priest walking down Franklin Street towards her.

There wasn't time to go back into the Car Park, so she pulled in at an empty parking meter and waited until Torres had walked past her car. Then she got out and used a smart phone app to set the maximum time permitted on the meter. Her mark was about half a block ahead when she settled into a steady step behind him. He made his way to the next MBTA Subway and went in.

This time he boarded a train on the Green Line and went as far as Health Station, which was the last stop on the city's western perimeter. Outside he took the first of several waiting cabs and handed the driver a slip of paper. "Take me to the closest intersection to this address please," he added.

At 5:45 pm the taxi let him off. He began to walk south on Jamaicaway. It was getting dark, but Jamaica Pond could be plainly seen on the other side of the street. The Pond was actually a sizable lake, located in this western suburb of Boston. The house he was looking for turned out to be situated on a corner with a hedge running along both streets. A vehicle was parked at the end of the driveway near a garage.

He had to check the plate number on the vehicle with the list on his phone. Hopefully, there was no dog. What would he say if someone came out? Thinking quickly, he would say he was looking for the house number.

Su saw him disappear up the driveway. She couldn't figure out why he was going into that yard. How could he know those people, she wondered? She didn't see him check the license plate number of the crossover parked beside the garage with the list from the reserved parking spaces at Seahorse Marine in East Boston.

**

Rafael Torres received an email from Sister Stuart when he logged on next. It wasn't long. She was only giving him her electronic address as he had requested when she telephoned the previous morning.

Rafa didn't have much exposure to women outside his family. He thought for a moment about Sister Stuart. This nun certainly wasn't the type of person one would expect to come to America looking for the Crucifixion Relic. In fact, to him, her character was better suited to teaching young people as she was currently doing.

Yet, after listening to her during the visit, he had to admit she was a first class Relicoligists. Also, it was she who had discovered Carney O'Sullivan. Perhaps she could be of more help to him. He turned back to the email program and, sent her a short message.

Reverend Sister Angela Stuart,

Thank you for calling to let me know about the Injunction Notice you found in the Globe. I spent a good part of yesterday running down two leads on the name Carney O'Sullivan mentioned in the publication. One was a place of work and the other a private residence. I also came across a third item for someone of that name in my Internet searches. A Carney O'Sullivan was the victim in a drive by shooting out along the coast this past July.

You have certainly turned this investigation around for me. I was beginning to wonder how I'd ever make any headway. Last week I went to the Boston Medical Centre unannounced to visit Doctor Samuelson. He was like stone and warned me if I came back, he would call security.

I don't know if this Carney I've located was the subject of Samuelson's article. However, it's possible, he may also be the shooting victim. Would you be willing to contact the Carney O'Sullivan I have located and ask him if he was the patient in Doctor Samuelson's article?

Respectfully,

Father Rafa Torres S.J.

**

The following day Carney left Seahorse Marine at 12:15 pm and drove to a restaurant where he had arranged to join his brothers, Jonathan, David and Paul. He and Jonathan wanted to tell David and Paul that their father's troubles weren't over. The brothers were all different. Jonathan was a lawyer, David owned and operated several hotels with a group and Paul, who had done a Ph.D. in Education, was a Director of Program Development with the Massachusetts Department of Education.

Over plates of pan-fried scallops, salad, and sourdough bread, Carney and Jonathan explained the incidents on Devonshire Street in the City and how the FBI had staked out the location in Chinatown where they found the machine gun that had fired the shots the terrible day in July at Nantasket Beach. Over coffee, Carney told them about the Injunction issued against him. They all thought it was a joke except Jonathan who worked at the District Attorney's office in Boston.

"Come on Jonathan," Carney chided him. "That Dr. Samuelson at Boston Medical said there was no miracle. He said it was only another example of Post Traumatic Release or (PTR). He even wrote it up on the Internet. I can email you the link if you want."

"Yes, you can send me the link, but don't forget an Injunction is a serious matter. If you don't follow the order, it is considered Contempt of Court. You can be charged."

"I'll be extremely careful, big brother. Don't forget, I have Dakota to think about."

That evening Carney received the call from Sister Angela Stuart. At first, he thought she was calling about Dakota's school work.

"No, Mr. O'Sullivan, I'm not calling about your daughter; I'm calling you."

"Me, do I know you from somewhere," he queried suspiciously?

"You don't know me, but I know you."

"From where?" He asked.

"From the Injunction Notice in the Globe," she replied.

"What do you know about that," he prompted.

Sister Angela decided to go for a long shot, "I've read Dr. Samuelson's review and I think there's more to what happened to you than just PTR."

"Listen, Sister, I'm not in the habit of discussing my personal life with strangers over the phone."

"I could meet you someplace," she suggested.

"How would you like to come have supper with my daughter and me on Friday evening?"

"This Friday Mr. O'Sullivan," she asked.

"Yes, this Friday," he replied.

After the caller hung up, he keyed a three digit sequence into his phone, to get the number of the person who had just called. On the computer in his home office, he used Reverse Lookup to secure the address attached to the number. The address turned out to be the Mother House of the Sisters of the Sacred Heart in the Boston suburb of Roslindale.

At 5:30 pm on Friday afternoon, a nun walked up the driveway of a home on Jamaicaway. The front door was answered by a man in his mid-thirties. He was smiling and extended a hand towards her,

"Welcome to the O'Sullivan's, Sister, we've been expecting you. Come right in."

She entered, and the door closed behind her. A young girl stood at the entrance to the living room, clasping her hands in front of her.

"Dakota, come and meet Sister Angela," her father encouraged. The girl approached shyly and the pair shook hands.

"Sister, you have a charming accent," Dakota exclaimed.

"Yes, of course, I'm from Scotland," the Nun declared.

"Well come and sit down. Let's all get acquainted," Carney urged as he dropped down on a leather couch.

Dakota was very taken by the religious who was visiting them and could not stop talking, "Soon I'll be making my First Holy Communion." The two talked of nothing else for fifteen minutes.

In the middle of the meal, she started to leave the table and her father asked, "What's up kitten? Where are you going? You haven't finished eating your supper."

"I'm going to put on my dress, to show Sister Angela," his daughter replied.

Her father intervened, "Wait until we're finished eating. You can go up and put on your outfit while Sister and I drink coffee."

When Dakota was upstairs putting on her First Communion dress and long veil, Sister Angela, and her father had the serious discussion they had been waiting to have all evening. The nun told him about herself, about Father Torres and the Crucifixion Relic. Carney was just saying he would like to meet with Father Torres when his daughter appeared.

"Oh you look like Tinker Bell from Peter Pan," the Nun laughed out loud clapping her hands together. It was just the cue Dakota needed. She did ballet steps back and forth across the kitchen floor in front of them as if she was on a runway at a fashion show.

After Dakota had changed back into her ordinary clothes, she and her father gave Sister a ride back to the Mother House in Roslindale. On the way back home, he and his daughter talked about everything. He hadn't been so animated since his wife's accident and death. When Dakota went to bed, he sat in the living room and mused for a long time about his life since the July First weekend in Nantasket right up to what had occurred this evening.

He distinctly remembered waking up in the hospital and going into the washroom. He hadn't even been aware of what he was doing until he looked in the mirror. He thought about that whole day and the visit he had made to Gate of Heaven, with the hospital volunteer, Mrs. Brown.

At that moment, he knew he had to contact her, even risking the possibility of her reporting it to the hospital and maybe someone there interpreting his actions as stalking. He remembered she didn't have a regular schedule of visits, but she did leave around 5 pm. That weekend after phoning the hospital and being refused information as to where volunteers parked, he drove to the area where he figured she would park and waited between 4:30 and 5:30 pm both Saturday and Sunday afternoon; however, he didn't catch the slightest glimpse of her.

***

Chapter 05

Louisburg Square

Martha's Vineyard is an island located off the southwestern tip of Cape Cod in Massachusetts. It's roughly 100 square miles in all. The permanent population is about 15,000, but it more than quadruples during the summer. There are three main villages – Tisbury, Oak Bluffs and Edgartown, as well as several smaller concentrations of the population such as West Tisbury, Chilmark, Aquinnah and South Beach. The island has an airport, which is serviced from Logan Airport in Boston, Kennedy Airport in New York and Regan Airport in Washington.

Ella Bowdine had not shown up in the volunteers' parking lot at the Boston Medical Center, on the weekend Carney watched from a distance because she had gone to Martha's Vineyard. Her architect father had designed several homes in the wealthy summer colony. As a teenager, she had gone with him for the site inspections. Her daydream was to own a house on the Island. It had been the subject of term projects while studying architecture.

Ella lived at home until she married. Her mother passed on from pancreatic cancer while she was studying and she started to take care of her father, who was still very actively involved in his architectural firm.

She was an only child and a daddy's girl. The bond strengthened after her mother's death.

The Bowdine family were Masons when they came over from France. French Freemasonry was much more receptive of women than their British and American counterparts. Ella's parents were American and were both Masons. Her grandfather had taken his daughter over to France for a vacation and she was initiated at the same time at his old Lodge. In America, they belonged to a mixed lodge, even though it didn't have full recognition of the Grand Lodge Ella mother had done the same think with her. When she married, Freemasonry had been put on the back burner. When the marriage failed and headed towards a divorce, she moved back home and resumed going to a mixed Lodge regularly with her father who was a Deacon. During this time, she became a substitute Tyler and on several occasions had been called to mind the door, while the Lodge was in session.

When she finally fell out of love with her former husband, the still young woman decided it was time for her to become more independent. To do this, she would have to move out of the family home on Pond Street, in Boston's Jamaica Plain neighborhood. It took about six months to progress from decision day to moving day.

Her father approved of the two-bedroom condo she purchased, on Louisburg Square, in the city's Beacon Hill area. He even came and stayed in the guest room several times, during the first few months. On these visits, they went out together to wander through the nearby Boston Common. He reminded her of the dream house she had talked about building when she was younger. On one of these strolls, she asked him to help her find a building lot on Martha's Vineyard.

Jack Bowdine was a tall, aristocratic man of seventy-five years. He had many connections both in and out of architecture. He still had an office in the firm but didn't work on any projects. He didn't have any regular office days; however, when he went in the team always sought out his advice concerning what they were working on. He proposed six different sites on Martha's for Ella's consideration. They visited each one together and compiled a list of pros and cons.

She still remembered going through each site with him.

"I really like this lot on Menemsha Pond" he insisted. "I could really design a great get-a-way on a spot like that."

"It's too far away from everything," she protested.

"What are you talking about, too far," he continued. "If you come over by the ferry, N Road leads directly here from Vineyard Haven. If you fly in, just take S Road and you're here.

"It's so far from everything. Every time I need a cup of sugar I'll have to drive across the island."

"Why didn't you say you were looking for convenience in the first place," Jack responded." Just look at this place in Oak Bluffs. You could do a great reno. Put a couple of dormers in the roof and bingo you have cozy little you, right in the middle of all the action."

"Dad, Oak Bluffs is where all the tourists go. I don't want to be a tourist," she insisted. "Tell me what you think about this lot on South Beach."

"That's a good price for that much land on this island, Ella," the elder Bowdine encouraged. "You could pedal a bike into Edgartown for your needs. However, for me, the chief attraction is the beach."

Ella's lot on the Vineyard was located not far from South Beach on Edgartown Road. The property extended down to the edge of Katama Bay. An old boat dock extended out into the water, beyond the low tide mark. An old wooden frame house had burnt to the ground and the owner decided not to rebuild. The location was protected from Atlantic swells and storms by Chappaquiddick Island and a sand barrier known as North Point.

The house turned out to be vastly different from the ideas she had submitted as coursework. In the end, she designed a cube structure. It sat on a square concrete base about fourteen feet off the ground. She became her own general contractor and did as much of the work as she could do. In fact, during the weekend Carney had looked for her in the volunteers' parking lot at the Boston Medical Center, she was busy taping and sanding drywall joints at her Island hide-a-way.

The construction resembled a sugar cube with one of the corners set into a six-foot square, above ground foundation attached to a concrete pad. The super-structure of the cube was made of steel beams bolted to the concrete base. Wood planks were strapped to the beams. A framing contractor put up the walls and floors. Thick, plastic film was stapled over the plywood exterior then the whole was clad with shingles. Solar panels were fitted on the southern exposures and there was a skylight in the living room.

During the building phase, the structure was equipped with a camp cot, hot plate, and bar fridge. She also owned an electric minivan and a ten-speed bike. Most days when she was there, the young woman drove several miles north into Edgartown for her main meal.

Inside the cube house, the floors were perfectly level. While taping and sanding the joints between the plasterboard, she thought about how she would equip and furnish this unique residence. A preference for rubber wood furniture from Thailand developed in her mind.

Bowdine Associates was located on the top floor of a renovated building on Battery Street, not far from Burroughs Wharf in Boston. The windows along the entire back wall looked out over the Harbor. There was always marine activity on the water. In the distance, planes could be seen landing and taking off at Logan Airport.

Although Masonic ritual varies between jurisdictions, a consistent message conveyed to every candidate is that aid is an essential part of Freemasonry. Masonic charity comes in many forms, both large and small. Little things mean a lot. A friendly smile, a warm handclasp, an embrace and a kind word can do as much for those who are isolated and depressed in a hospital as all the medicine the doctors can prescribe.

Hospital visitation had become a significant aspect of Masonic ritual for Ella. After Carney left, she had taken on a new veteran as a regular. On Thursday, she phoned the volunteer coordinator at the Boston Medical Centre to say she would be present Sunday afternoon.

On Friday at about 2:30 pm Ella stopped working on drawings for the conversion of an old brick warehouse on the waterfront into a microbrewery, restaurant, and bar. She drove to the entrance of the Callahan Tunnel, which carries vehicles from the North End of the City, under the Harbor and over to Logan Airport in East Boston. The plane for Martha's Vineyard left from Terminal C. There were two small bags in the trunk. Her volunteer smock and a pair of flat shoes were in one and the things she would need for an overnight stay on the Island were in the other.

The flight was forty minutes. At Martha's, she boarded the first taxi and told the driver to take her to the building supplies store, in Edgartown. There she ordered six gallons of primer, two paint rollers, a package of roller skins and an aluminum extension pole to fit into the handle of the rollers. Working alone, it was a long weekend for her; however, when she stopped to take a shower late Sunday morning, before going to catch her plane, there wasn't a drop of primer left.

**

Carney O'Sullivan drove back to the Boston Medical Center on Sunday afternoon, again hoping he might catch sight of the volunteer Mrs. Brown leaving. He found a parking spot one car length from an intersection which just enabled him to see the entrance and exit to the parkade. It was a long shot. He had come equipped with a pair of high-powered binoculars.

Cars leaving the parkade turned right and then stopped at an intersection where they either turned right or left. Several times he was sure the driver of a vehicle leaving the gate looked like her; however when he focused in with the glasses, it wasn't.

At 5:20 pm a silver Mercedes convertible stopped for a second at the exit and then proceeded up to the intersection. The car turned in his direction, and he got a close look. The driver was wearing sunglasses, but he was sure it was her. As she passed, he scribbled down the license plate number and then pulled out to follow.

The Mercedes continued to Massachusetts Ave and turned right following this main artery towards the St. Charles River. At Beacon St., one stop before the river, she veered right again and continued as far as the Boston Common before going into the Beacon Hill neighborhood, at the Massachusetts State House.

She parked on Louisburg Square, a grassy boulevard surrounded by a black iron picket fence. The sidewalks and parts of the street are made of a mixed pattern of bricks and round stones. Mrs. Brown removed a small overnight bag from the trunk and proceeded to enter Number One.

It was a four-story townhouse built of red brick, with black shutters. Each level had French wrought iron balconies. Carney waited. A few minutes later a woman swung back the French doors behind the balcony on the second level. Ten minutes passed. Then he went up to the door. There was no index of units and buzzers. He would have to check out the address in a City Directory.

The following day he stopped at the Public Library on the way home and learned there were four owner-occupied condominiums at # 1 Louisburg Sq. Each occupant was a woman. The second level was owned by an Ella Bowdine. That was close enough to Ella Brown for him.

He would have to be careful. She had warned him. Communication with patients after they left the hospital was against the rules. If he contacted her, she would have to report it. He couldn't chance a stalking charge. He would have liked to swing by Louisburg Square just to have a look, now that he knew it was where she lived but he didn't want Dakota to be alone.

Rosa, always stayed until he arrived home. She had been with them when his wife was alive. Before Dakota went to school, Jenna had the older woman come in around 8:30 am and wait until one of them arrived in the evening. About a year ago one of the Guatemalan's daughters started a part-time position, five mornings a week. Now Rosa only came to the O'Sullivan's around 2 pm. She would straighten things up a little, and prepare dinner. This way Dakota never came home to an empty house.

That evening, as usual, he listened to his daughter say her evening prayers before climbing into bed.

"Glory be to the Father and the Son and to the Holy Spirit. As it was, in the beginning, is now and forever shall be. Amen"

"Okay Kitten, that's a wrap," her father signaled. "Under those covers."

When the lights were switched off, he returned to his downstairs office to pen a note to Ella Bowdine.

Dear Ms. Ella Bowdine,

We met several months ago at the Boston Medical Center, where I was a patient. At that time, I knew you as Mrs. Ella Brown. I know the hospital has strict rules about communication between volunteers and patients after they leave. Hoping you will excuse this intrusion into your personal life.

I was the patient you met in the Trauma Unit, who was paralyzed below the waist by a piece of metal grazing my spine. One day you and I took a wheelchair taxi to visit Gate of Heaven parish church in South Boston. That night my condition changed dramatically, and the following day I was able to walk again. Some people called it a miracle. Others said it was post-traumatic release. Dr. Samuelson even published a research paper about it on the Internet.

The Internet article raised considerable interest on several fronts, and a number of people think that I am in possession of a relic having the power to heal people. As a matter of fact, last week a not-for-profit specializing in assisting handicapped people had a local Justice issue an Injunction, ordering me not to export or transfer the "Boston Relic" out of the Commonwealth of Massachusetts. I've also had a visit from a nun who transferred from Scotland to Boston, so she could find the relic. She informed me there is a priest here too, who was sent, by the Catholic Church, in Rome, to find the relic. I haven't met him yet but will soon.

You were the only person with me at the Gate of Heaven. Then, within 24 hours I defied medical science and walked. I know it's a lot to ask, but I was wondering if it would be possible for you to meet with me, the priest and the nun to tell them there is no relic and they are wasting their time.

He thought for a moment whether he should write his address, but he decided to offer only his email address. He would send this at the downtown Post Office on his way to work in the morning. Much to his surprise, he received an email from her two days later.

Dear Carney,

Why don't you, your daughter, the nun, and the priest come for dinner this Sunday at 5:30pm, so we can all have a chat about the magical wishbone everyone seems to think exists? You know the address!

Ella

**

Brian Robertson was elated. An Injunction had been issued. Not only were the Doctor and O'Sullivan ordered not to transfer or export the Boston Relic out of the Commonwealth of Massachusetts; they were also ordered to deposit it at the Court Registry when it came back into their possession. This was definitely reason to celebrate; however, the rejoicing should not come to the attention of anyone in or associated with the organization.

Robertson was sure he had saved the emails Sharon Harris had shown him when she first informed him about the relic. Perhaps they had been sent to a personal address. Her name came up quickly on an In Box Search and he found her private email address. He logged into a private address he had for personal messages and began to type.

Good afternoon Sharon,

Hope you're having a fantastic week and raising lots of dough for us. I'm extremely pleased with the results we had with the Board and with the Court on this Relic issue. In fact, I'm feeling as if there is something to celebrate and thought I'd treat myself to a weekend on the Cape. Then I remembered. I wouldn't have anything to celebrate if it wasn't for you.

If you don't have anything planned, how would you like to go over to Provincetown? I'm taking care of the bill. You would have your own room. There's lot's to do out there - walking, biking and eating. This time of the year, there won't be any throngs of tourists. I plan to leave the City at 8 am Saturday and be back here by 4 pm Sunday.

Let me know how your schedule is and if I should swing by your house Saturday morning!

Brian.

That evening he checked his personal In Box. There was a Reply from Sharon. "Delighted, I'll look for you out front Saturday morning!"

Provincetown is located at the extreme tip of Cape Cod. The population is approximately three thousand. It's a summer place, and when the season passes, the village makes a perfect get-a-way destination.

P-Town would be empty this time of the year, Brian thought. Several companies offered cheap flights from Boston, but he preferred the car. Depart and return on your own schedule. Besides, once you left interstate #93 at Braintree, it was a straight run down Pilgrims Highway to the Cape.

**

Sargent Gordon Nash and Corporal David Craven both cooperated with the DA and testified at the trial of the two Columbians who pled guilty to the charge of causing serious bodily injury. Both were sentenced to three years' incarceration, with no chance of early parole. The judge agreed with the defense since it was a case of mistaken identity, pre-meditation was ruled out.

Once the trial was over, the State Troopers completed the closing documents for the case and moved on. Since the pair had been illegal immigrants, Sargent Nash recommended the file be transferred to the FBI for follow-up in Atlantic City as the two Columbians had made contact with the party who hired them to kill Art O'Sullivan in AC.

The Bureau assigned the file to a junior agent who had recently been transferred to the South-East New Jersey Division, named Adam Wainwright. He was busy on another case but did have the two artist sketches from Boston digitalized and emailed to undercover agents working the casinos and boardwalk in the gambling mecca. The face didn't ring a bell with anybody.

About a month later, a casino reported a murder in one of their hotel rooms. Hotel security found counterfeit bills on the deceased. The FBI was notified. The investigator who responded to the call discovered security was also holding a prostitute named Bonnie, who had been in the room.

The FBI investigator entered the room where Security was holding the woman. She looked frightened, almost as if she would cry. Ms. Lui decided not to act like a moron.

"Hi there Bonnie," she said with as neutral a look as she could muster and then sat down in the chair across the table from the detainee. "My name is Emily Lui. I'm with the FBI. Would you like to tell me in your own words what happened here."

The young woman coughed once to clear her throat and began to speak, "He wasn't mean to me or anything and after we were finished he paid me. I asked if he would mind if I had a shower before leaving and he said 'sure'."

"When I came out of the shower, he was lying on the floor with a large patch of blood on his forehead. I knew my DNA was all over the bed. It's also in the police database, so I called hotel security. It was security who discovered I'd been paid with counterfeit money. They're good at spotting it around casinos.

"Okay Bonnie," the investigator started. "I'm not here to hassle working girls, and since you called this in, I'm even willing to overlook the counterfeit he paid you with."

"What's the catch?"

"There's no catch, but maybe you could help me out with another matter."

"What kind of other matter?" the woman asked suspiciously.

"You must see quite a few guys around these casinos?"

"I see a few, what of it?"

"I have a few sketches here with me. I'd like you to take a look and tell me if you have seen the fellow."

"That's all?"

"That's it," he replied bringing the first file onto his cell phone screen.

"Oh yeah, I've seen him before."

"Do you know his name?"

"They never give us their names."

"So he was a client?"

"That's correct, as a matter of fact; he was a client in this same casino."

"Recently," the investigator pried?

"Last week, I think on Tuesday."

"Do you remember the room?"

"I don't have a very good memory for numbers, so I write down the room numbers where I'm supposed to go."

"Do you have the room number written down?"

"It'll be in my purse there beside you."

Hotel security went through several computer screens, before pulling up Room 1178 for the previous Tuesday. "There you are, Ms. Lui. The bill was paid with a credit card belonging to Eduardo Romares. The mailing address attached to the card was in Philadelphia."

When she returned to the office, Emily went in and informed Adam Wainwright, "I got a potential ID for the two sketches you had sent around, at one of the casinos."

"That makes my day. Now the file can be transferred to the FBI in Philadelphia."

Eduardo Romares turned out to be a naturalized Columbian who was President of a company called Automatic Banking Corp. The company owned about eight hundred ATM's in locations between Philadelphia and Providence. A file was opened at the Philadelphia office, and an agent assigned the task of starting to gather basic information on him.

The CIA in Boston was not having as much luck as the FBI. Tom Reardon sat at his computer reading the comments his men had written with regards to Mustafa Hadad and Su Nam. There was still not even a hint of why the pair was in Boston. However, since they were often spotted near the same places at the same time, it was now suspected they were both in the city for the same reason. Reardon was tempted to have their hotel rooms searched, but didn't want to give away that they were under surveillance, just in case they had set a trap, which could be as simple as a human hair on a door casing.

**

As soon as Carney O'Sullivan received Ella's email he called Sister Angela, "Yes, she has invited both you and Father to come on Sunday with Dakota and me at 5:30 pm."

"It's certainly kind of her," the nun exclaimed. "I'll email Father Torres and would get back to you when I hear from him."

Rafa was delighted! "It's great news Sister. I'm finally going to meet the miracle man. Tell Mr. O'Sullivan I'll be ready and waiting outside my hotel on Franklin at five o'clock. And Sister may I ask a slight favor of you?"

"Ask away Father, I can only say no!"

"I was wondering if you could come up with a clerical collar for me. Even if it's a bit worn, it would be more appropriate for me to be wearing a collar, especially since you will be in a habit."

Once he had confirmed the dinner invitation, Torres opened a new message screen to send an email to the antique dealer in Madrid. He told him he would be meeting with the man who had the vintage object, in a few days. The broker forwarded the message to Cardinal Abbas in Rome, who was the Prefect of the Congregation for the Doctrine of the Faith.

Cardinal Abbas heard the computer signal an email message arriving. He finished what he was doing, before opening the software to see who was contacting him. At first, he didn't remember the name of the business and wondered if some spam had got through. Then he read the first line and a rush of excitement swept over him. The message read, "Our man in Boston has located the person who has the rare pearl."

The Cardinal began to tingle all over. His days were such an effort to keep the faith pure and straightforward. It was encouraging to learn this project was on track. Many weeks had passed since the Relicoligists had been dispatched. The Pope's advisor must be informed. He calmed himself, picked up the handset from its cradle and drew in a deep breath.

The phone in the outer office sounded three times before being answered. "Father Moreno, would you happen to have a number for Father Beal, here in the Vatican?"

"One minute Cardinal, I'll check the directory. No, I'm sorry, it's not a number we've called before."

"I'm finishing a report, and I must confirm something with Father Beal. Would you see if you could get his number?"

Not a problem Excellency, it's a number we should have in any case. What are his functions?

"I think he's an advisor to the Pope on matters of faith. Please put the call through to me, if you reach him."

"By all means," his assistant replied. It took ten minutes to track down the cell phone allocated to Father Beal.

Cardinal Abbas waited for the phone to sound a second time, before answering.

"Excuse me Excellency, I have Father Beal on the line for you."

"Put him through please."

Ordinarily Father Moreno would have hung up when he heard his superior say hello; however, this time he didn't. He was curious. How did the Cardinal know an advisor to the Pope?

"Yes, Cardinal Abbas," Beal's voice sounded in the ear piece. "How can I help you?"

"I'm calling with regard to the Crucifixion Relic issue his Holiness referred me to some time ago."

"Oh yes, I remember the matter. There was a chance it may have surfaced again in America...... in Boston," he added after a long interval of thought.

"Exactly Father, you were the correct person to call."

"Has it been located?"

"Father Torres whom we sent on a reconnaissance mission has messaged back via Madrid. A meeting with the man who was the subject of the miracle is to take place this week."

"Good news! I'm sure his Holiness will be delighted to learn of these developments."

"I thought the same myself."

"Cardinal, please keep me informed about all developments. You have my number now."

"I will Father and give my regards to the Pope."

"I definitely will, your Excellency."

Father Moreno hung up at the same moment as his superior so the red light on the latter's phone would go out. He couldn't believe what he had just overheard. It was fantastic news. He had read up on the relic since the name came to his attention. It certainly would be a win, win for the Church, if the relic could be repatriated to Rome, where without a doubt it should be.

Two nights later, eight hooded men met at the entrance to a small stone building, just outside the Vatican. When everyone had arrived, the door was unlocked and then re-locked from the inside after all had entered. The way led down a flight of well-lit stairs and along a passage to a central chamber. It looked as if it might have once been a crypt. Recently the room had been used as a storage area for files, waiting to be shredded.

The clergy assembling here this evening were comprised of five Cardinals and three Bishops, all members of the Illuminati. When everyone was seated, Cardinal Broscotti thanked them for coming and then went immediately to the purpose of the reunion. "As you know, we haven't met as a group since we learned a Relicoligist had been sent to America to explore the possibility the Crucifixion Relic had reappeared after an absence of one hundred and fifty years. Tonight I have news for you concerning him."

"Has he found the relic," one of those seated asked.

"Not exactly; however, he now knows the identity of the young man who was the subject of the Internet reporting that tipped us off. In addition, he has a rendezvous with him this weekend," Broscotti replied.

An older man with a slate gray, close-cropped beard spoke, "I think it is time to discuss why we are interested in the Crucifixion Relic and what possession will lead to."

"I agree," an overweight Cardinal seconded.

"Fair enough," Broscotti agreed. "How many don't know why we are following the happenings of this relic so closely?" No hands were raised. "Well," he continued, "it seems the cat is out of the bag, and we must discuss our intentions more clearly." This time there was a nodding of heads and some murmured affirmations from everyone.

"Cardinal, perhaps you would like to start the conversation," Broscotti stated, holding an outstretched hand towards the man with the beard.

"Fine," the older man agreed. "I'll start!" He stood and faced them. "We have all lived the ups and downs of the Vatican and for most of us; there have been more downs than ups. If our philosophy is going to survive in this City and in the Church, for that matter, we must do everything possible to ensure that one of our Society is elected the next Pope. Put simply, control of the Crucifixion Relic would give us a leading edge in the College of Cardinals."

"That's it in a nutshell," Bishop Sergio agreed. "If we had the Relic, we would have the power and would be able to keep it for a long time to come."

"Excuse me Cardinal Broscotti," another Bishop, who was named Schmidt exclaimed. "Might we know the source of this new information concerning the subject of the miracle in Boston?"

"It came from the Mother Superior in Edinburgh. Her charge has reported in and we intercepted the message sent to Rome."

"How long would it take us to locate Father Torres, if need be?"

"He has a Wi-Fi equipped computer to communicate with Madrid," a tall, gaunt Cardinal added.

"Why Madrid," Schmidt pressed.

"That was the Pontiff's decision. It helps his team keep control of the investigation," the same man replied.

"It was the bearded Cardinal's turn again, "If we had to make direct contact with Father Torres, do we know where he is."

No one replied so the question was repeated. "If I wanted to hop on a plane tomorrow and go pay this Torres a visit, does anyone really know where he is?"

"We don't know his exact location," Bishop Sergio intervened, "but we can obtain it very quickly."

"How?" Broscotti demanded.

This time it was an American Cardinal who spoke up. He was involved in the financial administration of the Church in Rome, "Father Torres uses credit cards we issued to him for almost everything. We only need to check his card account on the Internet to get the name of the hotel where he is staying. We can also learn where he eats and can ask to join him at his table if that would be more appropriate."

"I think we've fooled around with this Torres long enough," the overweight Cardinal exclaimed. "One of us needs to go to see him and find out exactly what he knows and tell him as soon as he has the Relic in his possession, he is to give it to us."

"I agree one hundred percent," Broscotti declared. "Now we need to decide who among us is going to go to Boston."

"I would like to volunteer," the American said; "however, I am required here, and it would look suspect for me to go running off to Boston."

"Yes, I agree," the Church official with the beard affirmed. "We don't want to tip off the other side."

"Perhaps one of the Bishops would escape their curiosity," the American suggested.

"I speak English," Bishop Sergio volunteered. It didn't take long for the other seven men in attendance to agree that it would be Bishop Sergio who would go in pursuit of Father Torres. All that remained was to devise a plausible cover story for him.

The eight who had attended the meeting left as stealthily as they had arrived. Each participant had his hood pulled up and each disappeared in a different direction.

**

After picking Sharon up on Saturday morning, Brian drove to the Southeast Expressway and later took the Exit for Pilgrims Highway. They crossed over the Cape Cod Canal on the Sagamore Bridge connecting the Cape with the mainland of Massachusetts and continued on to Provincetown. The whole trip took two and a half hours. The Inn where he had made the reservations looked out on Provincetown Harbor. By the time they were checked in and bags were unpacked, it was time for a light lunch.

"I'm not from New England," Sharon giggled. "I never know what to order."

"Just be daring," he urged.

After several minutes she responded, "Okay I've decided, I'm having deep fried clams and a Greek salad."

"Good choice," he praised. "I'm going to follow your lead. I'm ordering crab cakes with a side dish of corn on the cob."

With lunch past, they opted to explore the town and the many little roads leading off into the bogs and dunes on bikes. It was the right choice. Both were tensed up from the week, and the physical exercise helped them mellow out. Sometimes she pedaled ahead. At other times, he took the lead. When they had something to say to each other, they traveled side by side. She braked to let him catch up and then proposed,

"Let's stop and get a selfie beside that wrecked hull sticking out of the sand!"

"Roger Dodger," he replied pulling over to the side.

Daylight was fading when they arrived back at the bike rental shack.

Back on the main street, there were still a lot of people out walking. "Look," she exclaimed, "Most of the stores were still open. Let's find a souvenir shop. I'd like a little memory, just something small and inexpensive."

"I saw one when we were coming into town," he advised. "It should be on the next block, yes there it is, that little gray shingle place with the anchor out front."

The tiny one room building was jammed packed. The choice was overwhelming. Finally, Sharon held up a sand candle resembling the Cape's Long Point lighthouse and called out, "This is for me, Brian!"

"Nice," he commented. "I've decided on a small jar of wild Cape honey for my tea."

"Going off sugar?"

"No, simply a bit of variety," he replied and then asked, "Are you starting to feel hungry?"

"A little peckish, but would like to take a shower first. I worked up a sweat several times on that bike ride."

"Perfect, well let's go back to the Inn and get cleaned up. After that, I feel like a lobster for supper."

"Oh, yeah" she agreed. "With plenty of hot, melted garlic butter to dip the meat into.

"Spoken like a true New Englander," he replied smiling.

The following morning she phoned his room and woke him for breakfast. While they ate, she had approving thoughts of him. Yesterday he hadn't winked at her once during the bike ride and at the end of the evening, she hadn't been obliged to say, "Down Boy!" at her door. He played fair and so she decided to pay him.

"Did you have anything in particular planned for today?"

"I thought we might go walking in the dunes for a few hours or rent a small sailboat and go out on the harbor."

"Do you ride horses?" she asked.

"It's been a while, but I can ride. Why do you ask?"

"While waiting for you to come down, I looked through the brochures in the wall rack. There's a small farm not far from here on Blueberry Road where horses are for hire. Riding in the dunes and along the beaches is permitted. I thought we might pick up some takeaway and go off into the dunes. At noon we could have a picnic."

He was pleasantly surprised and replied, "Sounds like fun, I'm in."

It was twelve thirty when they stopped in a large crescent-shaped sand dune opening towards the beach. The wind was noticeable, but not unbearable. He tethered the horses on the spiral sand screws the attendant at the stables had given them while she spread out a blanket borrowed from the Inn and began to unpack the wraps and soft drinks they had purchased.

While eating they talked about the relic, which they now called the Boston Relic and wondered how long it would be before it came into their hands.

"You know Brian, sometimes I lie awake at night and think what it would be like if we acquire it!"

 "What sort of thoughts do you have?"

She considered his question a bit and then questioned, "Can I trust you?"

"Absolutely" he exclaimed.

 "Have you ever thought of how much good there is to do in the world, Brian?"

"Often," he replied, wondering where she was going.

"So many worthwhile projects are passed over because there is just not enough money to go around," she added.

He nodded his head in agreement and prompted, "Keep talking."

"I'd like to have my own foundation. I'd like to decide which wilting flowers got watered."

"You could also decide how much you would get paid," he joked.

"There's that too," she agreed and continued, "When we get the Boston Relic, we should make a switch and keep the real one for ourselves. Then we could go off someplace, maybe to a Caribbean Island and set up our own cure-clinic for the rich. They would pay us by making a donation to our foundation. Then we'd have the money to help all kinds of neglected causes."

He smiled and exclaimed, "You want me to go away and live on an island with you?"

She laughed too. "I haven't thought it all out yet, but I suppose we'd have to look respectable for our generous benefactors."

"By all means," he giggled. "We'd have to look respectable for the millionaires?"

Just before mounting the horses, she came up to him and said, "You'll never tell anyone what I said here today."

"Never, I promise," he swore crossing his heart with his right index finger. "Better still, one confidence deserves another."

"What are you talking about?"

"I'm going to give you one of my secrets.

"Which secret is that? Do you have another woman?"

No, nothing like that, it's my degree. The degree I needed to get the Executive Director position at The American Handicap Society. I bought it online. I've never been to a university."

"There it's a sealed secret," she declared brushing her lips softly against his cheek.

**

Rafa had told Sister Angela he would wait to be picked up in front of his hotel. Mustafa saw the Priest getting cleaned up through the hidden camera and surmised he was going out. On Sunday afternoon Dakota and her father drove over to Roslindale to pick up the Nun at 4 pm. The three of them continue on to the city, to get Father Rafa, before going to Beacon Hill for evening dinner with Ella Bowdine.

Earlier during the morning, Su Nam had followed the priest to Sunday services at the Paulist Center. Now she watched through high-powered binoculars from the second level of the car park just down the street. She couldn't figure out why he was standing at a side doorway of the hotel and why Mustafa had just walked by him. She wondered if the cleric was on to the Syrian and was playing a game of cat and mouse himself. Mustafa wondered the same thing and kept checking him with short sideways glances, but the Spaniard didn't follow or pay him any notice.

A few minutes later a black crossover came down the street and stopped in front of the entrance. Rafa climbed in and the vehicle continued on, passing Brother Hadad walking along the sidewalk. Su recognized the automobile. It was the same one that was parked near the garage the evening the priest had gone up the driveway on Jamaica Way. She refocused the binoculars and copied down the plate number.

The Syrian had also seen the priest enter the crossover and began immediately to look for a cab. Nam passed him still waving his arm at a taxi going in the opposite direction. He disappeared from her rearview mirror just when she spotted the SUV in traffic ahead.

During the following week, the assassin made sure this would not happen again. When the Priest went into the toilet to take his morning shower Mustafa went to his room with the specially adapted door flash card. It only took a few seconds to lift the inner sole and plant a GPS compliant tracking device in the toe of Priest's left shoe. Then he was gone, without making a sound.

While they were driving, Sister Stuart handled the introductions. "Mr. O'Sullivan and Dakota I'd like to introduce you to Father Torres."

"Pleased to make your acquaintances," Rafa blurted out.

"Hi Father," Carney greeted. "We'll shake hands when I stop driving."

"I can shake hands now," Dakota beamed, sticking her hand through the space between the front bucket seats."

Sister handed him a collar. "I borrowed this from one of the priests at Sacred Heart parish." In spite of the movement of the vehicle, the Spaniard was able to get it around his neck and buttoned at the back.

Ella had been watching for them in her front room window. When she saw four people approaching, on foot, it had to be them. By the time they mounted the stairs up to the large black door with the heavy brass knocker, she was standing in the open doorway. For this special evening she wore a light cotton blouse, gray flannel leggings and flat shoes.

She greeted them and declared, "Follow me, everyone. We'll save the introductions until we're in my place."

Once the front door closed behind them, all knew they had just entered another world. There wasn't one square inch that didn't bear her mark. Dakota became excited. She knew this was a woman's place. She was determined to take note of everything. Both Rafa and Sister Angela were delighted to be inside an American home.

Outside Su was by herself. Brother Mustafa hadn't made it. She only caught a glimpse of them as they entered the doorway at the top of the stairs. It appeared the Priest was wearing a collar. She waited a full five minutes and was rewarded. They walked past the front room window of the second-floor dwelling. She would have to learn the identity of the occupant. It had been a long day. She was not far from where she was staying. It was time to go find some dinner.

Ella had prepared a large pot of tea and a pitcher of sparkling water while waiting for her guests. She placed a tray on the coffee table and urged politely, "Help yourselves."

While the others were fixing their tea, Ella and Dakota looked each other over from top to bottom. The woman was about to speak when Dakota's young voice crossed the space between them, "I really like your home."

"You do," the woman said with a soft smile and added, "I really like your name."

"Me too," the little girl gushed. "I like your name too. I've never known anyone with a name like yours before."

"Well now you do, or at least soon you will."

"Really," Dakota said smiling at her.

"Really," Ella replied and then turned her attention to the girl's father.

"So, is your tea okay Carney?"

"Everything is fine," he replied shyly and then asked the other two guests. "Sister, Father, are you finding everything okay?" They nodded their heads in the affirmative.

It was the prompt their host needed. "Sister, Father, have some appetizers with your tea. There are two kinds of cheese, brie, and montery jack, and crackers to go with them. You too Dakota, help yourself."

Dakota came over to the coffee table and kneeled on the carpet so she could access the appetizers. When she had two crackers loaded with each kind of cheese, she turned to Ella and asked, "Where did you meet my dad?"

Immediately the woman looked at Carney with alarm, and he replied, "Didn't I tell you, dear? I met Ella in the hospital after my car accident last summer. She was a volunteer at the hospital and came to visit me whenever she was in."

Their hostess stood up and said, "I'll just be gone for a minute. We're starting with butternut squash soup. It should be put on simmer."

"May I come too?" Dakota inquired.

"Sure, come on, I'll show you my kitchen!"

When they were gone, the priest commented, "She's a nice little girl!"

Her father agreed and added, "She's smart in school too."

Sister Angela relaxed and cleared her throat. "I had supper with them last week. She showed us her first communion dress and veil. Her aunt helped her chose it."

"That's all she talks about," her father agreed. "You'd think it was Spring Prom!"

"Boys are the same," Father Torres informed them. "In Italy, the whole congregation joins in. Last year I had 15 boys and 11 girls do their first communion. It was as if the Pope was coming to visit."

Out in the kitchen, the conversation continued between Ella and Dakota. "Sister Angela has a very strong accent."

"I know," the girl agreed. "She comes from Scotland."

"Do you know her well?"

"She came to our house for supper last week. It was the first time I met her."

"What does she do?"

"She's a teacher, Grade four."

"And do you know the Father too?"

"No, I met him for the first time, when we picked him up at his hotel about half an hour ago."

After giving the soup a stir, they returned to the living room, and Dakota asked their host, "Can I tell them what we're having for supper?"

"Be my guest!"

Later, when they had finished the Spinach Lasagna Ella suggested, "Dakota if you want to watch TV until we're ready for the dessert, feel free, it's in the den, which is the first door on the left, before the bathroom."

She turned to her father, "Is it, okay daddy?"

"I don't see why not. We're going to have a conversation about things which wouldn't interest you."

When the girl left, Ella broke the ice by saying, "Pardon me if I seem a bit confused, but Carney told me you thought he came into contact with some sort of magic wishbone, and both of you came all the way from Europe to find it."

Sister Angela saw the look of shock on the priest's face and intervened, "That might be the way one would say it in America, Ms. Bowdine; however, I promise you, in reality, it's much more complicated."

Ella looked at Carney and asked, "Can you tell me how much more complicated it is?"

"Perhaps I can help," Rafa Torres offered, "and please call me Rafa."

"Please do," Sister Stuart invited but didn't say anything about calling her, Angela.

Rafa began to speak slowly, "Many years prior to the Crucifixion of Christ there lived an ordinary woman in the vicinity of the tomb Joseph from Arimathea provided for the burial of Jesus. Her name was Joanna. Like all women of the time, her daily chores included carrying home water for the family."

"One day she walked with a large earthen pitcher on her shoulder, and the shifting weight of the water inside caused her to fall. She landed on her back. When her back healed, Joanna had a permanent stoop."

The Spaniard looked at them and continued, "After the tomb was given back to Joseph, he asked Joanna to sweep it out so it would be ready, should it be needed. The boulder was then rolled over the entrance, to keep the interior fresh and clean. While she was sweeping, she found a small piece of linen cloth, in a crack on the floor, with what looked like a splinter of bone attached to it. She knew the history of the tomb and hid the item in the folds of her clothes."

"The woman awoke one morning to find she no longer walked with a stoop. Her daughter was the first to see the change in her mother. It didn't take the two women long to figure out the cause of this transformation, and they used the small fragment of rib bone to heal others in their group. Thus began the long history of the Crucifixion Relic."

"It has surfaced again and again across the centuries. The last occurrence was in Ireland, where it was used to bring a man back to life so he could testify against his murderer. Afterward, thousands of people prepared to travel to Ireland hoping to pay for cures with pure gold. A loyal monk of the Church took the Relic into hiding."

Ella was the first to speak, "So you two think Carney's recovery last summer can be attributed to a sliver of a rib found attached to a fragment of cloth in a tomb over two thousand years ago."

"We do," the Nun and Priest replied in unison.

"As a Mason, I understand the importance of relics for their historical significance and their ability to unify a group; but we tend to think of them more as artifacts. Many of our lodges include past Grand Master's aprons and jewels. However, we don't ascribe any inherent power to them," Their host continued, "Although I'm not a Roman Catholic, I do read the newspapers, and I have distinctly read several times the Church forbids relics."

"It's the official position," Rafa assured her, "but there are always some members of the faith and even some clergy who deviate from accepted doctrine. In these cases, the Vatican must investigate and shed sufficient light on the object. That's why I was sent to Boston."

Carney turned to Angela, "Did you also come to Boston for the same reason Sister?"

"I must admit it is not," the nun replied. "I'm not a Relicoligist like Father Torres. I'm a Scottish nun. I think the relic was part of a group of sacred objects taken to St. Andrews in Scotland thirteen centuries ago by Bishop Acca. Somehow a Monk spirited the Crucifixion Relic off to Galloway in Ireland. My main interest is to ensure the relic is restored to Scotland's National Heritage."

Both Americans were stunned by this response. "Then you're not working together," Ella surmised.

"Not exactly", Torres replied. "Sister Angela reports to her Mother Superior in Edinburgh who in turn has been in contact with Rome. Officials at the Vatican have requested we give mutual support."

Carney smiled and murmured, "Damned if you do and damned if you don't."

"So, what is it you would like from me," the architect pressed, "and of course from Mr. O'Sullivan?"

"To help us find the Relic," Sister Angela replied with obvious excitement.

"And what happens if we find it," Carney asked?

"I'm to take it to Rome," Rafa started to say but was interrupted by the nun. "I'll return it to St. Andrews in Scotland."

Ella could see differences of opinion exist between men and women, even if they are clergy in the same religion, so she stopped what could have become a nervous war of words, "Let's wait until we find it and then decide what to do because if we start arguing about what will happen to something we don't have, we'll never get around to looking for it."

"Then you will help us," Sister Stuart urged?

Carney looked at Ella and shrugged his shoulders. She shrugged hers back in response.

"Father Torres could see what was coming and headed off their answer to each other, "Perhaps you can start by explaining to us how Ms. Bowdine has become involved in this adventure?"

Everyone relaxed. Carney and Ella began to piece the story together for the two religious. They were just finishing when Dakota came back into the living room, "Is it time for dessert yet?"

"Yes honey," her father exploded. "Com'on and have some dessert."

"How many for coffee with their dessert?" Ella asked. It was unanimous all around, except for Dakota. "Good, I'll make a full pot."

While they were eating chocolate and almond bread pudding, which their host had prepared during the afternoon, Rafa decided to up the ante, "I'd like to go to see Gate of Heaven Church. There has to be something there."

"I agree," Sister Angela seconded. "I'd like to come with you."

"You won't find anything there," Carney protested. "It's just a church."

"This time it's me who agrees," Ella added.

"Sister, perhaps you and I could go there together this week?"

"I'd love to Father, but I must teach the children Monday to Friday; however if you could wait until the weekend."

"If you can wait until the weekend," Carney interjected, "maybe I can fit it into my schedule too. Dakota, do we have any plans for next weekend?"

"I'm supposed to go and stay with grandma and grandfather Cosgrove next weekend. It's Thanksgiving break. You were going to take me to their place at Hyannis on Saturday morning," his daughter reminded him. The Cosgrove's were his late wife Jenna's parents. They had retired to a large house at Hyannis on Cape Cod, after their only daughter Jenna's untimely death.

"Ah, Wednesday is Thanksgiving," he exclaimed.

"That's right dad, and you're supposed to come back on Wednesday to have turkey with us and take me back home."

"Listen, Father, I should be driving through South Boston on my way back from the Cape on Saturday at about 1 pm. I could stop and show you around the Gate of Heaven. It was the parish I grew up in. I was an altar boy there for five years, but then they caught me drinking the Mass wine and Reverend Father O'Malley decided I had become too old to be an altar boy."

"I could meet you some place in town Father Torres," Sister Angela exclaimed. "We could go to meet Mr. O'Sullivan together."

Now it was Ella's turn. "Are you driving to the Cape next Saturday morning Carney?"

"I cannot tell a lie," he laughed.

"Would you and your daughter mind if I hitched a ride to Hyannis with you? I was planning to go out to the Vineyard on the weekend, to close up my house there for the winter. There's a foot ferry from Hyannis. It would save me airfare from Boston."

"I'm sure there will be room for you. What do you say, Dakota?" The girl and the woman looked into each other's eyes momentarily. There seemed to be some stardust floating in the space between them.

"Oh, I'm sure there will be loads of room dad!"

"Then it's all settled," Carney exclaimed, draining the end of his cup.

"All settled except for where we'll meet you," the Spaniard interjected.

"Oh, that's right Carney agreed," looking sheepishly at the two religious. "Sister, where are you going to meet Father?"

"Well, I don't know yet," the Nun sputtered.

This time it was the Spaniard who looked uncomfortable. "Do you know the Boston Common Sister?"

"I do. It's a large park in the downtown area. I've been in town several times Father. I can find the Boston Common, but it's a large park. Can you be more specific?"

"Let's say at the main entrance to Boylston Station. It's in the southeast corner of the Park, just below the baseball field."

"I know the Station Father. It comes out on Tremont St."

"Okay, I'll meet you there at noon next Saturday. We'll take a taxi to South Boston."

"Well, that settles it," Carney agreed. "Now, where am I going to meet you two?"

"Why don't you meet us at the Church," Sister Angela replied.

"Sounds good, I'll meet you both at the Gate of Heaven at 1 pm."

"Give me a call as you're leaving home with Dakota," Ella said smiling at him. "I'll be waiting out front for you,"

***

Chapter 06

The Bishop

In Philadelphia, the FBI went quietly about its business building a simple ID file on Eduardo Romares, the man whom the call girl in Atlantic City had recognized from the sketches the two Columbians had helped prepare. Agents learned Eduardo built his business by buying out companies with established networks of ATM's. They tracked down some of the former owners.

At first, similar patterns seemed like a coincidence, but then they developed into a *modus operandi.* Two or three of the previous owners had been terrified into selling their businesses, after receiving telephone and mailed threats. Since the amount paid more than compensated for the machines, profit and goodwill, no one had complained.

At the FBI Randal Bergman was in charge of the investigation. He was a seasoned specialist who had acquired a canny understanding of the criminal mind through exposure to multiple fields of activity. After Law school at a state university, he joined the Marines and spent six years with the Marine Corps Police. During the last two years of Service, he had been preparing for the SEC's Office of Compliance Inspections and Examinations. At the end of his contract with the Military, he wrote the exam and worked as a Compliance Officer in financial fraud prevention and investigation. Around this time he met his wife and after five years of protecting American investors, decided to join the Bureau.

When his analysts put it all together and presented it to their supervisor; there was only one question on their mind. Why would someone intimidate an owner into selling and then give him top dollar? It just didn't fit. There had to be more to it than they could see. Romares could go out and open up new ATM routes, for a lot less than he was paying. However, the locations he was acquiring were established and that was the name of the game.

Bergman brought the file into the next team meeting of senior agents in Philadelphia. "Does anyone have anything on this Eduardo Romares?" he called out over the murmur of multiple conversations.

Most present shook their heads no indicating they didn't know Eduardo. "He wasn't on any 'persons of interest' list." Jerry Modi acting secretary for the meeting exclaimed. "However, I agree it looks odd."

"So do we," several others in attendance called out.

"I would like Bureau budgeted funds to allocate surveillance to Romares," Randal proposed.

Senior agent Crofton objected, "I also have a red hot suspect I want for surveillance. Are there funds available to support two fishing trips?"

Bergman assigned Lorne Andersen and Wally Sorensen to the surveillance project. Wally's strength was with the camera. He had snapped "the" picture in more successful cases at the Bureau than anyone. Andersen was known as the Jedi because he had been in so many tight squeezes and still didn't even have a scratch wound.

"I made a deal with Crofton," Bergman explained. "You have a week. If you have nothing then the funds swing over to his suspect."

"Should we work together or do two different shifts," Lorne asked.

"The choice is yours," their superior officer instructed. "However, if you have nothing capable of creating a reasonable doubt by the end of a week, I'll have to call it off."

Eduardo Romares, his wife Paulita and their three children lived in West Philadelphia, in a house built by a Professional, belonging to the previous generation. There weren't many Hispanics in the neighborhood. On both sides, the neighbors were African-American. To the west, the father had a Ph.D. and was a manager at a company where robotic controls were produced. The other neighbor was a logistics specialist with the Regional Commuter Rail Lines. The Romares were Catholics while their neighbors were Baptist. Both neighbors had been born and raised in Philadelphia while the Romares had emigrated from Columbia fifteen years ago.

Andersen and Sorensen decided to work together. They attached a tracking device to Eduardo's car and obtained a copy of his cell phone records. Sometime during every day, he visited Automatic Banking Corp. It might be a fifteen-minute break or a four-hour stay. There were a lot of stops in a day and a lot of people at these short halts. If possible, Wally shot pictures of everyone he met or spoke with in the open.

"That's it," Wally declared at the end of day five. "I've put all the photos shot today through face recognition software. Nobody in those pictures had a criminal record. Everything looked legit."

"It's the same thing with his cell phone records," Lorne sighed. "Every number he has called in the past six months was put through a full access computer scan. Not one of them has shown up in an active case during the period."

On Saturday afternoon, the Romares family came out of the house about four forty. Edwardo was a tall man with an athletic build. He had a full head of thick black hair which grew low and on the sides of his forehead. He also sported a close-cropped, filled beard. Today he was wearing a white shirt, powder blue tie and a grey V neck sweater. His wife Paulita was an attractive woman in a flower pattern dress, high heels and a belt that accentuated her narrow waist. The three children looked scrubbed and polished. Eduardo drove them to the local 5 pm Mass. They all entered the Church together.

It was the opening Lorne had been waiting for all week. He wanted to talk to the neighbors. Wally went into the Church, and Lorne drove back to their street. The car was no longer in the driveway at the Robotics' Manager's house, so he was obliged to walk up to the Logistics Specialist front door and ring the bell.

A ten-year-old boy answered the door. "Hi, my name is Anderson. Is your father around?"

"Dad, there's someone to see you," he called out and then turned back to the agent. "Do you want to come in?"

"No, thanks," Lorne replied. "I only have a few questions for him." A middle-aged African-American man appeared behind the boy.

"Good evening, Mr. Johnston," the FBI agent began. "My name is Lorne Anderson. I work for the American Mortgage Corp. Your neighbor Mr. Eduardo Romares has applied for a second mortgage on his house. They're planning on doing some renovations. Would you mind if I asked you a few questions about Eduardo?"

"No, not at all," Johnston replied. "Would you like to step in?"

"I won't bother you. This will only take a minute."

"On his application, Eduardo indicated that he works for Automatic Bank Corp."

"That's correct; he's been with them ever since he's been living next door."

"Has he ever mentioned anything about wanting to leave the company?"

"No, he seems quite happy with it. Sometimes I'm a little envious."

"Why's that Sir?"

"Where I work, I sit at a desk for 8 hours a day, every day, all year long." The neighbor continued, "Mr. Romares is a Field Manager for Automatic Bank Corp. There's a lot of flexibility in the position. He's out roaming around a couple of days out of every week. Some days he even stops in for lunch with his wife."

"I think you have answered my question. We always like to check out an applicant for risk of flight. I think Mr. Romares is going to be at

Automatic Bank Corp for a long time yet. Thank you for answering my questions. I won't keep you any longer."

On Monday morning, the two agents had a scheduled pit stop with their supervisor, Randal Bergman. "Don't tell me you have nothing," Randal grimaced as they sat down.

"We don't have anything we can show you pictures of," Wally replied honestly.

"But you have something" Randal barked. "I know that something look, and you two are wearing it this morning. It better not be a hunch."

"It's not a hunch," Lorne said, breaking the tension. "It's two items that contradict when placed side-by-side, but which may be explained away."

"Explain it to me," their superior demanded.

"The report says Eduardo is the President of Automatic Bank Corp and we checked out the three companies owning Automatic's equity and Eduardo owns all the shares in them."

"So the guy is the owner and the President," Bergman concluded. "There's no law against that."

"He told his neighbor the Johnston's he was a Field Manager at Automatic," Lorne replied.

"That's it," Randal demanded.

"How would an alien from Columbia get to own and be President of a company like Automatic? Why would he hide the truth from his neighbors? It would give him status," Lorne returned.

Then Wally added, "I read over everything transferred to us from Boston. The victim's father who they think the drive by was intended for told the investigating officers from the Massachusetts State Police he received an anonymous letter at his office, which contained a threat "Take your ATM machines out or else! It's our territory now."

Bergman drummed his fingers on the desk and thought about having to explain this spending if they got nothing. However, he had to admit, Lorne was keen. He wouldn't have thought to go back and interview the neighbors on a Saturday afternoon. "Okay, I'll give you next week, but forget about Eduardo. Concentrate on the company. Get pictures of everyone who's working there. Follow the armored car, when it goes out to fill machines. Get a sample of their money. Maybe some of it is bogus. Take a counterfeit dog with you to sniff out the machines."

**

On Monday morning when Father Torres went downstairs for breakfast at his hotel, he noticed someone who was obviously clergy, sitting in one of the large lobby armchairs looking in his direction. Not only was the man wearing a full collar shirt and cassock, there was also a violet zucchetto on the back of his head. It was the sign of a Bishop.

Rafa observed the Bishop begin to rise, and he halted momentarily. It was all the invitation the other person needed, and he exclaimed, "Father Torres!" in Italian.

The priest was stunned and sputtered, "Yes!"

"Are you going in for breakfast?" the Bishop asked.

"Yes, as a matter of fact, I am."

"I've been waiting for you Father," the stranger declared. "May I join you?"

"By all means," Rafa replied beginning to recover from his initial shock. "Come let's go in."

Mustafa saw the priest getting dressed on his laptop and arrived in the lobby a few minutes before him. The first thing he noticed was the Bishop. Unfortunately, he didn't understand Italian. He decided to wait until they came back out to see where the Bishop would go.

Over breakfast, the higher clergy introduced himself as Bishop Sergio. "We are almost neighbors," the stranger said. "I mean neighbors in Italy. I was born and ordained a priest in Naples and you are just down the coast at Amalfi."

"Which parish are you attached to in Naples?" Torres inquired politely.

"In all, it's been 20 years since I was ordained." Bishop Sergio explained. "During the first 17 years I was with Santa Chiara then I was made a Bishop and transferred to the cathedral Duomo di San Gennaro. I was only there three years when I was asked to serve in Rome."

"You knew my name," the Priest from Amalfi tested, "so you can't be on vacation."

"You are very observant Father Torres," the cleric from Rome praised, "but actually I was sent by the Vatican, to inquire about the progress being made with the Crucifixion Relic."

"You know about the Crucifixion Relic," Rafa exclaimed.

The Bishop became more dominant. "I understand you have made contact with the man whose spine was so miraculously restored."

"That is correct," Rafa replied.

"And have you found the Relic yet," was the next question?

"No, not yet," the Relicoligist declared. "The man involved has no knowledge of it."

"But it shouldn't be long now?" The stranger pressed.

"I couldn't say for sure Bishop, but anyway are you in Boston for long?"

"As a matter of fact, I've been sent here to help you. Yesterday I took a room in this hotel."

Father Torres was hesitant but continued, "Are you a Relicoligist?"

"No, but I'm learning."

"What sort of help does the Vatican want you to give me?" Torres inquired with a whiff of suspicion lurking in the back of his mind.

"Well, actually, they want me to take the Relic back to Rome when you find it."

Rafa was skeptical but didn't show a sign. He remembered Cardinal Abbas had told him not to take the Relic straight back to Rome if it came into his possession. The Cardinal feared there were too many self-serving factions in the Eternal City. Torres had been told to take the Relic to an Abbey, south of Boston in a town called Hingham. It was a place where Catholics went for a retreat. Upon arrival, he was to tell them he had a reservation and he should stay there on retreat until instructions were given to him by the head Benedictine monk.

The Relicoligist had heard and read of Vatican scandals and tales of mismanagement and greed, such as sainthood causes costing half-million dollars. A monsignor allegedly broke down the wall of his next-door neighbor — a sick, elderly priest — to expand his already extravagant apartment. In addition, there were stories of worldwide donations to help the poor winding up in an off-the-books Vatican account. He decided to play it safe.

"Very well Bishop, hopefully, you won't have to wait long. I could recommend some first-rate sites to see while you are in the City."

"And you," the Bishop asked, "What are you going to be doing?"

"All of my contacts have normal lives here and must work during the week, so I thought I would go to the Boston Library. They have an excellent section of books on relics, some of which I have never heard of. You can come along too if you like."

"I would prefer to see the sights of this City if that's okay with you. Deal with your contacts as you have been doing. A Bishop might not be an appropriate fit."

"As you wish Excellency," Torres replied feeling relieved.

"I'll be fine on my own. You locate the Relic and then I'll take it back to Rome."

They left the hotel restaurant together and boarded the same elevator. Mustafa went to his room and opened his notebook computer. The Priest was alone. This could only mean the other clergy was also staying in the hotel.

**

The FBI was not the only organization making headway with its files. In an unmarked office at One Center Plaza, in Government Center, the Boston office of the CIA worked quietly, but efficiently. Mustafa Hadad and Su Nam had not been allowed to remain in the city unobserved. Tom Reardon was pleased with what his agents had learned about the pair, even though they weren't actually an active investigation for the team.

Hadad and Nam seemed to be involved in some sort of cat-and-mouse game with each other, with two American citizens, a UK citizen, and a Spanish national. Hadad was the prime mover. Nam was mostly shadowing him, but she did occasionally engage in some observing of the others on her own.

For some reason, Hadad was following a Spanish national named Rafael Torres who had entered the US at New York and was supposed to be interested in antiques. However, Interpol informed them Torres was actually a Catholic priest, who was attached to a parish in Amalfi, Italy. The priest met up with a nun from Scotland named Angela Stuart who was on a teaching assignment in a Boston suburb. These two made contact with a Bostonian named Carney O'Sullivan, who was a successful entrepreneur. Lately, a second American, Ella Bowdine had joined the group Hadad and Nam had under surveillance.

Of the four being watched, only Carney O'Sullivan had an active file with the FBI and the local authorities. He had been the victim in a drive-by shooting the previous summer, a short way down the coast. In addition, he was mentioned in an Injunction local authorities had recently issued concerning something, called the "Boston Relic". It was not to be taken out of the Commonwealth of Massachusetts.

Reardon decided it was time Hadad and Nam became persons of interest and put them on the next day's briefing sheet. He added a note in the margin, requesting more information be provided on the Boston Relic.

**

It was the third Friday of November. Randal Bergman stationed himself in the open doorway of his office with a cup of black coffee looking out over the open concept office where most of his staff had their cubicles and desks. When he spotted Lorne Andersen and Wally Sorensen leaving the elevator, he waved vigorously until he caught their attention then exclaimed. "When you have a minute boys!"

He only had enough time to get seated behind his desk and they were standing in front of him. Lorne turned and carefully closed the door behind them. When their superior saw this he knew they had something and declared, "I'm all ears!"

"What do you want?" Wally asked with a wide grin and continued, "The quick and dirty or the long winded version."

"Give me a taste so I'll know what we're talking about then you can fill in the details at your leisure before going to your desks to type your reports into the system."

Sorensen began talking, "You told us to forget about Edwardo and concentrate on the company, so that's what we did. We looked at automatic Bank Corp. from the operations side and from the corporate side. I'll start with the ops and Lorne will cover the corporate."

The company's physical operations are located in an old bank. The building has been reinforced with heavy concrete bumpers on all four sides. Concrete filled pipes have been set into the ground in front of the main and rear entrances. There's a garage door at the back with a steel plate set into the ground that can be lowered to allow a vehicle through. The building is equipped with an auxiliary diesel generator. There are cameras everywhere. It's wired into the panel board of a local security monitoring firm and the police. All the wiring into the structure is underground."

"Everything that's standard with other ATM company headquarters," Randal commented.

"Yes and no, the firm employs six people besides the president. Every one of them is a relative of Edwardo's from Columbia. He sponsored them to come here to work. They got green cards and have all become citizens. Everyone, including the receptionist is licensed to carry an arm while working."

"Sounds like a real nest of rattle snakes," Randal laughed.

"Their armored car is state of the art. It's fortified with 42mm bullet-resistant transparent armor multi-layer glass with polycarbonate inner layers to prevent spalling upon ballistic impact. The armor plate is the thickest available. The cab is equipped with a filtered air system, a tear gas emission system, gas masks and oxygen cylinders. When two of the Romares saddle up to go out into the field, they cruise in a mobile bomb shelter."

"We followed the truck several times to check out the money drops," Wally explained. "They have procedures down to a fine art. The driver stays in the vehicle. The truck is loaded with racks of pre-counted cash to refill the machines. It takes the other operative less than a minute to do a service stop. It's like changing a cartridge in a computer printer. The driver is always positioned to watch the whole process. There are gun ports on all sides that he can open at the first suspicion of trouble."

Lorne interrupted his partner. "Romares' first job in this country was with an armored car company in Miami. He got it because of his record which included an honorable discharge from the Columbian Army and a first rate reference from his commanding officer."

"How many machines does he control," their Captain asked.

"The State Banking and Finance Commission requires quarterly reporting on a host of variables. Automatic Bank Corp.'s last filing indicated eight hundred machines in the field." Anderson replied. "They are all in little patches between Philadelphia and Providence, wired into the Internet and cash levels are flagged automatically twice in a 24 hour period online. We witnessed them fill a machine on Tuesday and then they went back yesterday. The racks that were brought back to the truck were almost empty."

Wally came back to expand on what he had already said. "We checked out a few of the machines ourselves after they were filled. We made several small withdrawals using our personal ATM cards. Anything under a hundred dollars has a $3.50 admin fee attached to it. Lorne did one withdrawal for $120 and the admin fee was $5.00."

"And Sir," Lorne interjected, "Like you advised us, we brought a counterfeit sniffing dog with us. Each time we did a withdrawal the dog was beside us and showed obvious interest in every machine; however, we had the lab check out the cash we withdrew and the bills are not counterfeit."

"Okay, that's enough about the machines," Randall said. "What did you find out about the corporation?"

Anderson cleared his throat and began to speak, "This is where it really starts to get interesting. Automatic Bank Corp. is owned by three numbered companies having Delaware registry. Edwardo is the President and only shareholder of each. Up until about eight years ago Automatic was a small struggling concern here in the Philadelphia area with about a hundred machines. In eight years it has grown eight hundred percent, mostly in the area between New York and Boston."

Bergman was curious. "How did he finance all that?"

"The company's financial statements are all on file with the regulators," Lorne declared. "About eight years ago he changed banks, if you want to call them that. Bitcoins have spun out a number of innovative start-ups on the Internet. Automatic Bank Corp. went in with one of them for its financing and kept its old bank for transactions."

Randal interrupted him. "Don't tell me they have Bitcoin banks now!"

"Oh, they have more than banks Sir. There are Bitcoin exchanges, outfits that will convert your cash into Bitcoins and others that will convert Bitcoins into cash."

"I don't blame you Sir," Wally exclaimed. "I didn't even know what a Bitcoin was before this case. Now I know it's a crypto or digital currency that's used on the Internet. Not only that, it was invented on the Internet.

It's not easy to steal the stuff and even if someone succeeds there's not much they can do with it. Every coin is registered on an electronic ledger called a Blockchain. As soon as someone would try to use the stolen Bitcoin, the transaction would immediately be flagged as its transfer to the person trying to use it would have had to been registered on the Blockchain."

"How is the financing being done?" their department head inquired.

"It's all written up and filed with the regulators," Andersen continued. "Automatic Bank Corp. has a Bitcoin wallet. The Bitcoin Bank of Miami Inc. transfers coins to Automatic's wallet and then Automatic transfers them to an exchange where they are converted into US dollars. These dollars are transferred to Automatic's regular bank. The loan is for one year plus one percent interest. Automatic then goes onto a Bitcoin exchange and purchases a forward contract for the amount of the loan plus the interest."

"The Bitcoin Bank of Miami accepts deposits in Coins and pays a half of one percent interest on them. We went through the Florida Regulators to get the names of depositors, but nothing looked suspicious. They were all small deposits. Then we found out the bank in Miami also issued half of one percent interest bonds that could be paid for with Bitcoins. Some very sizable bonds were taken by numbered companies all over the US. We're just getting started on checking out the shareholders and investors in the companies which purchased the bigger bonds.

"What's your gut feeling guys?" Bergman demanded.

"We think it's a money laundering operation, probably drug money. We're not doing ethnic profiling, but possibly it's the profit from cocaine sales in the US, considering the fact that Edwardo is a Columbian.

"Good work men," Randall exclaimed. "I can't believe a counterfeit bill from a prostitute in Atlantic City has led us through to this. Take all the time you need to file your reports into the system and let me know when it's done. I'm going to pass the Bitcoin operation on to our electronic crimes division. They have much more experience with this sort of thing. If it's a money laundering operation, they will find it."

"Isn't this Eduardo a piece of work?"

I'll say," Wally piped up. "Cheating on his wife with the Pros in Atlantic City and then feeding counterfeit bills in with the good ones that he's borrowing at one percent interest."

"That's what you two are going to crack," their superior boomed. "I want you to find out where the counterfeit is coming from and then take down this crook!"

**

Carney and his daughter were up early Saturday morning and left for Beacon Hill, without even eating. Friday he had emailed Ella the time they would pick her up and also told her they would be stopping at Dakota's favorite pancake house on the way to the Cape for breakfast.

From Louisburg Place, they circled around behind Government Center and entered the Interstate tunnel passing under the city. Driving south the sky was clear, but it was difficult to keep a constant speed, because of the strong headwind. They stayed on the Expressway until the exit for Pilgrims Highway.

The New England Pancake Palace was located in a large, white, wood-frame house, with multiple dormers in the roof and a wide, closed- in-veranda, all along the front of the building. Two massive Stars and Stripes blew savagely in the wind from their tall white masts. When the three climbed out of the Carney's vehicle, the loud snapping sounds coming from the flags frightened Dakota.

"I thought something was breaking and was going to fall on me," she gushed, "but when I looked up, it was only the flag."

"Here take hold of my hand," Ella prompted. "I won't let you blow away."

The restaurant was full, but the waitress found them a square table for four out on the veranda. A rack in the middle of the table contained a bottle of syrup and a squeeze bottle of honey. Dakota ordered a Belgian waffle with two eggs, two hickory-smoked bacon strips and blueberry topping. Ella tried their classic breakfast crepes and Carney settled on an omelet.

Ella felt a strange nurturing feeling towards the young girl who ate with glee across from her. Suddenly she exclaimed, "Dakota you have icing sugar on your cheeks."

The girl looked at her father and asked, "Do I, dad?"

Ella leaned forward with a cloth napkin in her hand and said, "Here let me brush it away."

Dakota let her touch both cheeks with the soft cloth and then declared, "Thank you! You're kind."

It was the architect's lead, "So you're off for a few days with your grandparents."

"Yes, they're kind too! They're my mother's parents. I don't see them as often as my grandmother and grandfather O'Sullivan, but I always try to see the other side of the family around Thanksgiving."

"What do they do?"

"Before they retired, they both had successful jobs, they were managers. Now they do different things."

"What sort of different things?" Ella coaxed.

"My grandmother makes quilts on a large loom and sells them on consignment through a gift shop in Hyannis. My grandfather has a small boat and some lobster pots. He sells his catch to restaurants and says he does it more for the exercise than the money."

"They sound interesting!" The ice was broken. Ella and Dakota talked almost continuously from there through to Hyannis.

Hyannis is the commercial and transportation center of Cape Cod. Its big safe harbor makes it the largest recreational boating and commercial fishing port on the Cape. In addition, the village has the primary ferry boat service for passengers and cargo to Nantucket Island and provides secondary passenger service to Martha's Vineyard. The Cosgrove's house was located on Old Colony Road, a short drive from the port.

Once Dakota and her bag were safely transferred to Ken and Nina Cosgrove, Carney and Ella headed for the ferry. It was a little past eight-thirty. She would be in time for the 9 am sailing of the walk-on-only boat out to Martha's Vineyard. When they arrived at the dock Carney suggested, "Go get your ticket. I'll park and meet you in the waiting room."

"You really don't have to wait with me," she said politely.

"I know, but I'll wait until you're on board. I'm not scheduled to see Father Rafa and Sister Angela until 1 pm, so I have plenty of time."

"Very kind of you, I accept your offer," she said, trying to open the passenger door. "I can't seem to get it open. The wind is too strong."

"Wait a sec; I'll swing around so you won't be opening into the wind."

Ella was in the waiting room when he arrived. The first thing she said was, "There's no ferry!"

"What, what do you mean, there's no ferry?"

"Those are gale force winds. The Coast Guard has ordered all boats to stay in port."

"Com'on, I'll drive you over to Woods Hole."

"There are no sailings from Woods Hole either. They said this could last all weekend."

"You should have flown as you usually do."

"They also said there are no planes to the island today."

"What do you want to do then," he asked?

"I might go along to Gate of Heaven if you don't mind."

"Didn't you have enough of relic talk when they came for dinner?"

"I don't believe any of it," she smiled, "but I'd like to see what happens at the church."

"Well, it's your choice," he consented. "I'm about ready for my second cup of the day. There are lots of small Java shops in Hyannis, let's go find one."

"So, we're going for our first coffee," she taunted. "See why they want us to report all incidents of stalking." He looked at her sheepishly and headed towards the parking lot wondering what had happened to the wedding ring she had been wearing at the hospital.

**

Torres left his hotel a little after eleven on Saturday morning and walked to the southwest corner of the Boston Common where a solid gray concrete building called Boylston Station, was located. There were hundreds of pigeons everywhere under foot. In the distance old, weathered gravestones were sticking up out of the grass.

He arrived several minutes before Sister Stuart appeared on the sidewalk peering in all directions. When he called out, she waved and walked towards him.

"How was your week Father?" Angela inquired.

"It was uneventful. The waiting game, you know, and how was yours"

"Oh, it was hectic. The children are off part of next week for Thanksgiving recess."

"Are the children giving thanks to the Lord?"

"No Father," she replied with a laugh. "Thanksgiving is an American holiday. They celebrate the three days the early Pilgrims feasted with the Native Americans."

"Pardon me, I'll get us a cab," the priest replied awkwardly.

"No trouble Father, if I wasn't in with all those children; I may have thought the same as you."

At that moment, a yellow cab pulled over to the curb. The back door opened as if by magic. The two religious climbed in pulling it closed behind them. "Where too folks," the driver exclaimed?

"We would like to go to South Boston," Rafa replied in his best English.

"Do you know Gate of Heaven," Sister Angela asked?

"Ah yes, it's a big church on East 4th," the cabbie replied, putting them at ease.

Mustafa had been following at a safe distance and hailed the next taxi.

Following a short drive through several small downtown streets south of the Common, they arrived at Boston's South Station where Rafa had arrived by train. Soon they were passing the Boston Convention and Exhibition Center on Summer St. The vehicle crossed over the Reserved Channel Bridge and entered a light industrial park.

It was twelve forty-five when they arrived at the Church. Mustafa was just behind them. He left his cab half a block past them and then sauntered back towards the Church. Today he wore dark sunglasses and the brim of his hat was pulled downward. Su spotted him as she drove past. She parked a reasonable distance past the Church and settled down to watch the Syrian, the Spaniard and the Scottish woman through her high-powered binoculars. A short time later the same black SUV she had followed into Beacon Hill the previous weekend, pulled up. A man and a woman got out and headed towards the Nun and the Priest. The four of them shook hands and entered the Church.

The Church was empty at 1 pm on Saturday afternoon. Confetti littered the floor at the entrance. Inside a faint scent of candles and incense blended together in the air. Obviously, there had been a wedding earlier during the day.

Ella sat in the same pew she had during the previous visit. Carney walked up to the front and then over to the nave on the left sidewall where the statue of Our Lady was located. Father Torres and Sister Angela followed him. He stood at the spot several minutes and then said to them in a low voice, "This is where I prayed until Ella came to take me and the wheelchair back outside. It was so relaxing. I dozed off for a minute or two. She woke me with a light shake. When we arrived outside, the van-taxi was waiting."

"Was there any apparition," Sister Stuart inquired?

"Our Lady's face began to glow," Carney answered. "It became almost flesh like, and I saw her lips move."

"Do you remember hearing anything while you sat here?" Rafa asked.

"Far away, inside my head, I heard a woman's voice say, 'Have faith in my son'."

"Sister and I are going to make a close examination around this area," Father Torres explained and then suggested. "Why don't you wait for us with Ms. Bowdine?"

In about ten minutes, the relic hunters joined them in the pew. "We've finished," Sister Angela informed them."

"Find anything," Carney asked curiously.

"We have a few clues we're going to follow up on," they replied together.

"Would you like to drive back to the city with us," Ella asked?

"That would be very kind of you," Sister Stuart answered and then they all rose and prepared to leave the Church.

Mustafa had been watching them from the vestibule. He was obsessed by the thought the nun and priest had found the relic at the statute. When the group started to leave, he moved quickly and slipped back outside. He hurried to the corner of the building and stepped into a recess formed where the two walls joined.

Carney was parked on the same side of the street as the Church, just beyond the "Passenger Disembarkation Zone", so they didn't have far to walk. He beeped with the remote to unlock the doors. The Priest and the Nun climbed into the rear while Ella waited to make sure their door had closed tight and then began to enter the passenger seat beside Carney.

At that moment, Mustafa appeared and pushed her onto the small armrest between the front bucket seats showing them his gun. The semi-automatic pistol had a silencer screwed into the end of the barrel.

"What's this?" Carney reacted with a roar.

"Keep your mouth shut wise guy. The rest of you don't try anything stupid, and nobody will get hurt," the Syrian growled as he pulled the door closed behind him. "Now wise guy, get us out of here." O'Sullivan did as he was told.

Carney sped past several blocks, headed in the direction of the City when Hadad suddenly commanded, "Turn right at the next corner and drive slowly." The street contained several one level warehouses.

"Pull up in front of the boarded up place over there," the carjacker ordered, "and then everybody out. If one of you tries to run, everybody gets it."

At the entrance to the building, Mustafa fired two silent shots into the lock and then turned the knob. The door swung open on its hinges. "Go in," their abductor ordered.

The warehouse was empty. Long shafts of sunlight streamed down into the empty space from several holes in the roof. Pigeons nesting inside the building cooed loudly. The concrete floor was broken periodically by posts holding up the roof.

"All of you put the contents of your pockets over there by that stain on the floor. Turn them inside out so I can see they are empty." The whiskered man barked. "If you have a purse, leave it there too."

When they had all done so, Mustafa opened his jacket revealing an inside breast pocket bulging with heavy-duty, plastic self-locking zip ties. They were used in industrial settings, to hold cables together. Some Police forces now used them as handcuffs when a number of people are being detained.

Mustafa demanded that Carney and Rafa come over to one of the posts holding up the roof. "You," he said pointing at O'Sullivan. "Stand close to the post and put your arms around it and stretching out with your wrists together." When he had done so, the Syrian handed a plastic tie to the Priest and said, "Secure his hands together with this.

When Rafa had secured his hands on the far side of the post, O'Sullivan was ordered to sit down and stretch out his legs on either side of the pillar the same as he had done with his arms. Then he growled at Rafa and shouted, "Now put this tie around his ankles, the same as you did with his wrists. Make sure you pull tight. I'm going to check both his ankles and wrists." The Priest obeyed without protest.

Next, Ella did the same to the Nun and Priest. Then Mustafa secured Ella himself.

While checking the contents of their pockets Brother Hadad used a small stick to separate the objects from any tissues that had been in their pockets and were also lying on the floor. After scooping up their ID and money, he left the warehouse with a loud bang of the door. They heard Carney's vehicle drive off and decided it was now safe to speak.

"We could be here until Monday," Ella exclaimed. "There's no one around this area on the weekend to hear our yelling."

"We better save our vocal chords," Carney suggested.

Suddenly the warehouse door opened and a woman entered. None of the four recognized her. It was Su Nam. She had been watching up the street and had seen Mustafa herd them into the warehouse. When he drove off, she decided to investigate.

As the woman approached them; they all began to speak at once. When she replied, it was in Korean and no one understood. She cocked her fingers to look like a gun then pointed towards the door.

Sister Angela spoke first, "She seems to be saying that she saw the man with the gun."

"We can't involve her," Father Torres protested. "He might kill her!"

"She doesn't have to be involved," Ella objected. "She just has to get us out of these bonds." They all held up their bound hands at once.

Su understood everything being said but gave no indication. She came and looked at the plastic ties and then made scissor motions with her fingers before kneeling down to rummage through her purse. Quickly she found a pair of stainless steel nail clippers and held them out for all to see.

"Oh praise the Lord," Sister Angela squealed. "I'll never say another word against cosmetics kits as long as I live."

The Korean woman chose the Nun to be released first and then handed her the nail clippers and fled the building. Minutes later they heard her car speed away.

"We've got to get out of here," Carney said loudly when they were all released. "He might come back at any time."

"He took all our money and ID," Rafa reminded him.

"Quick!" Ella screeched. "The Boston Convention and Exhibition Center is not far from here. There are lots of taxis there. I can use my office account with a cab company." They picked up the remaining contents of their pockets and left together. Outside, the four hurried up the street heading in the direction of the Convention Center.

**

When Mustafa left the warehouse, he drove back to Gate of Heaven. Since he hadn't found the relic among the contents of his captives' pockets, he thought maybe it was still at the Church. When he arrived, he entered cautiously. The Nun and the Priest had looked around the front of the Church, on the far right side, so he went there first.

He wondered how large the relic could be. Was it a perfect bone or just a chip? The only thing there was a statue of a woman. He examined it.

Its base was held down solid by two painted metal straps. The paint was cracked around the bolts holding the straps. There were chipped spots on the heads of the bolts. He needed to remove the straps so he could examine the statue. Perhaps there was something in Carney's vehicle he could use as a tool.

He left the Church and came back several minutes later carrying a tire iron concealed inside his jacket. Quickly he wedged the prying tip in under the metal band and pressed down. The bolts popped out of the cement easily. He was able to pick up the statue and examine it. There seemed to be a tight- fitted closure, on the bottom of the base. He didn't want to break the statue if at all possible. Breaking it would indicate an intruder had been there. Perhaps a motion-activated camera was watching him.

He turned the statue over and over in all directions and then heard something like a cantilever weight movement inside. All of a sudden the closure on the base slid open revealing a secret compartment. It was empty. This was all he had to know. One of them had beaten him to it. He needed to get back to where they were tied up. Hurriedly he put everything back in place and inserted the bolts in the straps, before dusting over the area with his handkerchief.

When he arrived at the warehouse, the door was standing open. He knew they were gone. I must go to the hotel he thought.

***

Chapter 07

Last Rights

When the escapees arrived at the Boston Convention and Exhibition Center they entered the first taxi waiting. "I have an account," Ella said directly to the driver. "I use it mostly to send architectural drawings around town, but it's also good for passengers."

"Which company is your account with Miss?" the driver asked, before turning on the meter.

"Boston Cab," she replied.

"That's us," the cabbie declared and then enquired, "Where too?" as he turned on the meter.

"I must get my passport," Rafa interjected. "It's at my hotel."

Ella told the driver to head for the priest's hotel, which was only a short drive from there.

When they arrived, all four exited the cab. Rafa was frantic and exclaimed, "I'll go in and retrieve my essentials as quickly as possible.

"Good," Carney agreed. "We'll wait down the street for you just inside the entrance to that Car Park."

Rafa looked everywhere for Mustafa before crossing the street and entering the hotel. The Desk Clerk at Reception recognized him. The distraught Priest explained he had left the plastic card to open his door, in the room.

"Happens all the time, Sir!" the Desk Clerk declared. "I'll check the register and issue you a second card straight away.

Immediately upon entering his room, he went to the safe inside the closet and spun the wheel of the combination lock. The door opened the first time. Inside were his passport and the ATM card he had been given at the bank in New York after landing. Mustafa had his credit card. The ATM card had only been used once to withdraw $1,000 in cash. Most of it was still inside his passport as he had swiped the credit card for regular purchases.

Mustafa paced back and forth in his room. He could see into the Priest's room which was clearly visible on his computer screen. The little rat wasn't there. Where could he be? Perhaps he had taken refuge with the Bishop he had seen him with in the breakfast room.

Brother Hadad was about to go downstairs to the Bishop's room when all of a sudden he noticed something move on his computer screen. It was the closet door in the Priest's room closing. There stood Father Torres with his back turned to the concealed wireless camera. The assassin grabbed his handgun and bolted out the door of his room heading for the Priest's floor.

At the same instance, Rafa also exited his room and ran for the stairs. When Mustafa reached the Priest's room, he slipped his universal pass card into the slot, tapped the lock app on his smartphone and turned the door handle. It took only a few seconds to discover his quarry had eluded him. Instantly he was back in the hall. The elevator door was closing. Quickly his hand shot into the remaining space. The door glided back open. The little rat wasn't there.

When Brother Mustafa reached the lobby, the Priest was nowhere to be seen. He advanced to the hotel entrance using quick long strides. The heavy oak door swung open. He stood at the top of three broad steps frantically scanning the street.

Sister Angela was hiding with Carney and Ella, a short distance down the street near the Parkade. Suddenly she sprang out onto the sidewalk waving her arms and jumping up and down while she yelled, "Father, Father over here! Watch out, he's just behind you!"

Father Rafa was hiding between two parked cars on Franklin. The huntsman didn't see him. However, the Nun did attract his attention. Without thinking, the assassin raised his gun and sent two silent shots in her direction. They were both dead on and penetrated her left chest near the heart.

Sister Angela made an unexpected movement resembling a ballet dancer's pirouette. Then she tumbled to the sidewalk. Several people ran over to examine the fallen Nun. A middle-aged woman began screaming, "She has been shot. She's bleeding all over. Call an ambulance. Call the Police."

Instantly Mustafa saw what he had done and began to worry. He couldn't see the Priest anywhere. After taking one last look in both directions, he bolted back into the lobby, slipping the gun and silencer into a holster inside his jacket as he moved. There was an emergency exit at the back of the entrance. Brother Mustafa hoped it wasn't alarmed.

From his hiding place between the two cars, Rafa could see Sister Angela was not moving. There hadn't even been the sound of a gun going off, but she had gone down. Already there could be heard the siren of an ambulance coming down the street. Suddenly he spotted Carney and Ella at the entrance to the Parkade motioning at him. He darted across the street then ran towards them.

Carney grabbed him by the arm and stammered, "We can't do any more for her. The ambulance is here. We have to go before the madman finds us."

As the three of them ran across the ground level of the parking garage towards the back wall, Rafa asked, "Where will they take her?"

Ella replied, "Accident victims from this area are taken to the Boston Medical Centre."

They could see a ground level gap in the half wall at the rear of the Parkade. Arriving at the spot, the trio discovered a long, steep, flight of cement steps leading down to a lane three levels below. Carney took charge, "Ella you go first and then you Father. I'll follow up at the rear."

Ella started down the stairs while the two men watched for their assailant. When she was about halfway down the second flight, Rafa began to follow her. He had only descended a few steps when suddenly the woman in front of him missed her footing and went tumbling forward down the remaining steps. The full force of her fall was stopped by her right foot. Under the skin, two of the metatarsals bones in her right foot snapped off and penetrated the membrane on the top of her foot.

Father Torres was the first to reach her. Huge tears were streaming down her cheek. She was shaking and kept repeating over and over, "My foot, my foot, it's my foot." Soon Carney arrived and knelt down in front of her. "Take off my shoe," she pleaded. "It's my foot, the right one!"

Carefully Carney removed her shoe and then the athletic sock already stained with blood. Two shattered bones were protruding about an inch above the skin covering the top of her foot. Blood was oozing from the wound and dripping onto the concrete pad where they stood.

"She can't walk," Carney said showing his concern. "We'll have to take her to a hospital. Give me a hand. We'll hold her upright between us."

"Wait a minute Carney," the Priest said calmly. "He's still out there hunting for us. We'll be easy to spot carrying an injured person between us and we won't be able to move quickly. We'll have to go out to the main street and hope to get a cab before he finds us."

"Well, what do you suggest," O'Sullivan growled angrily? "Can't you see; she's in extreme pain?"

Calmly Father Rafael replied, "Carney if you have it, use it to save your friend."

Carney looked at him with awe and exclaimed, "What are you talking about?"

"I saw the statue back in the Church," the Priest continued. "The paint was cracked all around the bolts securing the bottom of the statue to the stone. It looked as if someone had recently removed them. That man with the weapon most likely went back to the Church when he didn't find the relic on one of us. He too would have seen the bolts had recently been removed. He just shot Sister Angela back in the street. If he finds us, he will probably hurt your friend Ella too."

Carney looked at Ella, and she asked, "Do you have it?"

The startled man answered, "It was in a tissue, in my pocket, back at the warehouse. It's a tiny fragment of bone. He missed it. I still have it."

"You'll have to use it to save your friend," Torres repeated.

"You do it, Father," he said, extending a crumpled piece of tissue towards him. "I'm not a priest."

"No, you'll have to do it yourself. It requires real concern. This is only the second time I've met Ella. I don't know anything about her. Hold the material on her foot and ask God's help to heal her."

Carney did as he was told. It took several minutes and then all three saw the two shattered foot bones disappear back under the skin, and the wound was soon covered over with new skin.

Ella felt oozy. She didn't want to look at her foot. She closed her eyes and seemed momentary to go elsewhere. She was in what appeared to be a cave. Suddenly she heard a scraping noise and light came streaming in as whatever had been blocking the entrance began to move away. She could see a body lying on a ledge which was cut into the stone.

Inside Ella's head, a woman's voice spoke from far away. She was telling her not to have fear. She must have faith in her son. Ella felt the urge to flee and ran towards the light. Suddenly she opened her eyes. The Priest was standing in front of her.

"Try to put your weight on it," Torres instructed her. She stood and was able to walk with no pain.

"Give me the relic please Carney, Rafa said. "It's why I came to America. It must be hidden inside the Church again, away from the eyes of the world."

"Give it to him Carney," Ella urged.

The stunned man extended the folded facial tissue towards the Priest who took it and slipped it into a small breast pocket on his jacket.

"Now I must leave. You'll be safer without me."

"Stay with us," Ella pressed. "You have no money. We'll take a taxi to my office where I keep an ATM card. We'll leave you at the South Street Station."

"I have cash and an ATM card too," he said stripping off a fifty dollar bill from his fold and passing it to her. "They were with my passport in the hotel room. Take a cab with it. I'm leaving you now. Please be careful. I'll pray for you both and the little girl." A moment later he reached the end of the lane, looked both ways and then was gone.

Once Torres had disappeared Carney sprang to life, "I'm sorry you became involved in all of this, but we've gotta get out of here." She looked at him with an air of desperation then took hold of his outstretched hand. They hurried to the far end of the lane themselves. Mustafa was nowhere in sight. They walked briskly to the nearest cross street and hailed the first cab coming into view.

Bowdine Associates was located on the top floor of a renovated building on Battery Street, not far from Burroughs Warf. Ella keyed in her pass code and a buzzer sounded indicating the door was unlocked. Once she had the ATM card she turned to Carney and said,

"We need to report what has happened to the Police!"

"Agreed! I also must report the theft of my vehicle," he exclaimed.

"We should go back to the warehouse and call the Police from there," she suggested as they rushed back to the front entrance of the building.

"Not to the warehouse," he protested. "We would involve Father Torres and Sister Angela. We should go back to the Church and report in a carjacking from there."

"Okay," she murmured, "That's our game plan."

It took the South Boston Police five minutes to respond to the call the pair made from a pay phone not far from the Gate of Heaven. Once the police had driven off, the duo walked to a nearby convenience store, used the ATM card and purchased a disposable cell phone with some of the withdrawn money.

When they left the store Ella confessed she didn't actually feel safe going back to her place,

"He has my wallet and keys."

"I'm with you on that score. You should avoid your home for a few days or until we learn something from the Police. I'd invite you to stay at my place, but he has my wallet and keys also. Perhaps you could go to your father's house?"

"Good suggestion," she agreed, "but he's gone for Thanksgiving. My key to his house is on my key ring. If only I had been able to get out to the Vineyard this morning."

"The wind seems to have died down here in South Boston," he encouraged. "It might be the same down the coast by now."

"There's an idea. I'm going to phone Woods Hole and see if the ferry service has resumed."

It took three calls to get connected, but persistence paid off. "The Coast Guard has just authorized the first boat of the day to leave, and it is loading now," the woman on the information line informed Ella.

When she hung up, he asked, "How are you going to get there? We can't even rent a car without ID."

"There are buses running out of South Station all day. There's always a last bus at 6 pm on Saturdays."

"Okay, then you'll take the bus."

"Why don't you come with me? It's not safe for you either in Boston with that stupid man running around carrying a gun."

"We hardly know each other!"

"You're the one who used the relic on my foot. The Priest said there had to be genuine feelings or the relic wouldn't work. He didn't know me. That's why he didn't try to use it."

"Rafa did say that didn't he."

"Yes, and it worked."

"Okay, we'll both go to South Station," he replied, smiling at her timidly.

**

It had been several months since Father Torres had been to the Boston Medical Center. He remembered the encounter with Dr. Roger Samuelson distinctly. Hopefully, he would be more successful today.

The Priest arrived on foot at the Emergency and walked through the double sliding glass doors. No one was waiting at the entrance, so he strode up to the Reception Desk to talk to the attendant keeping his fingers crossed.

"Yes Father, how may I help you?" the woman asked, looking at the collar he was once again wearing.

"I was asked to come here to perform the Last Rights on a nun who was shot in the street this afternoon."

She scrolled through the Admissions screen. "Yes Father, we admitted a woman with gunshot wounds this afternoon. It was just before I came on shift. Do you have her name?"

"Her name is Sister Angela Stuart," Rafa replied.

"She wasn't carrying any ID, but they found the name Angela Stuart on laundry tags sewn to the inside of her clothing. She has been transferred up to the third floor. Take those elevators over there and talk to the Desk Nurse on Level 3."

"Thank you!"

"You're welcome Father."

The Nursing Station was located across from the elevators, so it wasn't hard to find the Duty Nurse. "May I help you Father?" she asked, looking at his collar.

"I was notified to come here and offer Last Rights to Sister Angela Stuart."

"I'm afraid Sister Angela won't be able to accept your offer, Father. She died about an hour ago. We've disconnected life support systems. The Hospital Morgue has been notified. They are supposed to come and remove the deceased this evening."

"An hour isn't too long. The soul doesn't leave the area immediately. I can still give her Extreme Unction," he informed the nurse.

"As you wish Father, she is in Room 310. It's down the corridor on your right. Please close the door after you."

Rafa entered Room 310. A darkened TV was attached to one wall on an extendible arm. A medical monitor glowed with a blue light, but there was no movement on the screen. Near the bed, an IV trolley still held a bag of fluid, but the tubing was wrapped around the top of the equipment. The sides of the bed were down and it was raised at about a thirty-degree angle.

He found it hard to imagine the woman on the bed was Sister Angela. She was so white and drawn. He approached and began to pray quietly to himself as he prepared to give her the last rite of Unction. He had no oil to anoint with, and there was no sink in the room, so he put saliva on his thumb and made the sign of the cross on her forehead while saying,

"Through this holy anointing may the Lord in his love and mercy help you with the grace of the Holy Spirit may the Lord free you from sin and save you and raise you up."

The man of God reached down into the small breast pocket of his jacket where he had put the folded tissue Carney had passed him back in the lane. When he felt the soft paper between his fingers, he carefully withdrew and opened it. The sliver of bone was no bigger than a toothpick.

Both Sister Angela's arms were under the sheet covering her. Rafa slid his hand in under the bedding and withdrew one of her cold hands. Then he placed the tissue in her palm and squeezed her fingers closed all the while saying, "Please Lord save this woman. Bring her back among the living."

It seemed like a long time, but what was only a matter of minutes. Suddenly he became aware of movement in the hand he was holding. Then it became warmer. He knew what was happening. Carefully he took the tissue from her grip and put it back in his pocket. Her face was starting to regain its color. He wanted to leave her a message, but there was no pen and paper. Then he thought of his wrist watch and looked at it. It was 7:10 pm.

It had been his father's. This was the one worldly possession his father had left to him when he passed on. His father's name was Rafael. It was inscribed on the back of the case.

He slipped off the watch and wrapped it around her wrist. She would know he had come and would understand the Church was in possession of the Crucifixion Relic again. Once it was done he said, "Goodbye and good luck!" Then he turned and left.

**

Mustafa made it out of the hotel by the back door and tapped on the smartphone app for the GPS tracking device he had placed in the Priest's shoe, as soon as he was in the lane beside the hotel. He could see the general direction in which Father Torres was located, but he had no idea how far he was from him until they came within 500 feet of each other. At that point a red circle would form around the pulsating red dot.

How could the Priest and the others have got free and back to the hotel? He had their ID and money and credit cards. They couldn't even take a taxi. The signal was weak, but it indicated his prey was southwest of him. He didn't think the Priest had the relic. He had seen the condition of the bolts holding down the straps securing the bottom of the statue in the Church. It was the work of someone who had access to tools. Brother Hadad suspected the other one. The one they called Carney.

There was little chance the Priest was out there alone. He had to be with Carney and the woman. He would follow the signal being emitted from his quarry's shoe and catch all of them. Then the relic would be his. This time he wouldn't leave them alive. Because the signals kept getting weaker, he decided to go back to where he had parked their vehicle and try to find them by driving around.

Agent Nam watched as he drove off. This is an evil man, she thought. The North Korean had seen him take down the Nun in the street. She had done well to follow. She had to protect her people back home from this man and his Brotherhood. They had told her at home not to let the relic fall into the hands of the Syrian, if she couldn't recover it for them.

When Rafa left the Hospital, he thought about going to the South Station and catching a train or bus out of Boston; however, that would be dangerous. His pursuer might be a wild man, but like all predators, he was smart. The transportation hub was one of the places he would likely go to first. He also thought about phoning the hotel and being connected to the Bishop's room; however, he was suspicious of the man. He had indicated the Relic should be given to him and that he would take it back to the Vatican City.

He remembered Cardinal Abbas had told him not to take the Relic straight back to Rome. If it came into his possession, he was to go to the Benedictine Abbey located in a town called Hingham, a little south of Boston. There was a freeway not far from where he was walking. He hadn't hitchhiked since he was a student in Spain, but why not he thought.

The traffic sign in front of him had two arrows. One said North Bound and the other South Bound. He went to the right and kept walking until there were only two lanes of vehicles moving forward in the southbound direction. Up ahead a large sign warned "Hitchhiking Not Permitted". He removed the collar and put it in his inside pocket, before sticking out his thumb. Five minutes later a tractor-trailer stopped in the curb lane. The driver motioned for him to get in. As the door closed, the truck began to move.

When the driver had maneuvered the long trailer into the flow of vehicles on the Interstate, he turned to his passenger and asked, "Where're you going, buddy?"

"Hingham," the Priest half hollered to be heard over the roar of the engine.

"Good one buddy," the man at the wheel hollered back with a smile. "I go right by the exit."

Torres understood and tried to think of a way to signal it, without shouting again. Then he stuck out his hand with his thumb pointing up just as he had seen in American movies. The driver replied with the same gesture and they smiled at each other.

Mustafa could not believe his eyes when he saw the red circle appear on the GPS screen. He was only a short distance to the North of the indicator. He looked around frantically. There was nothing but a maze of turn signals and white arrows painted on the road surface leading to the northbound entrance of the freeway. Quickly the vehicle became boxed in by the flow of cars and trucks and the driver had no choice but to be in the northbound lane.

As he moved up the ramp the needle on his smartphone app began to swing around and leave the inner circle on the screen. Instantly Mustafa realized he had made a wrong turn. His prey was somehow heading south on the same freeway. There was no way to get off. He would have to drive to the first Exit and turn around. Who knows where the Priest would be by then.

Nam had been following the Syrian. When she saw him turn into the northbound entrance of the freeway she didn't know what to think but decided to continue the pursuit.

When the trucker let Rafa down at the Exit for Hingham, he walked off the freeway to a nearby gas station and phoned a taxi. He told the taxi driver to take him to the Abbey in Hingham. The driver called his dispatcher who said yes there was an Abbey and gave him the address

A community of Benedictine monks lived in Hingham. Retreats were an essential part of their program. Guests from far and wide come to spend time in the retreat houses and to share in the prayer life of the monks. The property was contained behind an eight foot high solid stone fence running along the street. The cabbie turned off and drove up the main driveway. Rafa could see stone buildings hidden behind the trees. One was the church and the other the monastery.

Father Torres said he would get off at the monastery, as he put back on the collar. "Forty dollars please Father." Rafa gave him fifty saying, "The extra is for you, my friend."

A few minutes later he signaled his arrival twice with the heavy metal knocker. Soon the entrance was opened by a short, slight monk with white hair who wore a black robe with an attached hood resting on his shoulders. He looked at the Priest intensely and then exclaimed, "Yes Father, may I help you?"

"I was told to tell you I have come for a retreat and I have a reservation," the Spaniard replied.

"Well come in. You don't have any bag."

"No, I didn't bring anything with me."

"Welcome, I'm Brother Albert. Please have a seat and write your name on one of the pads for me. Then I'll go to see about your reservation."

There were several polished, wooden chairs lining the wall with matching tables between them. A notepad and pen were arranged on each table. Father Torres sat down and printed his name for the Brother, who took the first sheet from the pad and disappeared through a solid wood door. About 5 minutes later the member returned with a large smile on his face

"We have found your reservation, Father Torres. We have separate rooms available in the monastery where visiting clergy stay when they're here on retreat. Follow me, I'll take you there. We eat supper at 6:30 pm, so you are just on time. Once I show you your quarters, you can follow me to the dining hall."

**

When Ella and Carney arrived at South Station, they made their way to the Bus Terminal. It was housed in a separate building above the train platforms along Atlantic Avenue. The ticket agent informed them the ferries were getting back on schedule after the high winds during the earlier part of the day and would be leaving the Woods Hole Ferry Dock at the regular time.

They purchased two tickets for the next bus departure then found themselves spaces on a bench near their loading Gate and kept watch in both directions. They wouldn't be surprised by Mustafa, should he show up. When the time came, they boarded the coach and sat near the rear. The trip took an hour and forty-five minutes.

The Woods Hole Bus Station was one street back from the Ferry Terminal, a low white building at the beginning of the wharf where the boats tied up. Already cars were loading into the last ferry out to the village of Vineyard Haven. The beleaguered man and woman hiked up the ramp for pedestrian traffic.

At Vineyard Haven, on Martha's Vineyard, a number of island shuttle buses were waiting as foot passengers came off the vessel.

"Over this way Carney," she directed. "We'll wait at the Edgartown Bay."

At Edgartown, they stopped at the supermarket and then took a taxi to her cube house at South Beach.

She turned on the TV and the computer on arrival. Carney collapsed into a large comfortable couch with a loud sigh, "Oh, it feels so good to be plugged into the world at large again. Look, our carjacking at Gate of Heaven was an itcm on the evening News."

She came to sit down beside him and declared, "That's not a bad sketch of the man the Police are looking for.

"I'll drink to that," he agreed. "We gave them good details and it is a close likeness to that madman."

"Would you care for a glass of wine," Ella asked as she stood and walked over to the breakfast counter?

He looked away from the large screen over his shoulder at her and smiled. "Thought you'd never ask."

"Red or white," she prompted holding up a bottle of each in both hands?

"White is fine for me!"

As she poured the wine she commented, "I hope that Priest got away!"

"Oh yeah, Father Torres," Carney murmured. "I almost forgot about him. I'm sure he is long gone from these parts. Once things settle down, I'll have to go to find out about Sister Angela."

"Let me know when you learn anything."

"I will!"

The couple hiding out on Martha's Vineyard were not the only viewers of the evening News interested in the carjacking. CIA agent Tom Reardon looked at his TV screen intensely. It wasn't a perfect match, but the Police sketch looked familiar. It was someone he had recently dealt with. He thought intensely but couldn't recognize the individual. He clicked on the remote's Pause Button, to keep the drawing on the screen.

Next, he grabbed the tablet resting on the couch beside him and logged into the CIA Website. The person in the sketch didn't look like anyone of the Wanted Portraits. He clicked through to Persons of Interest. When he saw the face of Mustafa Hadad, he stopped and looked a second time and then back at the TV. It wasn't a match, but it was near enough to have a second look.

Special Agent Reardon picked up his cell phone and hit speed dial. He hoped they weren't all logging off early for the weekend. The phone rang three times before being answered.

"Good evening Special Agent Reardon, this is Investigator Andrew Wallace speaking. How may I help you?"

"Good evening Andrew I'm sitting at home just watching the local News There's been a carjacking in South Boston. The Police have a simulated portrait of the suspect. I'm quite sure I recognize the individual. It looks like Mustafa Hadad, who I added to persons of interest list for our office."

"One minute Sir, let me pull that up. Yes, I have him. What would you like to know?"

"Have the agents filled in an address for him yet?"

"Yes Sir, the man is staying at the Great Eastern Hotel on Franklin Street in downtown Boston."

"Do we have anybody on duty this evening, Andrew?"

"There's me and two agents, Sir."

"Would you have the Agents go over to the Great Eastern, to meet with management and see if they will allow them to check out Hadad's room? Tell them to inform management he's a person of interest and if they need it, we can come back with a warrant in the morning."

"Is that it?"

"Have the Agents call me directly, once they have been through his room."

"I will Mr. Reardon and you enjoy your evening."

"Thank you, Andrew."

The phone call came an hour and a half later.

"Mr. Reardon, this is Field Agent Greg Sabourin speaking. I'm at the Great Eastern Hotel in downtown Boston with Field Agent Deborah Washington. We're in the suspect Hadad's room and have finished a thorough investigation, except for the room safe."

"Anything look to be out of the ordinary Agent?"

"Lots Sir, we found a notebook computer open on the desk. It's hooked to a wireless camera elsewhere in the hotel. We were able to locate the camera in the room of another guest named Rafael Torres. Both men checked into the hotel on the same day. They have been here almost a month."

"Anything else," Tom asked?

"There is more. We found an empty box for a GPS tracking device that is sold over the counter in most Spy Gear shops. They have a chip that can be attached to a moving target and then tracked with the GPS app on a smartphone. We also found a box of high caliber pistol shells, but there's no gun unless it's locked in the safe."

Lastly, there are two sets of ID lying in a heap on the bed. They're for a Carney O'Sullivan and an Ella Bowdine."

"They are the two who reported the carjacking," Reardon exclaimed. "Excellent work Agent Sabourin. I think we should leave the area under observation in case Hadad shows up."

"No problem Sir!"

When Tom Reardon hung up he immediately called Andrew Wallace, to whom he related the contents of the call from the Field Agents.

"Andrew, I'd like you to notify State and Local Police and Logan Airport Security. Tell them Mustafa Hadad should be considered armed and approached with extreme caution."

**

At 9 pm the Morgue Attendant at Boston Medical Center pushed a gurney into the service elevator and pressed for the third floor. The corridor lights had been dimmed. He made his way to Room 310. The woman's body was lying in the bed under the blankets. He pushed the gurney alongside the bed before setting the brakes on the wheels. Then he flipped the covers off the body. She was wearing a hospital issued night dress.

After Rafa's visit, Sister Angela began surfacing in what appeared to be a cave. She seemed to be floating and stayed in that state until she heard a scraping noise. The light came streaming in as whatever had been blocking the entrance began to move away. She could see a body lying on a ledge which was cut into the stone.

Inside Angela's head, a woman's voice spoke from far away. She was telling her not to have fear. She must have faith in her son. The Nun felt the urge to flee and run towards the light but resisted until she felt the bed covers flip back. Suddenly she opened her eyes. A hospital orderly was standing in front of her.

The Morgue man took hold of her ankles and started to move them towards the gurney. All of a sudden he felt them being ripped out of his grip. Abruptly the young woman sat up on the bed, holding the night dress tight around her legs and began to scream. He fled the room leaving the gurney where it was and bumped into the Duty Nurse in the corridor who had come to investigate the sound.

"They sent me for a pick-up in Room 310, but she's still alive," the man exclaimed

"Impossible, she lost all her blood from a gunshot wound. There was no heartbeat for over half an hour. She was pronounced dead. We removed the life support systems."

"Well, go see for yourself, nurse," the agitated orderly urged. "She's sitting up in bed as alive as you and me. I need to get my gurney out of there, but she just keeps screaming."

"Hold on a minute, I'll go in and get it for you." As soon as the floor nurse opened the door and saw the woman sitting up in bed, she knew the orderly had been telling the truth. She went in and fetched his trolley for him. After he was gone, she went back into the room.

"Hello Ms. Stuart, I'm the Duty Nurse. You seem to be feeling better."

"Where am I?" Angela asked still sitting up in bed with the sheet pulled around her neck.

"You're at the Boston Medical Center," the woman replied. "You were involved in a shooting on Franklin St. The Police said you were an innocent bystander who was hit by a stray bullet in some kind of a clash between two rival gangs."

"But that's impossible," the frightened Nun replied.

"That's what I'd say too, but blood doesn't lie. Your clothes are in the closet by the door, and they're full of dried blood. We'll send them to the laundry in the morning. The Doctors were convinced they had lost you. After surgery to remove the bullet, you were brought here. Your vital signs disappeared for over a half an hour. Life support systems were turned off."

"Do you mean I was dead?"

"We thought you were. You should sleep now. It's 9:10 pm. A doctor comes on at 7 am, and he will examine you. Do you think you will be okay until then?"

"I think so!"

When the nurse had gone, Angela noticed she was wearing a man's wrist watch. It had a large face and leather strap. She couldn't figure out where it had come from. Carefully she removed the time piece then turned on the bed lamp to see the engraving on the back cover, "Feliz Navidad Rafael, Su Esposa".

It was Spanish. She had taken Spanish at school as her second language. The inscription said, "Merry Christmas Rafael, Your Wife". How did she get this watch? Who was Rafael?

Angela could feel the bandage on her chest and pulled up the nightgown to examine it. The nurse said she had been shot and operated on, and yet she felt no pain. She peeled the edge of the dressing away, to look at her wound. Much to her surprise, there was not a mark on her body. She wondered if she was dreaming and decided to go to the closet to examine her clothes. They were covered with dried blood, just as she had been told.

The Nun was extremely confused. She tried to remember. Before the man had come and taken hold of her ankles, she had been dreaming. The sun was shining. Then she tried to think about what she had been doing before the dream. The nurse said she had been shot on Franklin Street. It was the street where Father Torres hotel was located. She had been there. She had tried to warn Rafa about the carjacker with the gun. The olive-skinned man with the short stubble beard turned and shot at her. She remembered the intense pain in her chest and falling to the sidewalk.

She thought of the watch and the engraving, "Your Wife". It had been on Rafa's wrist. It must have been his father's watch, a gift from his wife and Rafa's mother. Angela stopped thinking and sat on the edge of the bed. If she were wearing his watch, then he had been here. He had left the watch so she would know he had visited. Then she felt her chest. There was no pain. There was only one explanation. He had the Relic and had used it on her.

The Nun stopped thinking and could feel panic rising up in her. This was what had happened to Carney O'Sullivan. If word of her revival, after being dead for at least an hour was to get out, they would say it was a miracle too and come looking for her. She had to get out of here before the doctor arrived in the morning.

Carefully she opened the door to Room 310 and eased her head out into the corridor. Towards the end, at the left, she could see a light and what looked like a Nurses' Station. To the right at the far end of the passage was a set of glass doors, with a red EXIT sign above them. That must be where the stairs are located she thought.

Closing the door, she opened the closet again to see if her shoes were there too. Quietly she dressed in the semi-dark. The dried blood on her clothing scratched against her skin, but it was the least of her worries.

She had no money. The man in the warehouse had taken it. She was glad she wasn't carrying her passport. It was still at the Nun's House in Roslindale. There would be cabs outside the hospital. She would tell a driver she had money in Roslindale. She would promise him a $10 tip.

She looked at the watch. It was 3:30 am. The door to Room 310 closed behind her, as she tiptoed towards the EXIT. At the bottom of the stairs, there was a view into Admitting. An Ambulance had recently arrived, and a stretcher was being wheeled in. Two people were sitting in the Lounge area. A Security Guard was talking with the Desk Attendant.

The Nun opened the door trying to act as confident as possible, not giving the Security Guard even a glance. When she reached the sliding glass entrance, it opened automatically, and she walked out into the cold night air. Several taxis were waiting. The first driver said it was an expensive drive out to Roslindale, and he couldn't afford not to get paid. The second driver said he was a Catholic and would take her word.

Sister Angela took the spare key from under the doormat at the Nun's House and entered. The other occupants had retired for the evening. She went to her room and then returned to pay the driver. He told her to forget the tip. The fare was enough.

Tomorrow was Sunday. The whole house would be going to 9 am Mass at the Sacred Heart parish church. She undressed and got into bed but didn't sleep a wink all night. Over and over again she tried to think of why Father Torres had risked going to the Hospital and why had he brought her back from the dead? The Relic was not supposed to be used. He knew that.

Near dawn, she drifted off momentarily into an almost trance. She seemed to be looking in on a scene from above as if she was floating in the air. Two men are walking along a road, dressed as men did in Biblical times. They were discussing the events of the past several days, including Christ's crucifixion and the reports of his resurrection, but she couldn't understand the language they were speaking. As they walked, they were joined by a third man; however, they didn't seem to recognize him.

**

The Korean agent was one car behind Mustafa on the Freeway. She became puzzled when he signaled to turn off at the first exit. She signaled too and stayed well back so he wouldn't pick her up in the rear view mirrors.

Mustafa crossed over the top of the Interstate and then reentered the traffic heading south. Su decided she would eat later. She continued to follow her quarry. In the cab of Carney's vehicle, the hardened criminal saw the red light on the screen of his cell phone swing around and begin to move in the direction he was headed.

Half an hour later the red indicator light had moved east of the throughway towards the coast. A highway sign said Hingham 1 mile. He took the Exit. The car behind him also turned off. Nam had a vehicle between her and Mustafa.

It was getting late when Carney's crossover entered Hingham. Its driver was still following the blinking red light on his phone. As he entered the town, the 500 feet band appeared on the screen. All he had to do was drive around town until he found the source.

Within half an hour, he was parked outside the Abbey. There was no way to tell how many monks and others were inside. It would be foolish to simply barge in and try to take the Priest. Instead, he drove to a quiet residential street just outside the 500 feet circle and bedded down on the front seat for the night. When the woman who had followed him there saw this, she went off in search of a motel.

***

Chapter 8

Logan Airport

Carney's eyes opened. He was lying on his back. It was remarkably quiet in the house. Far away outside he could hear the surf pounding against the beach as it rolled in from the Atlantic Ocean. He started to remember where he was. What a day yesterday had been. He didn't even want to think about it. He felt for his watch and raised his right hand above his face. It was 5:30 am.

His thoughts turned to Dakota. She wasn't far away, across the water in Hyannis. He was glad she hadn't become involved in any of yesterday's chaos. How had a decent father and a respected member of the community let himself become implicated with guns, a carjacking and yes, the shooting of a nun? Then there was Ella. She was totally an innocent bystander.

This was her house. She had taken him in and shielded him from the craziness out there. He remembered her falling and her pain. Even if the maniac with the gun hadn't caught her and done the same as he had done to the Nun, she could have bled out on the concrete slab or had an injured leg and foot for the rest of her life.

He remembered holding the relic on her foot and praying hard and fast. He had begged God to help her. He hadn't pleaded with God since his wife's car accident. If only he had the relic then.

He realized he had wanted to help Ella as much as he had wanted to save his wife. He couldn't believe he was having such feelings about another woman. What would Dakota think? What would his parents think? He began to feel shy about the incident. It would never be mentioned to anyone.

The window started to brighten with the sunrise, and he could see around the room better. He was in a double bed with a rattan head and foot board. An ordinary rectangular wooden table and a straight back chair were set against one wall. A handcrafted solid cedar chest was placed under the window and a hand woven, coarse wool rug lay on the floor between the chest and the bed. On the far wall hung a large Masonic compass and square insignia. He remembered having seen one at her Beacon Hill condo. She told him it represented fraternity.

The house was different from any he had ever been in. On the outside, it appeared as if everything was on a slant; however, once inside all the floors were level, but the alignment of the walls and ceiling did reveal the reality of being in a cube standing upright on one corner. She certainly was talented to have been able to design and construct a house like this. There was even a clothes closet in the corner. He would have to ask her to show him the plans.

**

Nantucket Island is almost 23 nautical miles southeast of Martha's Vineyard. It's further out in the Atlantic than its sister island and more exposed to the sea. Like its sibling, it too is a tourist Mecca. The off-season population of ten thousand swells to fifty during the summer. The island is known for having the highest valued real estate in the US. It is linked to the mainland by ferry service from Hyannis on Cape Cod and by flights from Boston's Logan airport. The airport is used by a large number of private/corporate planes owned by wealthy summer inhabitants.

As Carney lay thinking about his life, a couple was greeting the day not far away on Nantucket Island, at the Easy St. Inn in the town bearing the island's name. Brian Robertson and Sharon Norris had just reached early morning ecstasy together and were now starting to come down. Brian shifted his weight and moved over onto his side.

"I love it when we're simultaneous," she whispered slyly. "Who would have imagined we would connect? It's so animalistic!"

"I find it hard to believe all of this is actually happening," he said in a low voice beside her ear. "So much has changed, so fast, since you came to see me about the Boston Relic."

"There will be lots more changes when we get our hands on the Relic," she reminded him. "We're going to be living in paradise, in the Caribbean. We'll wake up every day like this."

He kissed the nape of her neck then stretched out on his back beside her. His mind flooded with thoughts about all the money he was going to have when they did get the Relic. He could have anybody then. He knew he wouldn't want her around to remind him of what they had done. Little did he imagine the same feelings were running through her head as she lay beside him. In fact, she already had a plan formulated, which would be activated the moment he turned his back on her and the real relic.

He was silent for several minutes and then spoke again, "All the physical exercise has made me hungry."

"Me too," Sharon murmured, snuggling up to him. "Let's have room service bring up breakfast. We could eat it in bed or at the table in front of the window."

"I'd prefer eating at the table."

"Okay, you call and order."

Breakfast came on a trolley while she was in the shower. When she returned, two places had been set. They ate and smiled at each other, even clinking their coffee cups together, as if they were wine glasses.

"Can you imagine what the Society Board would think if they could see us now?" Brian asked as he watched a couple adjusting the saddlebags on their bikes on the street below.

"Can you imagine what they're going to say when they learn that we've switched the Relic and we're gone?" Sharon laughed as she looked out at Nantucket Harbor imagining it was the Caribbean.

After breakfast, they turned their attention to the Morning News that had just started on the television.

"Police are puzzled by the motive behind a carjacking yesterday in South Boston, outside the Gate of Heaven Roman Catholic Church," the News Anchor explained. "Occupants of the vehicle had just come out of the Church when they were accosted by a man wheeling a gun."

"He demanded the driver's wallet and the passenger's purse. Both the wallet and the purse belonging to Mr. Carney O'Sullivan and Ms. Ella Bowdine of Boston have been recovered. They are intact with no money or ID missing. The automobile has not yet been located." A picture of a vehicle similar to Carney's appeared on the TV.

"The incident has been linked to Mustafa Hadad, a Syrian national from Lebanon who is wanted for questioning by Interpol in relation to at least a dozen murders. Police do not think it was a random attack. Hadad either mistook the couple for someone else or believed they were in possession of something he wanted."

"The suspect should be considered armed and dangerous. If he or the vehicle is sighted, contact the Police at the number on your screen. Remember you heard it first on WYMO Channel 3 Boston," the newsperson declared with a broad smile.

Brian and Sharon looked at each other in alarm. He was the first to speak, "It looks like we're not the only ones trying to get our hands on the Boston Relic."

"I wonder if this Hadad got it?" she asked anxiously.

"They might have been picking it up from the Church, where it had been hidden," he groaned, suddenly feeling terribly weak.

She noticed the change in him immediately and knew she had to stay strong and exclaimed, "Maybe they hid it in the Church. We should get cleaned up, get out of here and go take a look in that Church."

He looked at her and knew instinctively, everything would be finished between them if there was no Relic.

**

Carney heard movements in the house on Martha's and called out, "Is that you, Ella?"

"Finally waking up?" she replied rhetorically. "The bathroom is to your right when you come out of your room. When you're ready, come on down and join me for breakfast."

He appeared at the bottom of the stairs about ten minutes later and looked about the room before venturing in. Not much had been noted the previous evening when after one glass of wine he started to nod off and she showed him his room. Off to the left, a black leather sofa and armchair encircled an expensive Afghan rug. Beyond them was a large window built into the slant of the outside wall. Straight ahead of him she was sitting at a dark brown wicker dining room table with an inlaid glass top. It was surrounded by four matching chairs.

"Come sit down, Sir!" Ella teased. "You're keeping the bacon, eggs, and toast waiting."

"How did you sleep?" he tested feeling a tad shy.

"Oh, I didn't have any trouble getting to sleep," she informed him. "The sound of the ocean is like a lullaby."

"I know, I heard it immediately when I woke."

"We're going to have to stop meeting like this," she joked, "people will talk."

"I'll never tell if you don't," he kidded in turn.

"Okay, it'll be our secret," she confided.

"This is a cool place you have here," he stated pulling out a chair. "I wouldn't mind seeing the plans."

"That's right, you build boats don't you. Sure, I'll show you the plans," she consented, setting a plate and a cup of coffee in front of him.

He ate half the plate before looking up. "I was hungrier than I thought."

"They found our ID," she informed him quietly.

"What? Where?"

"It was on the News while you were dressing."

"Gotta call the Police," he stammered.

"What for?" she inquired earnestly.

"To tell them where I am, just in case they find my vehicle."

"I'd rather you didn't tell them where you are. They haven't caught him yet, and he sounds extremely dangerous. Interpol is looking for him in relation to murders in other countries."

"How do the Police know who did it, if they haven't even caught the guy?"

"They must have found his fingerprints on our wallets."

"Where did he ditch them?" he asked while rolling a bit of egg and a strip of bacon up in a wedge of buttered toast.

"They didn't say. All they said was our ID and cash is intact."

"Okay, I won't call the Police."

"So, do you still go to services at the Gate of Heaven?"

"No, Dakota and I attend in Jamaica Plain."

"Catholics take a course from the church before they get married don't they?," she probed.

"Yes, it's called a Pre-Marital Course and it's almost unavoidable. That is to say, it's hard to find a priest who will marry you if you haven't taken it."

"Did you take it?"

"My wife and I took it together at the Gate of Heaven. Why the interest in the Pre-marital course?"

"Oh, just curious!" she smirked.

"Are you planning to marry a Catholic?"

"You never know. I saw what you did yesterday. The priest said your feelings had to be genuine or it wouldn't work."

"Now you're embarrassing me," he joked.

"Well, there's also Dakota."

"What about Dakota?"

"She's going to need a mother soon. A troubling period is just around the corner for her. A man can't see a teenage girl through it all. She needs a woman to talk with about things."

"I see."

"Thought you would understand," she exclaimed with another smirk.

"I'll find out when the next course is scheduled to take place," he jested.

"That would be very considerate of you."

"We'll take it together," he exclaimed with a broad grin.

"It's a deal but, not at the same place where you and your wife took it!" she scolded in jest.

"It'll be a clean start!" he laughed.

"Yup, a new beginning!" Ella exclaimed. "While I was sitting here waiting for you, I was thinking about a strange dream I had last night. I think it had something to do with our ordeal yesterday."

"Wanna tell me about it," he inquired, taking a sip from his coffee?

"I seemed to be looking in on a scene from above as if I was floating in the air. Seven men were fishing. They dressed as men did in Biblical times. Another man appeared and began talking to them, but I couldn't understand the language. After some discussion, the men in the boat threw down their nets again and they were full when they pulled them up."

**

Mustafa woke in Carney's vehicle outside the Hingham Abbey when the first rays of the sun began to emerge from the east. He started the engine, made a U-turn and parked on the other side of the street to escape the dawn. It took about two seconds to drop back to sleep. Su woke at 7 am and turned on the television in the cheap motel room she had rented. She listened to the story about the carjacking which had taken place the previous afternoon.

The reporting was different from the way things had happened. There was no mention of the Priest and the Nun. She knew she would have to be careful if the Police were looking for the automobile. The Consul would disavow all knowledge if she became involved in a Police incident.

At 8 am someone knocked on Father Torres door and informed him breakfast was now being served in the ground floor cafeteria. He had been awake a while and had taken a shower in the common washroom down the hall. When the knock sounded, he was kneeling on a wooden prayer bench.

It was a large cafeteria built to accommodate the many believers who came here for a retreat. While eating, he counted sixty-eight people not wearing a black hooded robe. They must be present for the Thanksgiving Retreat, he thought. As he finished counting, one of the Benedictine Monks sat down at his table and introduced himself, Father Horatio Johnson.

"I trust you slept well," Father Johnson inquired?

"Yes, it's very tranquil here."

"Father Jacob Burns is the Abbot here," the monk continued. "He asked me to tell you he can see you at 10 am this morning. The Abbot's office is located at the extreme eastern end of the building, on this level. You're welcome to circulate around the monastery and grounds while you're waiting."

"Please inform the Father Abbot I thank him for setting aside time to see me and I will be there at 10 a.m."

Abbot Burns was a tall, muscular man who had played professional football before he thought he might have a vocation. It had been many years ago. This was his fifth year at the Abbey. Prior to being elected he worked as an administrator for the Benedictine Order, Monday to Friday and assisted with the Masses in a nearby parish on weekends. When Father Torres knocked he heard a strong voice on the other side of the door call out,

"Come in please!"

The two religious introduced themselves to each other and then Abbot Burns focused on the purpose of the meeting.

"About a month ago I received a message from Rome informing me I might be receiving a visit from you. The communication said you would say you were here for a retreat and that you had a reservation. I must admit, I was quite surprised when they informed me you had arrived, last evening. I immediately contacted the Vatican."

"I don't know anything about you or what you are involved in; however, it's not every day I receive a request from the Holy Father to lend assistance. I have been requested to take you to Logan Airport in Boston. I was also requested to purchase a one-way airplane ticket for you, provide you with one thousand dollars cash and to give you a private message faxed to me this morning from His Holiness."

Father Torres looked the Abbot straight in the eyes and declared in a clear, crisp voice, "I'm not at liberty to say anything about what I'm doing here, but I do very much appreciate whatever you do for me."

"Alright Father," Abbot Burns boomed. "I don't need to know any more than I know already. As you could see at breakfast, we have many visitors here for their Thanksgiving Retreat."

"Yes, I noticed."

"All my staff is much occupied. I can't really spare anyone for the time required to drive you into Logan and then return here. Ordinarily, we could take you to the Ferry Dock here in Hingham but it's closed for a month for repairs. However, I do have a Plan B.

"There's a small town called Hull, about a fifteen-minute drive from here out at the end of the Nantasket Peninsula. Monday to Friday there is regular public commuter service by boat from Hull into Logan and Boston. On the weekends, up to Thanksgiving or the fourth Thursday in November, there is a private water taxi service between Hull and the Logan Dock with a stop here in Hingham and another at the Harbor Islands."

"We have three visitors for the weekend who requested in advance a visit to the Harbor Islands while they are here. They are American History teachers. There are some old Forts on the islands related to the Colonial period. I just called the water taxi company. They had one seat left which I booked for you. In addition, I have two envelopes for you."

"This envelope marked #1 contains your airplane ticket and ten crisp $100 bills. You are not to open it until you are in front of the Check-In Counter, at Logan's International Terminal. The second envelope marked #2 contains a fax signed by the Holy Father in Rome. You are not to open it until after your plane is in the air."

Father Torres accepted the two envelopes and thanked the Father Abbot.

'Our shuttle van will be leaving before noon. Probably the Chapel would be as pleasant a place as any for you to wait. It's at the other end of the building, exactly where this office is located. The driver will go there to contact you when he is ready to leave. His name is Father Young."

Outside the grounds of the Abbey, Mustafa watched the marker on his GPS screen moving. He knew the priest was walking around inside the building. He also knew he couldn't stay holed up in there forever. He decided to wait until dark. If his target didn't come out during the day, he would go in under the cover of the night to find him.

The issue soon resolved itself for the Syrian. Within an hour, the blinking red light on the screen began to move towards him. The priest was leaving the Abby. When the shuttle van reached the street, it turned north and drove towards the ocean.

Mustafa wheeled around and began to follow the steel blue vehicle. He could see three people sitting in the back and a passenger in front with the driver. The Carney's crossover came up close to the van. Brother Hadad could see the passenger in front was the Priest. Quickly he reviewed his options and decided to follow.

At length, the Abbey Shuttle turned into Nantasket Avenue. Rafa recognized the name. During his research in the newspapers at the Boston Library, he read the report on Carney O'Sullivan's accident. The drive-by shooting had occurred at Nantasket Beach in Hull.

Soon they were passing through the beach area. It wasn't a warm day, but the parking lot in front of the beach was over half full. In addition, there were many people sitting on the sand or walking along the edge of the surf.

When they passed the intersection of Nantasket Ave and Nantasket Rd., Rafa remembered the shooting had occurred on Nantasket Rd. Looking to his left he thought, it all started just up that road about five months ago. What a small world!

It wasn't long before they reached Pemberton Point at the extreme end of the peninsula where the wharf was located. The Abbey vehicle pulled up beside a Hull Police Cruiser at the entrance to the pier. Two burly officers wearing holstered side arms were surveying everything happening.

Mustafa cursed his luck and drove past them to look for a parking spot. By the time he returned at the entrance to the wharf, the steel blue passenger van was gone. He walked by the Police who looked at him casually and went out onto the wharf. Ferry terminals don't pride themselves on much on aesthetics. Pemberton Point was just concrete, then a metal ramp to a dock. It had a few "No Parking" signs and a wastebasket, but there really isn't much here to talk about. There is, however, one restaurant - Pemberton Bait and Tackle, which offered good fried food for lunch. He could see a rather large boat had just launched, leaving a deep furrow of white foam and churned water in its wake.

An old man was casting with his fishing rod at the spot where the vessel had been tied up. Mustafa went over to talk with him.

"What boat just left?"

"The ferry," the fisherman replied

"Did you see anyone who looked like a priest board it?" the assassin inquired.

"Yes, there was one fella wearing a Roman collar."

"Is it possible to have them come back to pick me up?

"You'd have to call their office. That's their number on the sign over there, but from what I saw, every seat was occupied. It's the holiday weekend."

"Where is it going?"

"It makes a brief stop at Hingham, the Harbor Islands if someone wants them, then goes on to Logan Dock and finally to the end of the line at

Long Wharf in Boston. There's about half an hour turnaround time then it comes back here after making the same stops."

"By Logan Dock, do you mean Logan Airport?"

"Yes, there's a ferry terminal not far from the runways. A shuttle bus visits it about every hour and then loops around by the airport Terminals."

"How long would it take the water taxi to reach Logan Dock?"

"At least an hour, probably a bit longer seeing it's fully loaded," the old man replied.

Mustafa turned and walked away without even thanking him. On the way back to Carney's vehicle he stopped at the takeout window of the Bait Shop and paid for a large order of deep fried clams. He went over everything in his mind while waiting for the food. The Priest must be flying back to Rome so he would be headed for the International Terminal, but he wouldn't get there for at least two hours. Brother Haddad was sure he could be at the airport in less than two hours.

**

When he reached the interstate going north, his progress improved rapidly. Soon he was at the Tunnel going under the Boston Harbor. He thought about going to Logan Dock but then discarded the idea. E Terminal was International. He headed for E Terminal parking. Agent Nam was two cars behind.

Arrivals were on the lower level. The shuttle bus between the other terminals and Logan Dock would stop on the lower level. Central Parking was connected to the terminal via an elevated passenger walkway.

As Mustafa entered the Parkade, a picture of his license plate was snapped and sent to Airport Security. Within a minute of being advised, the Chief of Security had Tom Reardon on the phone. The CIA agents at the airport were wearing communication plugs in their ears, and Reardon could talk to all of them at once.

"This is it, boys, Haddad is at the airport. He's just entered Central Parking and is most likely headed for a quick escape through the International Terminal. He's probably disguised and carrying false documents. If you can stop him, that carjacking is sufficient to keep him from leaving the country. Do I have anybody in the International Terminal?"

"Agent Pride here Sir, Agent Greer and I are in Terminal C, which is beside E Terminal. We can be in E in two or three minutes."

"Go ahead Agents and keep the rest of us posted."

Mustafa parked the SUV and headed for the pedestrian bridge, a moving walkway to the terminal. The Korean caught up to him at the entrance to Terminal E and stood behind him on the escalator going down one level to Ticketing and Departures. When he arrived in the lobby, he made straight for the Alitalia baggage and boarding pass check in lines. Su stayed near the bottom of the escalator. She could see Mustafa scrutinizing each face waiting at the Check-In Gates.

When he finished and turned to come back towards her, she knew he would be going down to the next floor where ground level transport arrived, so boarded the escalator ahead of him and then veered off towards the arrivals and baggage claim area when she stepped off the moving stairs. Brother Haddad arrived about a minute and a half later. He took up a position where he could see the Stop for the Airport Shuttle outside and the escalator going back up to the Departures area. He didn't have to wait long.

The shuttle arriving from Logan Ferry Dock and the other Terminals pulled in about eight minutes after he began watching. The last person off the bus was carrying no baggage. Hadad took one look and recognized Rafa immediately. He had tracked him too long.

The woman noticed the Syrian remove a weapon from a shoulder holster hidden under his jacket and start to screw a silencer into the barrel. It was her signal. She moved behind a large pillar between the baggage claim area and the Entrance and removed the pistol from the holster she was wearing between her thighs. She also screwed a silencer into the end of the gun's barrel.

Haddad didn't have a clear shot at the Priest until he was going up on the escalator. Then he moved with precision, looked twice around him, brought the gun up until his hand was in line with his sight and prepared to pull the trigger. Just as his finger closed around the trigger and squeezed, Korean Agent, came out from behind the pillar, brought her left arm up to serve as a gun rest, placed the silencer on her jacket at the elbow and also squeezed the trigger.

Her bullet was a fraction of a second in advance of his pressing on the trigger, and as his bullet left the chamber, her bullet came smashing into his gun and hand at 1,400 feet per second. It was enough to deflect the bullet leaving the end of his silencer and the gun flew out of his hand upon impact. Su ducked back behind the cement pillar just as he spun around to see where the shot had come from. She dropped her gun into her handbag and started to walk towards the Women's Restrooms at the back of the Baggage Claim area.

At this exact moment, the CIA's Pride and Greer came rushing through from Terminal C, and she almost walked straight into their path. They continued on towards the door for Ground Transportation. As soon as she entered the Restroom, she took the pistol out of her purse, grabbed a piece of paper towel from the wall dispenser, wiped the arm clean and then dropped it into the garbage receptacle. Quickly she walked to a stall and locked the door behind herself.

In the privacy of the stall, she pulled up her skirt and removed the holster. It went into her handbag before she straightened her clothes and opened the door. There were two travelers at the sinks. Once they left, she dropped the holster in the garbage container at the far end of the Restroom and left, heading for the passageway to Terminal C.

When Agents Pride and Greer arrived at the Ground Transportation area, they saw Brother Hadad fumbling with his left hand, trying to pick up his gun from the floor. Blood was coming from his right hand. The Agents immediately drew their service revolvers and barked a powerful command. "Drop your gun!"

Mustafa didn't straighten up but swiveled to see who had issued the order. From the way they dressed, he knew who they were and let the weapon fall back to where it had been.

"On the floor, on your stomach," Agent Pride ordered as he kicked Mustafa's gun away.

**

By this time, Father Torres had reached the top of the Escalator and was following the signs towards the Check-in Gate for Alitalia. He had seen or heard nothing of what transpired on the ground floor behind him. Since he had no bags, he walked up to where the Boarding Passes were being issued and removed the envelope #1 from the pocket inside his robe, to take out his Pass. It took a second to open the envelope and unfold the piece of paper upon which the Internet Boarding Pass had been printed. Much to his surprise, it indicated he was flying on Aer Lingus, which is the Irish National Airline. He checked twice to make sure it was his name and then wandered off to find the Aer Lingus Check-in Gate.

Once Su Nam was in Terminal C, she rode the escalators up to level three and entered the Pedestrian Bridge to the Central Parking. As soon as she had her vehicle, she left the Parkade and continued on towards the entrance to the Tunnel under the harbor and back to Boston. It was a short trip to her hotel where she checked out and then went to fill the car with gas. When the Committee in North Korea had approved Su's Mission, they told her if she couldn't secure the object for North Korea, then she should do her utmost to make sure it didn't fall into the hands of the Brotherhood of Eternal light or as she referred to them BEL.

While the attendant was fueling her car she sent a short text message to the North Korean representative at the UN. "PLEASE FORWARD - BEL STOPPED – LEAVING U.S." Then she dropped the phone in the service station trash can. Her plan was to drive to New York City and purchase a ticket to Seoul.

Since carjacking is not a federal offense, Mustafa Hadad was turned over to the Boston Police for processing. This would give the CIA all the time they needed to contact Interpol and decide what was to be done with the criminal.

Father Torres had to wait in the Departure Lounge several hours for his flight, but ultimately it did lift off. A cabin attendant announced the seat belt sign would be switched off soon and they would be coming through the cabin with complimentary beverages for all. Rafa removed the envelope marked #2 from his inside pocket and opened it. First, he read the fax from the Pope.

"Dear Father Rafael Torres,

Congratulations on your successful retrieval of the Crucifixion Relic for the Church. We have decided not to bring it back to Rome. There are far too many factions here who would compete with each other for control of such an object. We have decided to have you deliver it to a Benedictine Monastery near Murroe in Ireland. That's not far from Limerick, where you will be landing. When you arrive at the Abbey, seek out Father Abbot Erikson. He's a Dane. Tell him what you have and put it directly into his hands. He will be pre-instructed as to what should be done.

The Benedictines in the US were asked to provide you with $1,000 US$. If you have family still living in Spain, I suggest going there for a visit, before returning to Italy. In addition, I ask you not to use the credit or the ATM cards issued in your name. We believe they have been compromised. The hounds must be kept off your scent as long as possible, so the Relic can be secured in a safe place.

Your Holy Father and Pope of the Church of Rome"

There were also ten new US $100 bills. A thousand dollars wouldn't go far, but it would take him to the continent. He also had what was left of the $1,000 he had withdrawn from an ATM and kept folded inside his passport.

Before putting them back in the envelope and into his inside pocket he thought of the Bishop who showed up at the hotel in Boston. He may have been one of the hounds. At that moment the complimentary beverage cart stopped beside him. He accepted a glass of white wine.

**

As soon as she arrived back at her place in Boston from the weekend on Nantucket, Sharon Norris went on line to see if there was any chatter in the blogs and Chat sites about the Boston Relic. Three hours later she was rewarded. It wasn't much, but an anonymous poster in Miracles Chat left a short script, "There's been another one at BM". She wracked her brain. BM had to be Boston Medical.

She scripted a short, "Thanks for sharing about another at BM!"

She waited fifteen minutes, but no reply came so she decided to go take a shower with the plan to come back later and re-post exactly what the anonymous poster had said on other sites with the hope that she would draw someone out.

An hour later Sharon was back on her computer. Currently she had logins for a dozen sites, some blogs and some chat rooms, where miracles and paranormal phenomena were discussed. Once in the young woman surveyed the current discussions and if none were a fit, she would start a new thread before posting, "There's been another one at BM". Once bread crumbs were sprinkled in the twelve locations, it was time to go out and pick up a few groceries.

The following morning she had time to check her posts before going into work. There had been a small amount of activity on some sites but none on her threads until she hit the Miracles Blog where a poster named Brother Andre had posted, "By 'BM', R U referring to Boston Medical and by 'another', R U referring to that spinal cord recovery that was reported in their online Journal about six months ago?"

"Sort of," she replied and then logged off. It was a busy day and she went straight from work to a function she had been invited to at Radcliffe College in Cambridge. The guest speaker examined the impact of private philanthropy on the organizational structure and academic culture of colleges and universities in the Greater Boston Area. It was 10 pm before she was able to go in and check what had transpired on Miracles.

Much to her surprise the poster had been online five minutes previous and had typed, "There has been an incident reported and discussed among those who know concerning The Boston Medical Center, but it is nothing like what happened back during the summer."

She couldn't help herself and asked, "What are they discussing?"

As luck would have it, Brother Andre was still on line and she saw three dots start to go around in a circle indicating that he was typing something. After more than a minute it appeared below her comment.

"Nothing has been confirmed as of yet, but it seems the Police were called to Franklin St. recently concerning a Nun who had been shot in the street. She was taken by ambulance to Boston Medical. It was reported on the News as a stray bullet in an altercation between two rival gangs. Several concerned groups did follow up and sent volunteers in to visit the Nun, but she had disappeared. There was no record of her being discharged, but hospital staff were not authorized to discuss the incident with the media."

"A break came when someone reported overhearing a morgue attendant talking about the incident with a friend in a bar in South Boston. It seems he had been called to remove a woman's body from one of the rooms. He had been told she had been pronounced dead several hours before he went to retrieve her. Much to his surprise, she sat up in bed and began screaming. The duty nurse told him she was the Nun who had been shot during the day."

"When this started going around the BMC issued a Press Release saying the Nun had a visit from a priest who wanted to give her Last Rites and then the following morning it was discovered she had vanished during the night. Apparently the Hospital has filed a missing person's report and the Police are continuing their investigation."

Sharon couldn't believe what she was reading and exclaimed out loud, "The Catholics got it! The Catholics have the relic!" That night she resolved to meet with Brian Robertson as soon as possible to give him an update.

Brian had a lot to deal with when he arrived back from Nantucket but did finally accept her invitation to buy him lunch on Friday. She chose a restaurant in a restored brick warehouse on Long Wharf. The original beams were still visible in both ceilings. A bronze American Eagle clutching a Stars and Stripes in its talons looked down on their table.

"No alcohol for me," Brian said to the waiter as he passed him a drink menu. "I still have a full afternoon, which includes a one-on-meeting."

"I'm the same," Sharon seconded. "We'll simply order now.

"I've been here before and had your Seafood Tacos," he told the waiter. "They were delicious, so I'll have them again. No bread or fries, please, I'm watching my carbs."

"I'll try the deep fried halibut," she decided after a quick look at the menu. "I'm the same. I'll replace the fries with a salad."

"So, what did you want to talk about Sharon?"

"It's about the Boston relic!"

"Oh," he tweeted. "Did they turn it in to the Court Registry?"

"Not quite, there has been another incident at the Boston Medical Centre."

"What sort of an incident?

"A woman was dead for two hours after her life support systems were turned off. She had a visit from a priest who gave her Last Rites. Sometime after that she made a full recovery and walked out of the hospital in the middle of the night."

"How do you know all this," he demanded with anger showing in his voice.

"I got it from a regular on the Miracles Blog at the beginning of the week."

"Can you show me?"

"I brought you a print out."

"May I see it please," he asked stretching out his arm.

He scanned the sheet of paper she passed him and then exclaimed, "The Catholics got it!"

"That was my exact reaction," she declared.

"How can this be? We had an Injunction. What's a Priest doing with it?"

"I don't know. The doctor and patient were supposed to deposit it at the Court Registry."

Brian's face went sullen and his eyes narrowed as he looked directly at her. "Sharon, you have missed something. I relied on you to follow all this Internet chatter. It was you who brought it to my attention. I expected you to be diligent. My meeting this afternoon hinges on us having possession of that relic."

"I'm sorry Brian. I'm just as surprised as you."

At that moment the waiter arrived with their meals. It helped them change the conversation.

"Let's eat Sharon! These look so good!"

She had seen the anger in him and was glad to have a diversion. When they were finished she tested the topic which had motivated this lunch once again.

"What are we going to do about this Priest? Do you think we can ask the Judge to expand the Injunction to include him?"

"I'm not sure. My immediate concern is about what I'm going to say to the person I'm meeting later this afternoon. I apologize for over reacting before we ate."

"Accepted! I'll see what I can find out over the weekend and give you an update on Monday. I don't think it's wise to leave any discussions about this latest development in our email, given the way email communications are getting so many people into hot water."

"I appreciate your candor!"

Brian gave Sharon a light kiss on her cheek as they were leaving.

***

Chapter 9

Niddrie Mains

On the 30th of November dawn began breaking on the Atlantic horizon, a hundred miles or so off the western shores of Ireland. Rafa had slept a little. During the night, he dreamt he could feel warmth radiating from the Relic and awoke suddenly. He dozed off several times afterward and then woke again abruptly, from a dream where he thought he had lost it. As they flew across Ireland towards Dublin, cabin attendants came through serving breakfast. He had a second coffee and began looking out through the window.

The countryside was a brilliant pattern of multicolored fields. Here and there he distinguished houses and roads. This was going to be his first time in Ireland. He found it hard to believe the Church was sending the Relic back to where it had resided over a hundred and fifty years ago. He also found it hard to believe he had acted so similarly to the people in that distant time. They had been motivated by love for someone who had been murdered. What had motivated him to bring Sister Angela back among the living?

He would have to come to grips with the reason sooner or later, but for now, he didn't need to think about it. Both he and Sister Angela were so lucky nobody but them knew he had used the Relic to return her to life. He hoped she managed to get out of the hospital before being confronted by the doctors. There would have been a lot of explaining for her to do if she hadn't. He remembered reading the time of her death on the chart. She had been dead for over two hours when he brought her back to life.

The seat belt light came on, and the Captain's voice was heard throughout the cabin. "Good morning folks. I've switched on the seat belt sign as we have begun our descent into Shannon Airport. The time on the ground is 7:10 am and we expect to be at the terminal gate in twenty-two minutes. The temperature at the airport is fifty degrees Fahrenheit and a light rain is falling. There are various methods of connecting with Limerick, but there is no train. I'd like to thank all of you for flying Aer Lingus and we look forward to serving you again in the near future."

After showing his passport at Immigration, a Customs Agent found it odd that he was traveling without luggage. His English had improved since being in America. Father Torres explained he would be well taken care of by the Benedictines he was visiting at an Abbey, just outside of Limerick. The passport was stamped. The priest made his way outside to the bus loading area and boarded the coach to City Centre.

The Abbey was located eleven miles west of Limerick, close to Murroe. Many people from the village worked in the city, so there was a daily bus connection. Residents didn't think anything of seeing someone wearing a Roman collar riding the same bus home as them, after work. The taxi driver in Murroe said he had taken many monks to the Abbey from the bus.

The Abbey was in the center of a 500-acre estate which enclosed streams, lakes, woodland paths and a Norman style castle. It was founded in 1927 and was a community of approximately 50 monks. They ran a boarding school for boys, a farm and a guest house for retreats. They belonged to one of the Benedictines' twenty worldwide congregations. Each congregation is composed of many abbeys. The abbeys are run by an Abbot who is elected by the monks for an eight year period.

The abbey was located in a Normanesque castle with a Windsor-style round tower, all fronted with an impressive facade and Norman gatehouse. The main buildings were facing south and commanded an unbroken view of some thirty miles towards the Galtee Mountains. This Abbey was presided over by a monk from Copenhagen named Father Abbot Erikson.

He was the man Father Torres sought out upon arrival and was invited to an evening meeting after supper. The first thing the Abbot said to him was, "Good evening Father, I see a collar, but I can tell you are not a Benedictine."

"No, I'm not a Benedictine, Father Abbot. I am a Spanish Jesuit."

"Ah yes, I remember studying about the troubles of the Jesuits of Spain. One of your Kings expelled your Order from Spain and its South American possessions in the seventeenth century."

"True, our Society lost over 200 missions in South America. It was a serious setback for the continent as we ran the only schools. Afterward, the people lived and died there without ever learning to read or write. Pope Pius VII restored the Society of Jesuits in 1814."

"But anyway Father, you're not here to talk about the past. I have been told you will be giving me something. It must be very small. The monks told me you arrived without any luggage."

"I have no bags. What I have is a Relic, which I've been asked to bring to you for safe keeping."

"A Relic, I see, we already have several of them hidden somewhere on the property. Even I don't know exactly where they're located. This estate is 500 acres large. As you can imagine, there are many places where a relic could be concealed."

"Probably why I was asked to bring it to you," Rafa surmised.

"May I see it?" the Abbot asked.

"Certainly," Rafa replied removing the cloth handkerchief from his inside pocket and unfolding it in the palm of his hand.

"Oh, it's so small, only a tiny chip of a bone," Abbot Erickson exclaimed. "I have never taken much interest in relics. They seem to be more of a

Catholic culture from the past. A practice associated with southern Europe. I was raised in Denmark."

"Correct, the Church has even forbidden relic worship, and I agree," the Spanish priest replied.

"So how is it you come to be in possession of this relic?" Abbot Erickson continued.

"I'm a trained Relicoligist," Rafa replied. "Sometimes Church authorities send me to investigate the surfacing of a relic. I must try to determine if it's genuine or not. If it's some kind of scam being used to manipulate innocent believers, we expose it to the public. If it seems legitimate, the Church tries to get it out of circulation and hide it away some place where it will be safe and not cause any irritation among believers. I've even been to Russia to investigate an object thought to be a relic."

"I know you can't tell me anything about this One, but I must assume, in your expert opinion, it's authentic."

"Yes!" he declared, thinking back to when he watched Carney restore his friend Ella's foot. "This One is very genuine!"

"Very well, I have been told it should be given Catalogue number 'C01' and when you leave it with me, I will receive further instructions."

Father Torres folded the handkerchief and placed it in the Abbot's hand before saying, "This Relic is your responsibility now. Its journey with me is finished."

"Thank you, Father, I will take excellent care of it. About your accommodation, I have decided to assign a God Pod to you. God Pods are private hermitages, located on the Abbey grounds. They are equipped with a small fridge, electric hob, and microwave oven. Bed linen, bath towels, and tea towels are also provided as well as some of the usual necessities such as tea, coffee, milk, and sugar.

"Main meals may be taken in the Monastery. The monks assemble in Church four times a day for the Divine Office and the Mass. Benedictine worship emphasizes beauty and harmony, celebrating God's presence, while it evokes a response of loving reverence in the monk. Pods are generally used for personal retreats. When you feel ready to go, we will provide you with fresh clothing in line with what a Jesuit would wear."

"That is very kind of you Father Abbot."

The Abbot picked up the phone on his desk and informed his assistant, "Father Torres is ready to be shown to God Pod #3." A minute or so later a monk entered the office. After shaking hands with Father Erickson, Father Torres followed the assistant.

As they walked down through the seventeenth-century Italian-style, walled terraced garden the assistant took pride in telling the visitor about where they were. "This was the first garden of its kind in Ireland. It combines a large variety of herbs, plants, vegetables, flowers, and trees, which are named in the Bible."

"I can see that it's very advanced," Torres commented.

"Benedictines live a monastic life but there are nothing horse and buggy about us," the monk assured him.

"What's your name, if I might ask?" Rafa enquired politely.

"Not at all Father, my name is Barry O'Neil."

"Pleased to make your acquaintance."

"Do you mind if I ask you a question?"

"Not at all," the Irish monk replied. "Ask away!"

"What is the Benedictines secret?" Rafa questioned hesitantly.

"Oh, that's simple Father. It's the Rule!"

"And what is the Rule?"

"The Rule is what St Benedict wrote down for us. The Rule is a wonderful harmony of wisdom, good sense, and firmness."

Father O'Neil continued, "The Rule of Benedict is a style of life for those interested in living with and in God. It is a no-nonsense, unembroidered handbook for those who want to join the rewarding school of the Lord's service. His rule contains directions for all aspects of community life, but there is an in-built diffidence and flexibility allowing for adaptation to different countries, climates, centuries; which is why it has lasted for over fourteen hundred years."

"Thank you for your candor, Father Barry."

"Not at all," the monk laughed. "And here we are at God Pod #3."

**

It had been two weeks since Philadelphia FBI agents Lorne Andersen and Wally Sorensen had been instructed by their superior, Randal Bergman, to concentrate all their efforts on finding the source of the counterfeit bills that Edwardo Romares was putting out through the ATM's that Automatic Bank Corp. owned. They were glad Randall had transferred the investigation of the Bitcoin operation to the Bureau's electronic surveillance unit.

Their job involved a lot of old fashion police work. They didn't think Edwardo would keep a stash of fake cash at home as it might implicate his wife and family if ever the scheme was discovered. All the stops they had recorded that he had made, had to be checked out. They decided to start with places he visited more than once to narrow the field; however that wasn't tight enough. Finally they settled on places he had visited more than once where no ATM was installed.

Late Thursday afternoon of the second week in December a needle came out of the hay stack. Lorne was looking out the window at a few early season snowflakes fluttering through the cold air outside the pane. Wally was analyzing the print-outs of the activity the wireless GPS on Romares car was sending back to their headquarters. The reports gave them a lot of information such as longitude and latitude, street name, civic addresses within a radius of 100 feet of where he parked, as stop and start times. Suddenly he exclaimed, "Bingo!"

"What, what have you got?" Anderson wanted to know.

"We have two more metrics," his partner replied. "Now in addition to more than two stops and no machine on premises, we need to consider day and time. I have found a location where Mr. Smart Ass stops every Thursday at 2 pm for ten minutes and there is no ATM located there."

"Where is it?"

"Over in Camden."

"Did we ever record that stop when we were following him?"

"Sure did!"

"Them we should have an address?"

"Sure do!"

"Feel like going for a ride this afternoon Wally?"

"Thought you would never ask."

Camden is a city in New Jersey. It is located directly across the Delaware River from Philadelphia, via the Benjamin Franklin Bridge. The Camden Waterfront, a mixed-use community, is home to a 1.5-mile beautifully maintained promenade lined with regional attractions concert venues, a minor league baseball stadium, and Adventure Aquarium. The Waterfront is a safe, family-friendly destination.

"So where are we going to, Buddy?"

"A small business on North 6th Street, not far from City Hall."

"Not a dead end, people coming and going wouldn't be noticed."

"Exactly, a car parked less than fifteen minutes wouldn't even be noted."

"So, what kind of business is it?"

"The name we recorded was Walden Printing. While we were waiting I looked it up on my smart phone. Their main line was silk screening T's, hoods and athletic wear, but the Web page said they also did off set and digital printing"

"I remember that place. It wasn't far from Rutgers University. We thought Edwardo was looking for T-shirts for his kids"

"Now we're going to see who else goes there beside Mr. Romares."

After crossing the bridge they followed the freeway to the first Exit which was N. 6th. "Let's take a drive by first," Lorne suggested.

"No problem," Wally agreed. "There it is up there on the left."

"I'm seeing more this time than when we were here before."

"Me too, there's a loading dock on the side and it looks like they use the two levels."

"Silk screening takes a lot of space. There are pneumatic tables and at least one dryer. I worked in shipping for a small place in Philly one summer when I was in high school," Sorensen informed him.

"What do you say I go in the retail part and sniff it out?"

"Sounds good!"

"I don't know what I should be looking for though."

"Check out the T-shirts and maybe get one for your son.

"Thanks, I'll meet you up the street."

The two agents ended up spending the next day and Monday to Thursday of the following week in a stake-out van positioned so that they got a clear photo of anyone entering Walden Printing. The vehicle was also equipped with silent witness video cameras on the outside to monitor anyone approaching and to get snaps of any customer's license plate if desired. The camera feeds went to an inside monitor that allowed Lorne and Wally to see everything that was happening in the street.

Their first break came about 2 pm Friday. A tall thin man in his fifties approached the firm after leaving a car parked down the street. Wally snapped a frontal and side view portrait of him and sent a digital image to headquarters for a scan by facial recognition software and then a data base search for a match.

The operator got to their submission about 4 pm. At 4:30 Lorne received an email. The man in the photo was a known felon, Dewayne Ross. He had served time ten yours ago for passing counterfeit. Mostly small stuff like putting a fake $5 or $10 in someone's change at a gas station where he worked.

"Maybe Dewayne is up to his old tricks again," Wally commented. Lorne raised his eye brows and smiled.

On Monday, Tuesday and Wednesday the client entering Walden around 2 pm turned out to have a former conviction for counterfeit. On Thursday Edwardo showed up at his usual time. Lorne phoned Randal at HQ to let him know. Bergman was delighted.

"Lorne, you and Wally have done a wonderful job on this and now you get your reward. I want you to break camp over there in Camden and come back over to Philly. Go directly to Automatic Bank Corp. One of our teams will meet you. They will have a portable counterfeit scanner with them. Wait until Edwardo is parked. Then you and Wally take him down. Don't spook him before he's parked. We don't need any high speed chase. As soon as we receive confirmation that he's carrying counterfeit a squad will move in Walden Printing in Camden."

**

Rafa woke from his first night in the God Pod after a deep, ten-hour sleep. He had no idea what time it was. Instinctively he raised his left arm to see his wrist watch, before remembering he had left it with Sister Angela. It was sunny outside, but what time could it be?

The restored man felt a shiver of excitement run through him and knew what it was. The Crucifixion Relic had been delivered. He was liberated. Now he would be able to fall back into his quiet, orderly life in Amalfi. Then he remembered the fax from the Pope. He wasn't to come back quickly. He could go to visit family if so inclined.

Gradually he noticed his hunger and threw back the bed covers. There was tea, coffee, powdered milk and sugar cubes. Within 5 minutes, the kettle was whistling, and he poured boiling water over two spoonfuls of instant coffee. The bells in the tower sounded unobtrusive, and he counted twelve chimes. It must be noon. The digital clock on the microwave was correct. He decided to go up to the monastery and arrived just in time for lunch. That day the main course was farmhouse soup, beef stew with slices of dark rye and apple caramel pudding.

For the rest of the day, he wandered along several of the many paths crisscrossing the five hundred acre estate. Contact with fields, streams, and woods soothed his soul as he re-lived, in his mind, the details of the months since leaving Italy. When he heard the muffled sounds coming from the bell tower toll six times, calling all to Evening Vespers, he decided he would stay at the Abbey a week.

During the first two days, he prayed and thought about God. His concept of the divinity had developed since the last time he'd been on retreat. Some aspects of his notion of God were better defined; however, he still needed much more introspection. Near the end of the fifth day, Sister Angela came into his thought.

On the plane, he had put her out of his mind, but now the slightly nagging issue of why he had brought her back to life, had to be settled. The following day he recalled every time he had been with her and every communication they had. He didn't find anything suspect in his or her actions or words until he arrived at her shooting.

He remembered he was hiding between the parked cars on Franklin Street in Boston. Carney, Ella and Sister Angela were huddled together at the entrance to the car park waiting for him. He had been looking at them and not back over his shoulder at the Hotel entrance. He hadn't seen Mustafa come out watching for him. He hadn't seen the gun in his hand, but they did. Sister Angela must have thought he was about to leave the shelter of the parked cars and join them. She jumped out to warn him about the danger, and she took a bullet meant for him.

Had he felt obligated to her for that warning? Was that the reason why he had gone to the hospital? Had she thought about what she was doing? Had she acted instinctively or emotionally or had she seen the opportunity to take the Relic back to Scotland slipping away? The desire to reclaim the Relic for Scotland had prompted her to leave her sheltered life in Edinburgh, and voluntary take up the teaching position in America. He went over and over her in his mind.

She had told him she had been a student of Scottish Literature in the Ph.D. program at the University of Saint Andrews in Scotland prior to becoming a nun. Her thesis centered on the life and writings of a Scottish Nun who belonged to the Society of the Sacred Heart. Sister Angela's interest in relics had begun with the writings of this religious.

That evening he went to have a brief chat with Erickson. "And so you see Father Abbot, in addition to this being my first time in Ireland, I'm finding my knowledge of the whole of Great Britain is slightly deficient."

"You sound like a man with a question," the Abbot laughed.

"You are perceptive," Torres remarked.

"You read relics, and I read men," the Dane replied seriously. "That's why they chose me to be the Abbot here. What do you want to know?"

"What do you know about Saint Andrews University in Scotland?"

"Actually I'm a little deficient on the subject myself," he conceded with a smile, "but let me run a search on the Internet."

"You have the Internet here?"

"Just listen to this fellow, would you," Erickson joked as he typed on his tablet's virtual keyboard. "Do we have the Internet here? My dear friend, we invented the Internet, well, the Irish did with a bit of help from the

Danes. But anyway, all joking aside, my Search for St. Andrews has returned five hundred articles. What exactly would you like to know?"

"Where is it?"

"Let me see," and he read from the tablet's screen. "The University of St Andrews is in the town of St. Andrews, in the District of Fife, Scotland. It is the oldest university in Scotland and the third oldest in the English-speaking world. It was founded in 1412 when Papal Letters of Patent were issued by the Avignon Antipope Benedict XIII to a school of higher learning formed by a small group of Augustinian clergy."

"And where is this District of Fife located?"

"From the map here, it seems to be located northwest of Edinburgh, which is the capital city. But tell me Father, have you acquainted yourself with our magnificent library?"

"No, I've been acquainting myself with your wonderful nature trails."

"You should make our Library your next stop. We have free Internet on two computers, and guests are welcome to use them anytime the machines are not occupied."

Rafa traded in his outfit for a crew neck black sweater with a square opening for his collar and wool slacks, a heavy duty windbreaker and a pair of crepe soled walking shoes. When he had purchased a rail ticket from Limerick to Dublin's Heuston Station and then from Dublin's Connolly Station to Belfast in Northern Ireland; he still had a combined total of fifteen US $100 notes being what the monks at the Abbey in Hingham Massachusetts had given him and those he had kept with his passport in the hotel safe.

It took a day of train and ferry travel, but when he landed on Scottish soil a fellow passenger offered him a lift as far as Troon. The kindness was exhilarating and he accepted. He had been obliged to break another 100 US$ to pay for the ferry to cross the Irish Sea and was very mindful that the finite amount of cash he had was slowly decreasing. He needed to conserve enough to at least get to London and then take the train across the Channel to Brussels.

To save notes, the Priest decided to hitchhike from the village of Troon to the village of St. Andrews. He prayed for God to lead him through the urban conglomeration of Glasgow. That night he slept in a tiny Inn on the main street of Troon. In the early morning, he left for St. Andrews, resolved to try and see what it was about the area that would have inspired Sister Angela to go to America and risk her life to bring back a relic for the town.

The trip by car from the west coast to the east coast of Scotland is only about two and a half hours, but when one gets in and out of rides every twenty miles and then must wait for the next ride, it does take time. When he wasn't talking to the strangers who picked him up hitching, he thought of the occasions Sister Angela had told him about St. Andrews, its relics and her opinion on the Crucifixion Relic while waiting for the next lift.

About the middle of the 10th century, Andrew became the patron saint of Scotland. Legend states the relics of Andrew were brought, under supernatural guidance, from Constantinople to the place where the present town of St Andrews stands today. They were brought to St. Andrews because it was thought to be the resting place of other valuable relics. Among the relics already believed to be in the town were those Bishop Acca had conveyed there sometime around 732 AD.

Sister Angela believed Acca's relics were split, and part of them went to Galloway in Ireland while part went to St. Andrews in Scotland. She believed a monk devoted to Acca went to Ireland and the Crucifixion Relic ended up in a monastery in Galloway. In her opinion, it was only right the sliver of Christ's rib should be returned to St. Andrews, to rest in peace with the relics of the Apostle Andrew.

**

In Boston the Police were nearing the end of their investigation of the woman who had disappeared from the Boston Medical Centre in the middle of the night. The lobby at the Hospital Emergency had been equipped with several cameras. Detectives took copies of the back-up video files from six pm of the day in question to six am the following day. They found several clear shots of the Priest entering the ER at 7:00 pm. His roman collar was distinctly visible. He wasn't carrying anything and he was only in the building about half an hour.

The duty nurse was shown a photo printed from a still extracted from the video file. "Yes that's him, that's the person who had entered the dead woman's room around 7 pm."

Video back from the next morning showed a woman entering the ER at 3:15 am. She had a cape on and a hood pulled up over her head. It didn't take detectives long to find out the taxis that were parked outside at that time. One driver had reported a fare to Roslindale but there was no drop off address. He did a 6 pm to 6 am shift. The Police contacted him during his shift.

"I remember the fare very clearly officer. She was a Nun. She wasn't wearing long robes, but she did have a white bib attached to her collar. I've had nuns in the cab before who wore the same thing. She wanted to go to Roslindale and she didn't have any money. She said she had money there. I'm a Catholic myself and decided to take a chance."

"Where did you take her," the detective asked?

"I don't have the exact address, but I remember where I let her off."

"Where was that?"

"It was a house where Nuns live who are attached to Sacred Heart parish and the school."

Detectives visited the Mother House in Roslindale and spoke to the Superior.

"Her name is Sister Angela Stuart. She came here from Edinburgh at the beginning of the school year to teach Grade one. She had taught in Scotland and had good recommendations. Shortly after Thanksgiving she informed us that she couldn't stay. An emergency had come up and she had been asked to return to Scotland. Everybody liked her. The Principal at the school gave her a good recommendation."

"To the best of my knowledge she only ever had one visitor here. It was a priest with a Spanish accent?"

"Did you get his name?"

"No, I'm sorry!"

"Tell me Sister, did Sister Stuart have access to a computer.

"Yes, we have a computer in the TV room. All the nuns staying here have access to it. Sister Stuart was given a login and a password."

"Would you mind if we examined the computer?"

"Not at all, I'll log you in on her account."

The detectives found copies of emails she had sent and received from Father Torres in the hard drive's cache. After that they had an ID for the Priest.

The Boston Police were well aware of the speculation circulating on the Internet concerning the woman who had disappeared Boston Medical Center. When they finished their investigation a communique was released to the media. They confirmed that both the Priest and the Nun had left the United States and that they were closing the file.

When Sharon Norris read the News Release from the Boston Police she went to Brian Robertson office. A copy of the Boston Globe was on the corner of his desk. It was folded so that the reporting about the Police News Release was on top. She saw it and looked at him. "So you've read it!"

"Yes, Sharon," he sighed with a tone of boredom in his voice. "Not only have I read it but four of the Directors and the Chairman of the Board have also read it and called this afternoon to give me their opinion."

She sensed the Executive Director wasn't in a good mood. "I should leave. We'll talk about it some other time."

"No Sharon stay, I insist. Have a seat. We have matters to discuss". Once she was seated he inquired, "So what do you think?"

"I called a lawyer this afternoon," she confessed.

"What did the lawyer say?"

"He said if we had of worded the Injunction to say 'Dr. Samuelson, Carney O'Sullivan and Others' we could have gone after the Priest the moment we knew of his existence."

"But how could we have gone after him if we didn't know who he was?"

"The lawyer said we could have used the back-up from the cameras at the Boston Medical Center the same as the Police must have done."

"That's easy enough for him to say; however, there's just one little problem."

"What's that?"

"We're not the Police!"

"I hadn't thought of that."

"There are a lot of things you haven't thought about Sharon."

"I don't accept that!"

"Sharon, I'm not the type of person who goes around rubbing on a rabbit's paw. It was you who came to me with this scheem in the first place. I relied on you to do the necessary follow up."

"For my part, I bent over backwards and got the Board to come in with the project. Then I went through all that Court and Injunction thing. That Priest didn't just come on scene at the Hospital and maybe the Nun has been in it for a while too. There must have been something in those groups where you followed all this that mentioned a Priest. Then there's that Ella Bowdine and Mustafa Hadad who were involved in the carjacking with O'Sullivan Gate of Heaven Church."

"Sharon, that's a lot of people who slipped through while you weren't watching."

"You could have been doing some of the watching too. I gave you the names of the groups and their URL's."

"You never asked me to help you out with that so I assumed you had the matter all in hand. Besides, you're the Director of Fund Development for this organization. It's your area that isn't pulling its weight. Last Friday afternoon I had to explain to a Gent from Virginia that we won't be opening a branch in his state because we're having money problems. If I was you I would have been putting in overtime, to make sure this Boston Relic thing was a success. The Board is going to have some questions about all these people who slipped through."

"It's not fair that you put everything on me like that. There might not have been one mention of the Priest, the Nun, Ella or that Hadad in those groups."

"That could be true my Dear, but you might be called upon for an explanation."

"Don't my Dear me, Mr. Robertson. I only came here to let you know what has happened. I think I'm done, so good afternoon to you."

"Don't forget to close the door after yourself," he called out after her.

When she left he pulled out a ruled pad and began to draft a letter to the Chairman and Directors of the Board. It was dated December 06.

**

When he was in primary school in South Boston Carney O'Sullivan had taken over a newspaper deliver route from his older brother. It was two streets, three blocks long and the cross streets. There was a lot of competition among the neighborhood boys for paper routes so they weren't long. The paper he delivered was the Boston Globe. There was always a spare copy in his bundle, just in case one of the papers got damaged. That's when he became a regular reader of the Globe.

On December the sixth he was browsing through the previous day's paper, while taking a short lunch break at work. On the lower half of a page near the end of the edition a title caught his eye. **"Boston Medical: Missing Woman Resolved"** He stopped and read the reporting. When he finished reading he thought back to that day momentarily. Then he remembered he had told Ella her would keep her informed if he had any news about Sister Angela. He picked up his smart phone but found he still only had an email address for Ella and so used the Web browser to look up Bowdine Architects.

"Hello, Ella Bowdine speaking!"

"Hi there, it's Carney O'Sullivan speaking!"

"Carney, oh my God, this is the first time I've heard your voice over the phone."

"I know, we're getting as bad as the kids, nothing but email communications."

"So what's up?"

"Did you read yesterday's Globe?"

"Afraid not, I'm rushing to finish a project and when that happens the newspaper is the first thing that has to wait."

"When we were on Martha's, you ask me to let you know if I learned anything about Sister Angela."

"I remember that."

"There was a report in the Globe yesterday. She had been reported as a missing person but the Police have taken her off the list. They said she has left the country."

"I'm glad to hear that. I was so afraid that she might not have recovered from that shooting in the street."

"Yes, she recovered."

"Listen, you mentioned you would like to see the plans for my house out on Martha's."

"If you're not busy Friday noon, why don't you come over for lunch? I'll order some wraps and we have great coffee here. You can tell me all about Sister Angela, see the plans, we'll have lunch and I'll give you my cell number."

"Sounds great!"

"See you at noon!"

"Thanks!"

"Thank you for calling me."

"See you Friday!"

Bowdine & Associates occupied all of what had been the upper loft of a dry goods warehouse. They had left the space open. Each architect had work station set-up along the wall where the windows were located. Everyone had a view of Boston Harbor. Individual locations were equipped with a large drawing board under which were wide shallow drawers where plans and drawings were stored. A desk was located behind each work area.

Three cubicle offices had been set up along the brick wall at the back which overlooked the parking lot. They were reserved for client meetings. Each cubicle was fitted with a door and a window looking out on the office. Clients in the work area were a familiar sight. Nobody even noticed Carney O'Sullivan when he came in at noon on Friday. Ella waved to him from her work station and he walked towards her.

"Hi there," he greeted with a broad smile when within hearing distance. "Good to see you again!"

"Likewise, come pull up a stool," she responded. "I have my Vineyard house plans all laid out to show you. Take off your jacket if you want. Put it on that desk. It belongs to me too."

"So this is the house that Ella built!"

"Sure is," she crowed, delighted to be showing him. "I know every inch of it from conception to plans to construction."

"Where do we begin?"

"First things first, so I thought I'd start with the concrete pad that the square enclosure upon which the house rests is built into."

"Fair enough!"

Fifteen minutes later she noticed a delivery man at the entrance. "That will be our wraps." She motioned to the driver to leave them in the first cubicle. "Number one Rule, No Food in the Work Stations. Even coffee can't be brought near the drawing boards. It must be left at the desk and consumed there. Come on, let's go to the kitchen and get a coffee then we'll go have our wraps."

When they were finally sitting and had opened their lunch she inquired, "So what have you been up to since last we saw each other?"

"I've accepted to do a sailing yacht. It must be drafted and then the materials determined. Following that cost of materials and cost of labor are estimated. I must arrive at a ball park figure and present that to the client. They make the final decision."

"Who drafts the boats for you?"

"I do that myself!"

She smiled and exclaimed, "Nifty!

"You'll have to come over to visit my boat shop sometime."

"You'll have to invite me sometime."

They continued bantering back and forth in the same manner until both cups of coffee were done. This prompted him to say, "Well, it has been fun!"

"Ah," she sighed. "I sense the past tense. Is our rendezvous finished?"

"I must get back to work."

"Likewise," she agreed then added, "When do you want to do this boat shop thing?"

"How about next Friday?"

"Perfect!"

"I'll email you directions.

"Your turn to provide the grub."

"I'll surprise you."

"I like surprises."

The following week, after a half hour tour of Sea Horse Marine, Ella and Carney sat down to platters, which contained an assortment of deep fried clams, lobster pieces, scallops, a small steamed cob of corn, dill pickles, a kale salad and a round of pieta bread. This was to be washed down with a large cup of chai tea.

"Excellent surprise Mr. O," she giggled as they sat down to the boardroom table. "All my fav's!"

"Then prove it by not leaving a scrap," he joked picking up a plastic fork.

"Your boat shop is impressive. I wasn't expecting to see a computer set-up in your design area and then another in the motor set up shop for balancing the engine and reducing the vibration."

"Every little bit helps! We aim for zero vibration when a motor launch goes out the door."

A little bird told my father that I had lunch with you last Friday." Carney looked at her oddly. "Nothing serious, he just asked me who the new client was."

"What did you tell him?

"I said you were a new friend. Then he wanted to know how I'd met you."

"What did you say?"

"I said completely by accident," and she was smiling.

Carney was suspicious. "What kind of accident?"

"I told him I was coming down the stairs inside the City Hall lobby when I missed my footing and went sailing forward. You were coming up at the same time and caught me in midair. We both would have gone tumbling down if you hadn't stuck out a hand and grabbed the steel railing just in time"

He looked at her seriously and declared, "If I ever found out Dakota had told me a whopper like that one week of detention with no TV, tablet or smart phone."

"My dad is the same," she laughed, "Reaching over to punch him lightly in the shoulder.

"What's your dad's name?"

"Jack!"

"What did Jack say when you told him that?"

"He hugged me and said he wants his little girl to be more careful going down flights of stairs. Then he scolded me with, 'No texting when walking' and he said he wants to meet you."

"Meet me, why?"

"He wants to thank you for saving his little girl," she exclaimed.

"I don't even know the man. How am I supposed to meet him?"

"What are your plans between Christmas and New Year's?"

"I don't know yet, why?"

"He has invited you, Dakota and me over for supper."

"He doesn't have to do that."

"So you don't want to meet my dad."

"The guys always have to meet a girl's dad.

"You know the drill, Mr. O."

"Okay, you and your dad discuss it and text me the details," he relented and then became serious, "but not while you're walking down stairs."

"There you see, she giggled. "It wasn't that hard was it?"

**

Rafa arrived in the North Sea village of St. Andrews at noon. To his immense surprise, he found a ruined cathedral overlooking the Bay. It had been Scotland's largest and most impressive medieval church and dominated the history of the country from the 12th century until the Protestant Reformation in 1560. The ruin occupied a site used for worship since the 8th century AD, when the relics of St Andrew, Scotland's patron saint, are said to have been brought here. A graveyard surrounded the ruins and the whole was encircled by stone walls.

The only relics the Spaniard found were in the Cathedral Museum and they weren't identified as being those of Saint Andrew. He felt a little deceived, but the situation had been all of his own makings. It was he who had imagined something here must have motivated the woman. When quite satisfied he had absorbed all the ruin had to give, the priest set his sights on the University of St. Andrews, where she had been a student.

In recent times the University had a student population of approximately eight thousand. Most came from the UK, but thirty percent of the enrollment was comprised of foreign students. Many were sons and daughters of politicians and wealthy businessmen who studied in English to help them become fluent, even if they acquired a Scottish accent.

The town of St Andrews spreads inland from the cliffs that are battered year-round by the North Sea. The Cathedral Ruin, the out buildings, and wall occupy the furthermost point east in the town, running out to where the land ends. The University is sprinkled here and there around the town, occupying at least ten different sites.

Rafa picked up a tourist map but didn't get to know much more about the school than the locations of Lecture Halls, Student Residences, and the Administration buildings. By then the town residents were hastening home for supper, and he had to go in some place for the night again. In the back of his mind, he kept a mental tally of the money he had and noted every time it decreased. After finding a room in a bed and breakfast, he went out to hunt down something for dinner and wandered around the town thinking about what he was doing.

He would never be back this way again and decided not to miss the opportunity to visit Edinburgh. He'd like to see the Mother House where Sister Angela had lived and would possibly also visit the Community Kitchen, where she had worked, before leaving for America. Afterward, he'd catch the night train to London. Sleeping in the train would help him avoid paying for a night's accommodation.

The following morning he learned St Andrews had no railway. The nearest station was at Leuchars a distance of 5 miles. It was on the main line from London King's Cross via Edinburgh, to Aberdeen. After a filling breakfast of boiled eggs, porridge, an orange, toast, and coffee, he set off to walk to the train, following directions the woman who ran the bed and breakfast gave him. It took an hour and a half and he felt happy about getting the exercise. The train from Aberdeen to Edinburgh was a shuttle, so he only bought a ticket as far as the Capital of Scotland.

Before boarding the train in Leuchars he bought a newspaper. Once the carriage began to move he took out the paper and noticed a small headline on the lower half of page one. He had missed it when scanning the publication on the newspaper rack in the station. It read, "The Pope Has Resigned". He read through the article quickly. Following several months of ill health, on the very best advice of three personal physicians, the Pontiff had called a press conference to announce he was resigning.

It was then that Rafa understood the warning he had received from the Pope in the fax at the Abbey in Hingham. The sick old man had stayed on until he received word that the Relic was once again safely under control of the Church. Now there would be a mad scramble among the Cardinals to find and gain possession of the tiny sliver of one of Christ's ribs. The Cardinals who controlled the relic would control who would be the next Pope.

During the trip, he thought about how he would find Angela's Mother House. The school where she taught in the Boston suburbs was attached to Sacred Heart parish. She had said her religious order in Scotland had arranged the situation for her, so there was a reasonable possibility the name of her order was the same name as the parish in the Boston suburb of Roslindale.

The Information Officer at Waverly Station in Edinburgh keyed Sacred Heart into the search screen on his computer. Several possibilities returned, and Rafa requested him to write down the address for the Society of the Sacred Heart. When he had the piece of paper in his hand and saw the address, the priest immediately asked for directions.

It took a taxi driver to find the Mother House in Lauriston Gardens since the cluster of buildings was located behind a stone wall. There were "No Parking" signs on both sides of a solid metal gate. He was about to say been there, done that and have the driver take him back to Waverly Station when a small gate opened, and a woman came through the stone wall onto the sidewalk.

"Please wait a minute driver," Father Torres said, opening the taxi door. "I'm going to ask for directions from that woman."

"Excuse me... "

The woman turned and looked at him then asked, "Me, are you talking to me?"

"Excuse me, but are you a Nun?"

"Yes, I'm a Nun."

"Then the Society of the Sacred Heart of Jesus is behind that wall."

"Yes, that's correct! Are you looking for someone?"

"Does your Society still run a Community Kitchen in Edinburgh?"

"We do. It's in Niddrie Mains."

"Could you give directions to the taxi driver?"

"No problem, Sir," she replied, walking towards the car.

When she walked on, Rafa asked the driver, "Do you think you can find the place?"

"Oh I can find it alright, but I'm not really sure you would want to be going to such neighborhood."

"What's the problem?"

"The problem is roughness. They're a tough lot. There are rumors of some people carrying a hatchet under their coat when they venture into Niddrie Mains."

The Sacred Heart Kitchen was located in a single level red brick building on Niddrie Mains Road. On one side there was a Laundromat and on the other, the building was burnt out and its windows were covered over with plywood. There was a Pub beside that and a Pub across the street.

The cabbie pulled over in front of a bronze statue that was bolted to the sidewalk. It was a young boy in short pants and wearing a short sleeve shirt. He had a violin cocked under the left side of his chin and his right hand was outstretched towards a woman who was passing him a violin bow.

Rafa paid the driver. It was four forty-five pm. He wondered if the kitchen was open. Only one way to find out he thought crossing the street and entering the red brick building. A tall muscular man stood just inside the door. He pointed to a line of men. "Get in the queue over there buddy, unless you're a tourist and in that case, get out." Then he laughed out loud.

Rafa joined the back of the line and picked up a tray, the same as the others. It took five minutes before his turn came. The woman behind the counter held a plate heaped with potatoes, turnip, and meatloaf in her hand. Without looking at him, she asked, "Would you like any gravy Sir?" when he didn't reply, she looked up and then exclaimed, "Rafa, can it really be you?"

"It's me," he replied in a low voice.

"How can this be?" she asked. "I must talk with you."

"Yes," he stammered, "I would like to talk to you too."

Somewhere behind him a formidable voice snarled, "Hey bud, cut the chit-chat and tell her if you want gravy."

"Yes, I'll take some gravy please!" he exclaimed not knowing where the words came from.

"Sit at the back near the wall. I must complete service. I'll come over to you when I'm finished."

"Where," he asked, still in a daze?

"Over there by the wall," she repeated and pointed with her outstretched right arm. He looked in the direction she indicated. The kitchen ended at a wall made of square concrete blocks. The area contained several heavy, rectangular wooden tables and chairs. Half of the places were empty. He set his tray down in front of an empty chair on the far side of one of the tables so he would be able to watch her work.

Two hours later they were sitting across from each other in a Tea House. They hadn't spoken in the street, except for her to tell him to follow her. She broke the space between them after he had his first sip of tea.

"How did you get here?" she asked impatiently.

"It's a long story," he drawled.

"How long are you staying?" she insisted.

"They gave me some money in Boston, but it's going fast. I'm not supposed to use the credit card. They think it may be compromised."

"Then we'll have to make your money last as long as possible," she declared solemnly, without asking for any explanations.

"That's easier said than done, Sister. Every time I turn around it's a little bit here and a little bit there."

"The meal you had today didn't cost you anything."

"No, and it was good."

"You can eat there once a day while you're in Edinburgh. I do the tea shift. Where are you staying?"

"Nowhere yet!" he replied. "And what is the tea shift?"

"Father, you're no longer in America," the Nun laughed. "Now you'll have to learn British English. Tea is refreshments or meal usually including tea and served in late afternoon."

"After we finish this cup, I'll take you around to the Men's Hostel. You can sleep there for free. They let the men in at 8 pm and they must be gone by 8 am. There's breakfast too. You see, your money is going to last longer than you think. What do you say?

"Why did you put yourself in danger to warn me on Franklin St.?

"Why did you sneak into the hospital and bring me back from the dead?"

They sat smiling at each other in silence until he said,

"Okay, I accept your offer of a bed and breakfast in the Hostel and one meal a day at your kitchen. The Pope told me not to come back to Italy yet and not to use the credit card. He said for me to take a break and suggested a visit to my family in Spain."

"The Pope has resigned. When were you talking to him?" she laughed with a smile.

"He faxed me at an Abbey south of Boston before resigning."

"I overheard Mother Superior and some of the older Nuns discussing the Pope's resignation. They said there are rumors the Illuminati are in Rome and there might be a power play by them in the College of Cardinals to have their choice chosen as the next Pope."

"You know about the Illuminati?"

"Only what I hear!" the Nun admitted.

"I may have had a spy from the Illuminati visit me at the hotel on Franklin Street," he confessed and then noticed the change in her humor. "Oh, I shouldn't have said that."

Sister Angela sucked in a deep breath, "It's okay!" Then she rolled up her sleeve showing him his watch. "This is how I knew it was you."

"I left it for that reason," he confided. "I wanted you to understand what had happened. There was no pen and paper available."

"You're going to need it to navigate the times at the hostel and the kitchen," she instructed

"You keep it. I'll get another someplace."

"That's spending money. I have a lot of things I want to discuss with you before your money runs out. Put out your wrist." she commanded.

He did as she said and she slipped the adjustable strap over his hand and let it settle around his wrist before saying, "If God would grant you one wish, what would it be?"

He thought for a moment before replying, "It's been a long time since I've said a Mass."

"Your wish is granted," she laughed. "We have a chapel at the Mother House. I'll reserve it for you."

"Thank you for granting me a wish," he laughed. "You're like a fairy godmother."

"Think nothing of it Father. I'll attend your Mass, I'll be your altar servant, and you can give me Holy Communion," she declared with pride.

"I'd like that," he replied with genuine sincerity.

"I would too," she assured him. "What time is it now?"

He smiled and looked at his watch. "Four thirty!"

"There you see, I finished in the kitchen at 4 pm. We walked here and had a cup of tea. I'll meet you here tomorrow at 4:15."

"Agreed!"

"Now come on," she laughed, "swallow up your tea. You must register at the Hostel."

"Won't they find it odd you bringing me there?"

"I've been around the Mains quite a while. You won't be the first person I've shown over to the Men's hostel."

"The taxi driver said I would need a hatchet around here."

"He wasn't joking," she replied seriously. "Mind your own business and don't talk to strangers."

"Yes Mum," he answered and they both burst out laughing like children.

"One last thing," she begged.

"Your wish is my command."

"What happened to Ella and Carney?"

"They are alive, at least they were the last time I saw them."

"What do you mean by the last time?"

"I left them in an alley in Boston behind the car park where you three were hiding. They had no money, but I was carrying the funds that I'd picked up from my room. I gave them $50 for a taxi."

"Why didn't you stay with them?"

"It's a long story!"

"We have time," she said.

"Okay," Rafa agreed. "After you were shot, we fled down a long cement stairway at the back of the car park. Ella went first. At about the half way point she missed a stair and slid down to the bottom. Her right foot stopped her forward momentum, when she reached the bottom. A bone inside her foot snapped off and penetrated the skin. She was in great pain and was losing blood."

"Oh the poor woman," Sister Angela moaned in her deepest Scottish accent. Rafa looked at her in amazement. She had been shot and still she could emphasize with another woman.

"What happened next, Father?"

"When we were in the Church, I noticed the paint on and around the bolts holding the statue in place was chipped and broken. It appeared as if they had recently been removed. I thought to myself, perhaps Carney has come back here on his own. I didn't mention my suspicions to anybody until I saw the predicament we were in. Ella couldn't walk. That madman with the gun was behind us. Carney and I would be hard pressed to carry her and flee at the same time. I simply told Carney that if he had the relic, he had to use it to save his friend."

"Oh my, it was used twice, once with her and then with me."

"Yes, he used it and her foot healed completely, almost instantly."

"How did you end up with the relic?"

"I asked him for it. He hesitated and Ella told him to give it to me."

**

That night Sister Angela was wrenched from a sound sleep and sat straight up in her bed. It was as if there were no walls or ceiling in her room. She could see a man rising up towards the heavens. He was dressed in clothing of Biblical times. She wanted to see his face and stood up from her bed before walking towards the apparition. As if from nowhere, a cloud floated in and blocked her view of the man and then the walls and ceiling came into view again. She got back into bed and fell to sleep, but remembered the incident in the morning.

***

Chapter 10

Spanish Teacher

Rafa settled into an almost regular existence in Edinburgh. Slowly the city began to open up for him. He liked it and quickly appreciated the Scots. Every morning after a cup of black coffee, two boiled eggs and a slice of bread he would put an apple in his pocket and go out to explore the town until tea time when he went to the Sisters of the Sacred Heart's kitchen for his main meal. There were no lockers in the Hostel so he carried his shoulder bag which contained his few possessions and an umbrella. If the weather was poor, he spent most of the day at the library or lost in thought at a church.

Sister Angela was always happy to see him. Some days she would say, "Cup of tea today sir?" This meant shall we meet for a cup of tea on her way home. He always accepted her invitation. Other days she would say, "It's a busy day for me sir." This meant something at the convent needed tending to and she didn't have time for a cup.

Rafa waited for her a block or so from the kitchen and they would walk to a Tea House or to her convent together. They talked a lot whether walking or drinking tea. He liked both types of day. Some days there was even an inch or so of snow underfoot but the City is not known for snow.

One day she asked him about the Pope. "When will they chose a new Pope?"

"Usually the College of Cardinals call for a Conclave fifteen days after the death or resignation of a living Pope. It shouldn't be long now. Why do you ask?"

"I had a visit at the Mother House from a Bishop Sergio two days ago."

Rafa felt the hair on the back of his neck stand up straight and asked in alarm, "What did he want?"

"He wanted to know about Boston. Mother Superior had notified the Vatican I was going to Boston to look for the Crucifixion Relic. He wanted to know if I found it. He even had a hospital report showing that I had been dead for over an hour and then came out of it. He asked me if I knew where you were."

"What did you tell him?"

"I told him I had gone into a coma in the hospital after blood loss but that the Lord wasn't ready for me and I woke up. I told him I hadn't seen you since Boston."

"Thank you, Sister!"

"Father!"

"Who is Bishop Sergio?"

"I'm not sure. He showed up at my hotel in Boston saying he had been sent to take the Relic back to Rome. I suspected him because those were not the instructions I was given before leaving. In the fax, I received from the Pope before he resigned he said there were too many factions in the Vatican who would compete with each other for control of the Relic. He even told me not to use the credit or ATM cards I'd been given. Bishop Sergio might belong to one of those factions. He may even be with the Illuminati. When I was in Italy there were rumors they would try to control the naming of the next Pope. Since you didn't have the Relic they will be looking for me."

"I think you should stay in Edinburgh for a while Father."

"So do I Sister!"

Before long they had staked out five different Tea Rooms. Sister Angela wasn't worried about being seen with him, it was the frequency at the same spot she thought might be noticed.

"So now you've got it straight," she chided. "We'll name each spot after a day. Here's a list so you don't get mixed up. Monday is High Street, Tuesday is Nicolson Square, and Wednesday is Fredrick Street, South Charlotte Street is on Thursday and Friday will be Princes Street."

"I'll soon know Edinburgh well enough to give walking tours."

"This is not a good time of the year for walking tours, but wait until tourist season. You have Spanish and English. I bet you could earn as much as the monks at the Abbey in America gave you doing walking tours. You wouldn't be able to let your clients know you live in the Hostel. Come to think of it, you'd probably do well not to become too friendly with anyone in that place. They might recognize you giving a tour and come up and ask you what you're doing."

"I'll remember your words, Sister. Thanks for the good advice."

"Now you have your list. Simply go to our spot for that day and wait for me."

He agreed, "It's a good system!"

"By the way, I've been invited to visit family and friends at Christmas. My family lives in a little place at the end of the land called, Armadale. It's right on the North Sea. The storms are something ferocious up that way. My friends live in St. Andrews. They're from school days. They've invited me for Hogmanay. You're welcome to come to St. Andrews. Several of my friends have brothers. I could get you a place to stay for free."

"I'd like to very much, but what's Hogmanay?"

"That's what the rest of world calls "New Year's Eve", but you'll probably be gone by then?"

"Oh no, I'm staying. I must make sure my money lasts until walking tours start up."

"I was only joking about the tours."

"I'm not joking," he replied. "Maybe I'll walk to St. Andrews to save the train fare."

"Suit yourself," she laughed. "I'm not walking back with you."

He could see Lauriston Gardens and said, "Okay, this is as far as I'm going. I'll see you next time, Sister."

"Goodbye Father, keep well!"

**

The next hurdle for him was saying Sunday Mass at the convent and her being his altar servant. Mother Superior had been hesitant at first.

"Sister, are you suggesting I give permission to a man who is living at the Men's Hostel and eating at our kitchen in Niddrie Mains to come into our sanctuary, to say mass?"

"He's just a priest Mother Superior."

"How does a priest end up in such dire circumstances?"

"He was on an errand for the Church and then the Pope resigned," Sister Angela explained. "He has been advised not to return to Rome for now as there is a struggle going on among the Cardinals who are charged with finding a new Pope. He thinks the Illuminati might be looking for him to help their choice for the next Pope."

"Sister Stuart, what do you know about the Illuminati?"

"Nothing Mother!"

"As I suspected," the older woman scolded. "Sister, I'll tell you what it sounds like to me. It sounds like paranoia schizophrenia, but I'm not a specialist"

Sister Stuart continued to explain who Father Torres was and how he had ended up in such a state of affairs without mentioning anything about her experience at the Boston Medical Centre.

"And what is he doing in Edinburgh," Mother Superior snapped with annoyance having learned the Priest was a Relicoligist who had been sent to Boston to look for the Crucifixion Relic.

"He was curious Mother!"

"Curious about what?"

"About St. Andrews!"

"He's been there too?"

"Oh yes, before he came to Edinburgh."

"And what does he think of our relics?"

"I haven't asked him, Mother. They were the subject of much study for me. I didn't want to act like a show-off."

The Reverend Mother went online while Sister Angela sat in a chair on the other side of her desk.

"There I have the Web site for the Cathedral at Amalfi on my screen. I can't understand all this Italian, but I see a Father Rafael Torres is listed among the pastoral staff."

"Do a Search under his name Mother," the younger Nun urged. "His Blog and some of his published articles will come up."

Mother Superior searched his name and found numerous articles he had posted about Relics, as well as his Blog.

"Now I understand why the Illuminati would be interested in him," she thought out loud. Sister Angela didn't say a word as she really didn't understand who the Illuminati were.

The older Nun looked directly into her subordinate's eyes and concluded, "As long as he lives at the Men's Hostel and doesn't use that credit card, there is no way they can trace him."

"That's what he says!"

"Sister, Father Torres has permission to say Mass for the nuns and you may act as his altar servant. Tell him not to eat before he comes and he can join me for breakfast at my table in our cafeteria at 8 am. There are many things about the Church I am anxious to discuss with him."

The first Sunday two nuns attended his Mass. Afterward, there were always at least half a dozen. He didn't come every Sunday, but on those days when he did perform the sacrament at Sacred Heart, he was always invited for breakfast and sat at Mother Superior's table. She was especially interested in discussing the choice of a new Pope and the Illuminati with him.

"So what are your thoughts on the Conclave Father Torres," Mother Superior asked at the first breakfast?"

"I'm sure the will of God will prevail," the Priest assured her.

"Do you have a favorite among the Cardinals?"

"No, they are all excellent candidates!"

"I've heard the Illuminati might try to take control of the election."

"That's why we pray for God's direction Mother."

"Did you hear dark smoke rose up from the Sistine Chapel this week?"

"Yes, I read the headlines at the street news vendors."

"Today shall be a day of prayer, reflection, and dialogue," Mother Superior continued. "In the following ballots, only the two names who received the most votes in the last ballot shall be eligible in a runoff election."

"Let us pray the College votes wisely."

The following day white smoke rose up from the Sistine Chapel and the Catholics of the world breathed a sigh of relief.

**

At 5:30 pm on Wednesday of the week between Christmas and New Year's, Dakota pressed on the door bell of a large house on Burroughs, not far from her father's place in the Jamaica Plain neighborhood of Boston. The door opened and Ella stood in front of them wearing a black woolen dress with three quarter length sleeves and a gray apron.

"Dakota," she exclaimed, "I thought you would never arrive!"

The young girl felt shy receiving such a warm welcome and raised her two hands in front of her holding up a bottle of wine. "This is for you, well your dad and my dad too. I can't drink wine yet!"

Ella took hold of the bottle and looked directly at her father. "Carney, good to see you again! Come on in, we've been expecting you."

Jack Bowdine was a tall, slim man with distinctive features and a full, gray mustache. This evening he was dressed in a white shirt with no tie, gray flannel trousers and a black coat sweater. He stood in the middle of the living room waiting for his daughter to bring in the guests.

"Dad I'd like you to meet Dakota and her dad Carney!"

Jack shook the girl's hand. "So pleased to meet you my dear. Ella tells me you only live a few blocks away."

"Just out on Jamaica Way Sir!"

"And Carney, I owe you so much thanks. If Ella had gone down those stairs head first, who knows, she might not be with us today."

"I'm very happy to make your acquaintance Mr. Bowdine!"

"Everything is almost ready," Ella explained. "I need a few more minutes. Why don't you three sit here in the living room and get acquainted?"

"Need some help," Dakota asked.

"Sure you come with me while the men discuss the problems of the world."

When they had gone, Carney looked around and commented, "I see you have a Freemason Fraternity symbol on the wall."

"Oh, you know the Masons," Jack enquired.

"Not really, I saw one on the wall at Ella's place and when I asked she said it was a symbol of Fraternity."

"Yes we are both Mason's. Our family has been Freemason for several generations, even before we came to America."

"How long have you lived in the US?"

"Both my parents were born in the New York City area. Their parents moved there from France. My wife and I as well as Ella were born in Boston. Both my daughter and I studied at the Boston Architectural College."

"I did an Associate Degree in Boat Construction at a private college in Maine."

"Sounds interesting!"

"Oh without a doubt, I use something that I learned every day."

"What do you do?"

"I own a company called, Seahorse Marine. We build wooden boats, mostly yachts with a motor but also a few sailing yachts. As a matter fact, we're starting one now."

"How long will it take to build?"

"Depending on scheduling and what else we have on the go, about six months."

"Getting back to the insignia on the wall, how much do you know about Freemasonry?"

"I must confess, really nothing!"

"I won't pretend to even scratch the surface with you, so here's a high level view. Modern Freemasonry broadly consists of two main groups. Regular Freemasonry insists that a volume of scripture be open in a working lodge, that every member profess belief in a Supreme Being, that no women are admitted, and that the discussion of religion and politics is banned. Continental Freemasonry is now the general term for a more liberalized version. Some, or all, of these restrictions have been removed."

"Which branch do you subscribe to?"

"Ella and I are among the latter. We belong to what is called a mixed Lodge. There are certain recognition issues between the Grand Lodge and our mixed lodge over the initiation of women. My wife was initiated in France while on vacation with her parents. She did the same thing with Ella."

"Sounds fine to me!"

"There's also a running feud between Masons and the Roman Catholic Church over the issue of revelation. My wife enrolled my daughter in a catholic girl's school for a number of years so she wouldn't form any erroneous ideas."

"Sounds like you had a good wife."

"She was excellent! When she was young, she fell for a Roman Catholic fella, but it never went anywhere because if he had become a Mason, his church would have excommunicated him."

Just then Dakota popped her head around the corner, "Gentlemen, your presence is requested in the dining room."

Ella was standing waiting for them. "Carney you sit at that end and Daddy, you're in your regular spot at the other end. Dakota you and I are on the sides. Everything is in serving dishes on the table, help yourselves. Since everybody has probably been eating too much turkey, I decided to mix thinks up a little. We're having, Lapin a La Cocotte, which is literally translated as Rabbit Casserole."

When they were seated Jack looked at Dakota and said, "So, Missy, will you honor us with grace tonight."

Dakota looked at her father and began, "Bless us oh Lord for these thy gifts which we are about to receive from thy bounty, Amen!"

During the meal their conversation went back and forth. As she was finishing Ella looked at Carney and declared, "Dakota was telling me that you will probably go skiing during the winter."

"We usually go up a couple of times during the winter."

"Where abouts do you two ski?"

"If it's a day trip we go to Wachusett Mountain or Pat's Peak in southern New Hampshire. If we're staying overnight, we might go to the Berkshires."

"I've skied all those spots," she laughed.

"You ski!" Dakota exclaimed.

"Sure I ski!"

"You should come with us some time."

"Oh, I wouldn't want to intrude."

"No intrusion," Carney declared. "Come anytime you wish."

"You'll have to let me know in advance, so I can make plans."

"I'll send you an email."

"That will be perfect, thank you."

**

Sister Angela Stuart left Edinburgh on the train December 23rd headed to Thurso, the most northern railway station in the United Kingdom. Her family would meet her there. Before leaving she made arrangements for Father Torres to stay with Colleen McElroy's brother Angus in St. Andrews December 28th to January 1st. She would stay with Colleen, who was married with two children. Both the McIlroy's worked at the University and invited their guests to attend a party with them on Hogmanay.

As prearranged, Sister Angela went around to Angus's flat to collect Father Rafa at 10 am on Thursday, December 29th. She had prepared a list of places to show him. At the top of the list was the Cathedral Ruin. The tour of the remains of the ancient church, it's out buildings and the cemetery was all inclusive. Rafa was shown the nave where pilgrims came in the day hoping to be cured. He was shown the altar under which legend held that relics were buried. So much detail and many short narratives about history and culture flowed from her in a seemingly never ending stream. He was astonished.

It took the better part of the day and then she simply said, "We're done, that's St. Andrews Cathedral!"

"Sister," he gasped. "I feel so animated. It's like I've been living inside a travelogue for the past five hours. You should give tours."

"I have a confession to make Father," she admitted shyly.

"What confession?" he asked curiously.

"Much of what I've told you comes from my Doctoral Thesis or something I came across when researching it."

"I'll have to read your thesis some time."

"And that you shall. Now I have another confession."

"You really are a sinner," he joked.

"The rest of your tour won't be quite so interesting, but I'll do my best."

"That's all we can ask of anyone Sister."

During the following two days she led him through university buildings, cafés she once haunted and the small shops only an insider finds. Saturday evening they went to a banquet hall along with a throng of the town's residents. Some brought their children. There were lots of games – darts, crocano, and cards. Three young men played the pipes and were accompanied on violins by three young women.

Some danced and some did a sort of jig. In between dancing, the gathering devoured ten dozen haggis, dozens of steak pies, two hundred Scotch Eggs, hams, potatoes, leeks, black bun and gallons of alcoholic beverages. Father Rafa and Sister Angela toasted tiny glasses of sherry at midnight. On Sunday, January the First, the pair caught the first train back to Edinburgh.

Rafa walked to their Monday tea room on High St. in Old Town the day after returning from St. Andrews and arrived about 4 pm. It was a long narrow room with a kitchen at the back. Once it had been a lane between two buildings but was now covered over with a roof. The building on the right was made of large clay bricks that had been painted over many times. The left wall of the room was the irregular stone masonry of the outside wall of the building beside. A raised false floor was covered with a thick woven wool carpet and there were tables and chairs for two along each wall.

It made Rafa feel nostalgic and left him with a warm fuzzy feeling. The tea was served in a proper china cup, and the sugar bowls were covered with quaint crocheted doilies keeping the sugar free from foreign bodies. He particularly liked the apple pie at this tea room.

Sister Angela appeared at 4:30 pm and started the conversation with, "Well, and how was your day after our exciting weekend?"

"It was a good day," he reflected. "Many names and places where I walked had more meaning because I knew some of the histories behind things I was seeing," the priest replied. "This city has always been the political capital and St. Andrews was only the **ecclesiastical** capital for a few hundred years, but it has left its mark on Edinburgh."

"Then my efforts were worthwhile."

"Very much," he agreed.

"So what else did you think about while trudging around today?" she wanted to know.

"How it seemed a little like we're playing house," he replied.

"I beg your pardon," she coughed, sitting up straight.

"I didn't mean to offend you."

Oh, I'm not offended, not in the least. Have you ever played house with anyone Father?

"No, have you?" He shot back without thinking

"As a matter of fact, I have and let me assure you, it's nothing like what we're doing."

"I didn't mean to go into your private life Sister."

"You didn't, I'm the one who is doing the offering," she assured him. "It was a long time ago. I was in my Ph.D. in St. Andrews. I had to have a Director for my thesis. His name was Dr. Glen Maclean. It just sort of happened once and then I moved in with him."

"He was fascinating. He had two doctorates, one from Oxford and one from The Sorbonne. I was a little girl from up where the land ends. I was mesmerized by a man of Letters. The carnal part was secondary. It was like we were linked in our minds."

"I see," he declared shyly, "but you became a nun."

"Well, you know what they say, Father."

"No, what do they say Sister?

"The Lord works in mysterious ways," she laughed.

He laughed and smiled at her, "It sounded more like someone's confession."

"Someday, I may come to you for confession, but for now I feel more comfortable with the old priest who visits the convent now and then."

"Even if what you say isn't under the seal of confession, it remains private," he assured her.

"Oh, I had no doubt about it Father. Besides, who would you tell, one of the men at the hostel?" she jabbed with a tinge of sarcasm in her voice

"Perhaps we should change the subject of our conversation," he offered feeling he was intruding.

"Not at all," she insisted. "There's still more."

"More, what more," he stuttered slightly confused.

"There I knew," she laughed softly, pouring each of them a cup from the pot that had just been set down on the table. "You want to know more."

"You don't have to," he protested, but she started again anyway.

"Glen and I were lovers for about a year. As Director of my Thesis, he knew everything. We talked about it day and night. It was a very different experience for me. I liked it and I liked him. He had a research assistant provided by the Faculty and one day she announced she and her husband were having a baby. She was giving up her position. I so wanted to become his research assistant as my thesis was almost done and I would be defending it soon."

"Did you get the job?"

"No, he was not an ethical person," she scoffed with disgust. "The Faculty published a Position Open Notice and interested were requested to send in a personal letter stating why we believed we qualified and a professional Curriculum Vitae to the Selection Committee. Unbeknown to me, he supplied the Committee with a detailed profile of what he was looking for and he also gave a copy of it to another graduate student who he was seeing on the side, at the same time he was living with me. That was also unbeknown to me."

"So, you became a nun?"

"Not quite, I didn't find out until after my Thesis was accepted. One day he casually mentioned he needed his house back. I said I wouldn't move out, so he told me what he had done. I was devastated. I couldn't move out fast enough"

"I left Scotland and went on to the Continent. I ended up going overland all the way to Australia. After working there for a year, I signed on to be kitchen help on a boat headed for the United States and landed in Los Angeles about a month later. I rode in a bus along Route 66 all the way across America and finally ended up in Boston. It was in Boston I knew I had a vocation. I was ready to come home and become a nun."

"I'm sorry Sister Angela!"

"Don't be sorry Father. The Lord works in mysterious ways. Have you finished your tea?"

"Yes"

"I had something I was going to talk to you about today, but then you brought up this playing house business and it had to be dealt with."

"You can still tell me. I don't need tea to listen."

"No, I suppose not, so here goes. I'm sure it has something to do with that relic."

"What are we talking about?"

"I've been seeing things. This time it was very much different than the first two times."

"Tell me about these visions."

"The first time was when I was regaining consciousness in the hospital. I was sure I was in the sepulcher with Him. More recently I saw a man dressed like in biblical times rising up to the heavens. When I tried to see his face, a cloud came and hid him from view."

"What was the other time you were going to tell me about?"

"It was very much different. It was almost in modern times. I was watching a weeping woman prostrate on the body of a man. She kept saying, "Oh my dear husband what am I going to do?" over and over. She had a very thick Irish accent. Then there was a knock on the door and a monk came in. He had his hood up so I couldn't see his face."

"What did the monk do?" The Priest inquired seriously.

"He put a cloth into her hand and said, "Touch him with this and ask God for his mercy." She did as he said and her husband sat up. The monk took the cloth from her hand and disappeared out the door. The husband asked her to go fetch his friends."

"Very quickly I found myself looking in on a Court Room. The man who sat up in bed after his wife touched him with the cloth was asking the Court to give him permission to intercede on his own behalf. Things seemed to be going poorly for the Prosecutor and he asked leave of the Judge to call the man as a witness."

"The Prosecutor received permission to call him as a witness and asked him if he saw the man who shot him in Court. He pointed at someone and said it was him. The Court Room exploded. There were Catholics on one side and Protestants on the other. The Protestants kept yelling it was some Catholic magic and they would get to the bottom of it"

The Catholics kept chanting, "Guilty, Guilty, Guilty!"

The Priest cleared his throat and said, "You must have been seeing what happened in Ireland 150 years ago."

"That's what it must have been," Sister Angela agreed and then inquired, "Father, I've been meaning to ask if you still have the Relic?"

"No I don't," Rafa replied.

Sister Stuart pressed on, "I simply assumed you had come directly from America when you arrived in Niddrie Mains, but now I'm wondering, did you?"

"No," Father Torres admitted. "The Pope sent me to Ireland."

"With the Relic", she pressed?

"Yes, with the Relic," the Spaniard affirmed. "It's all supposed to be Confidential. I left the Relic with a monk in an Abbey in Ireland."

"Then it must remain Confidential," she agreed.

"Thank you," he said.

"I think we should call it a day Father. I'll tell you in the kitchen the next time I'm free for another meetup."

"Would you like me to walk along with you?"

"No, I'll be fine. It was just a wee bit of reminiscing about Mr. Maclean. I now have what's in no man. I have the Lord!"

"Good evening Sister, I'll see you soon."

She smiled and left.

They didn't talk to each other for two days even though he took his main meal in the kitchen. On Thursday they did meet.

"Father, there's something I've been meaning to tell you, but I wanted to wait until we were past the holidays."

"What's that Sister?"

"I'm finished at Niddrie Mains today. School is starting Monday and it's my turn to teach the children. One of the other nuns will be taking my place behind the counter. We always switch around so everyone gets a chance to teach. But you can still come to say Mass on Sunday.'

Rafa was quite taken by surprise and didn't know what to say then sputtered, "Thank you for informing me of the change in your schedule. I know you will be delighted to be back teaching children and I'm happy it's your turn again."

The Nun's return to the classroom proved beneficial for Rafa. First, he had to decide if he was going to stay in Edinburgh and if he was, he should extend his social contacts beyond the Sacred Heart convent. After much thought, he decided money would be the key to his decision about staying in Scotland. If he couldn't find a way to replenish his treasury, the decision would be made for him.

The Circulation Desk at the Central Library told him he needed a bonafide civic address to apply for a Library Card. He couldn't afford to move out of the hostel, so had to be content with reading books while in the Library.

He missed not having a smartphone, but it would be too big a cost. There were a dozen public computers at the Library. One day he went online and registered for a free email address, rafa@scottsmail.org. Sister Angela gave him her email address one Sunday when he went to say Mass and they were able to stay in contact.

Given a choice between tea and coffee, his preference was coffee. Since he was no longer meeting the Nun in tea rooms, he began to explore some of the cafés in the city. Before long he had his spot and even engaged in conversation with a few of the regulars. On the back wall was a Notice Board.

One afternoon when there weren't many people in the Café, he stood for a while reading what patrons had pinned up. Someone was offering Spanish Tutoring, both conversational and written. There was an email and a street address for contact. He was curious where the person might live and wrote down the location.

The following day he went hunting for the address and learned the tutor lived in a rental mailbox. He had a flash of inspiration and saw this as a solution to the Library Card requirements. The same day a mailbox was rented near the Hostel. His passport was sufficient for identification.

His life changed when he had access to the Library. Now he could borrow books and read them where he liked. Within a week he had posted two ads to Edinburgh Free Ads on the Internet under two categories.

Free Walking Tours

Let an experienced guide show you around the City of Edinburgh. Tours conducted in English or Spanish. Pay by donation.

Contact Rafa Torres

rafa@scottsmail.org
55 – 166 Rose St.
EH2 4AT

Free Spanish Tutoring

Experienced tutor offering services in conversational and written Spanish. Pay by donation.

Contact Rafa Torres

rafa@scottsmail.org
55 – 166 Rose St.
EH2 4AT

It was Friday. It had been a successful week. He wanted to tell someone about it. There was only Sister Angela who would understand. He sent her an email asking if it would fit for him to say Mass at the convent on Sunday at 7 am. He also sent her links to his two ads. Her reply came Saturday.

"I spoke to Mother Superior about Sunday. She said there will be no problem. She also said to tell you not to eat breakfast at the Hostel, instead, come and sit at her table and tell her what you've been up to."

"I also had a look at your ads. You get an A for effort, but I'm afraid I must fail you on overall impression. Rafa, you can't work for nothing. You'll go broke. Nobody pays by donation in Edinburgh."

Near the end of January, he received the first reply to his Tutor Post. They were wanting someone to help their high school son with his Spanish homework. The tutoring would take place once a week in the family's kitchen. The woman said she didn't understand Pay by Donation. She would pay him £5 an hour for two hours of tutoring.

On Valentine's Day, he took English honeymooners, around the town for two and a half hours. The gent gave him £10 and she added a £5 tip.

The money inspired him with confidence and he wanted to share his enthusiasm with Sister Stuart. Through email, they arranged to meet at their Monday Tea Room, on Saturday afternoon.

"I don't know about this tutoring Father," the Nun squeaked after he explained about his student. "Seems more like cheating to me. I certainly wouldn't want an adult doing my students' homework and have the child turn it into me as theirs."

"It's not like that at all, Sister. I'm making sure the boy knows what he's doing. It takes a lot of prompting, but it's really him who is doing his exercises in the end."

"Anyway Father, I think I like your Tours business better, but you can't expect tourists to go hunting for you on the Internet. You need a card, something like a business card. You could leave it at all the hotels, hostels and B&B's," she suggested. "However, I wouldn't say Free Tours and then say Pay by Donation. Somehow it seems fraudulent to me."

"I've been thinking of doing something like a card," the Priest informed her. "What's holding me back is I have no phone for people to contact me."

"You don't need a phone. Simply say on your card your tours start from a certain spot every day at 9 am. You're out and about by then anyway, so go to your designated spot and hold up a little sign saying something like, "Father Rafa Tours".

"Excellent idea Sister, I'll look into it. Do you have any suggestions about where the Meet-Up place should be?"

"Tourists like the Old Town. Somewhere along High St. would be good. How about Parliament Square? The equestrian statue would be a good starting place."

"You've just paid your donation for a tour. Come any Saturday you like. I'll be leaving the statue in Parliament Square at 9 am." They both laughed together and she poured them another cup of tea.

"So it seems you will be staying in Edinburgh a little while longer Father?"

"I am, I can't simply abandon you here, and especially not when you are having visions."

"Let me assure you, Father, I'm not lost. The Nuns I live with wouldn't tolerate it. If anyone in the house seems too quiet, the others go and pick at them."
"I'm not exactly sure why I don't want to leave this city, but I suspect it has something to do with knowing you," the Priest confessed and added, "You're the closest thing I have to family."

"But I'm a Nun," she interjected.

"I'm not saying anything Sister, but some days I wonder if I still have my vocation as intact as it was when I left Amalfi."

"Perhaps we shouldn't see each other anymore," she suggested.

"Oh no, quite to the contrary Sister. May I ask you something?"

"It all depends on what you're asking," she fluttered.

"What would you think of me if I asked to be released from my vows?

"I don't know what I'd think, but why would you want to be released."

"Then we wouldn't be a Priest and a Nun."

"But I'd still be a Nun, even if you are released from your vows."

"Is this discussion distressing you, Sister?"

"I'm not distressed."

"Okay then, you asked me why I would want to be released from my vows."

"Yes, that was it."

"It's because we may have a vocation for each other."

"I'm glad we're having this conversation, Father," the Nun interjected. "I think we've been needing to have it since you arrived in Edinburgh. I know you haven't had such a vocation before, but I've been through this vocation thing with a man. It ended in sadness until I found I had a vocation with Our Lord."

"Something happened between us in Boston, but I'm not sure just what. In all honesty, I should tell you, at this moment I'm not having second thoughts about my vocation as a nun. It might be different if you were released from your vows, but I can't promise anything. I'd have to wait until you were free before I could even start to think about such a thing for myself."

"I wouldn't have it any other way, Sister!"

"Would you like to walk with me towards the convent Father Torres?"

"I'd be delighted to accompany you."

A week later Rafa received an email from Sister Angela.

"I spent part of Sunday after our last meeting reading the Edinburgh Evening News. As you are already aware, I read every last word in a newspaper. I came across an advertisement which might be of interest to you. It took me a week to decide whether or not I'd tell you about it. Then I decided, if you're going to stay in Edinburgh, you'll need a proper situation.

In the Saturday edition, down at the bottom of the Education page, there's a small ad from the Iona Co-Ed High School. It's a private institution. They're looking for a Spanish teacher for the fall term.

It's quite a complicated procedure. They prepare a short list of all applicants and then have interviews. Your university or seminary marks would need to be transferred to them."

Rafa logged out of his email and walked towards the Periodicals section of the Library.

On the last day of May, the Priest found one envelope in his rented mail box. It was from Iona Co-Ed High School. It contained a letter from the Selection Committee.

Dear Father Rafael Torres,

Thank you for your application to the Grade 9 and 10 Spanish Teacher position starting in September. There were many highly qualified candidates. It was not an easy task; however, we have short listed three people. Please contact us before June 15th to arrange for an interview.

Best Regards,
Helen McDougal, Secretary
Iona Selection Committee

***

Chapter 11

Epilogue

The American Handicap Society's Board of Directors held its first monthly meeting of the New Year on the second Wednesday of January. There were many items on the agenda and they had a full quorum. The meeting began with a call for acceptance of the Agenda. The Secretary intervened to add an item to New Business. Once the Agenda and the Minutes of the previous meeting had been approved they were ready to receive the various Reports that were standard items at every sitting. The Chairman gave his report and was followed by the Vice – Chair, Secretary, and Treasurer. They were followed by several committees – Operations, Strategy, Legal, Community and Fund Development. It was already 8:20 pm when they reached New Business.

"Mr. Chairman and fellow Board members," the Secretary began. "Most of you received two letters during the month of December. At the Chairman's request, I asked that these letters be included in New Business at the beginning of the meeting. Everyone is aware of their content; however, I motion they should be read into the Minutes of this meeting so that proper protocols and procedures are followed. First I will read the letter from the Society's Executive Director Brian Robertson dated December 6th. Mr. Robertson is present this evening and has reported for the Operations Committee. The second letter is from the Society's Director of Fund Development, Ms. Sharon Norris dated December 7th. Ms. Norris is also present and has reported on behalf of Fund Development."

"Mr. Secretary, I approve your motion to read the letters into the Minutes. Could we have a show of hands?" The Chairman declared. All hands were raised except Sharon and Brian. "Motion is carried. Please proceed with the reading!"

"Dear Chairman and Directors of the American Handicap Society,

It distresses me to be writing to you about this issue as we approach the holiday season; however, I would be remiss in my duty as Executive Director of the Society if I let this go unnoticed. Today I would like to convey a few thoughts I have concerning the state of our Fund Development.

We are almost at year end and again the Society has not met its fundraising targets. Granted, we are in difficult economic times but other not-for-profits such as the Whole Earth Society, the Homeless Children Institute, and Culture for Ex-Convicts, to name but a few, have met and surpassed their funding targets. I think the problem might lie with the leadership we have in this area.

As you will recall, earlier in the year I was approached by our Director of Fund Development, Ms. Sharon Norris concerning the possibility of the Society acquiring a relic. Whether it possessed paranormal powers or not, it would have been a key talking point for us in every area. I presented the issue to the Board and authorization to seek an Injunction on behalf of the Society was approved.

We all came to know of this potential opportunity for our organization because Ms. Norris learned about a relic in this city on the dozen or so blogs and chat rooms she was following on the Internet. Supposedly a Mr. Carney O'Sullivan had been miraculously cured of paralysis caused by a spinal cord injury while he was a patient at the Boston Medical Center. Mr. O'Sullivan was cited in our Injunction.

This week the Boston Globe published the results of a Police investigation of a new incident that occurred at BMC around Thanksgiving. This time a Priest walked into the same hospital, allegedly to give Last Rites to a woman who had been dead for at least two hours. The following morning she was gone and a missing person report was filed. During the investigation, Police found video footage of her leaving the hospital unassisted around 3 am. Both the Priest and this woman have now left the country.

When I questioned Ms. Norris to see if the Priest had been mentioned in any of the Internet sites she was following I learned that she wasn't even following them. I'm sure you will agree more is required than wishing on a rabbit's foot and hoping for an Injunction to do your job for you. She should have been on those sites every day. Had we known about this Priest the Injunction could have been expanded to include him.

This issue is an excellent window into our Fundraising effort and what is problematic with the department. In my opinion, the department needs a new head with fresh ideas and better analytical skills. Ms. Sharon Norris is a very personable individual and I'm sure she would do much better in a smaller organization than The American Handicap Society.

Best Regards,
Brian Robertson

"Thank you Mr. Secretary," the Chairman said. "Would you now please read Ms. Sharon Norris's letter."

"Dear Chairman and Members of the Board,

Yesterday I learned that the investigation of the second miracle in our city had wrapped up and the media published a report the authorities had released. This miracle was very similar to the one occurring around the 4th of July of this year which prompted the Board to have an Injunction issued to gain possession of a relic that we called the Boston Relic.

At the time, the Board authorized Mr. Brian Robertson to do whatever necessary to protect the Boston Relic for the Society and appointed me his Special Assistant. Apart from having the Society's lawyers seek an injunction, management of this project by Mr. Robertson was nonexistent. He didn't even ask me to continue to monitor the Internet Blogs and Chat Rooms.

This is one tiny example of what is happening at the head of this organization. I've been with it several years now and have never seen Mr. Robertson come up with standard management tools like a Strategic Plan or a Tactical Plan. These are part of the curriculum in any management program. The reason for this is that Mr. Robertson has

*never been to University. The management degree mentioned in his CV
is nothing but a piece of paper he bought off the Internet. If he had better
training he wouldn't be trying to open new territories when there is a
possibility we may be obliged to close some of our existing branches.*

Sincerely,
Sharon Norris

"Thank you Mr. Secretary," the Chairman said. "Brian and Sharon, we
are going to have an in-camera discussion of your two letters, so I ask
that you both leave the Boardroom.

Once the door had closed behind them Robertson exploded, "How could
you have done a thing like that to me?"

She half screamed in reply, "I don't have anything to say to you!" and
walked to the end of the hall where there was a lone chair.

Inside the Boardroom, all Directors were having their say. Some said
they must be having a lover's spat. One Director suggested that they kiss
and makeup. There was a lot of jovial laughing and joke making until
the Chairman called them to order.

"Gentlemen, I took the liberty of having our lawyers check out the
Executive Directors academic credentials," the Chairman informed
them. "He only has a high school diploma. The university that issued him
a degree in management was charged in Federal Court several years ago
with fraud after someone was caught practicing medicine with a degree
bought from them online."

"The man has cheated us," Director Dr. Louie Tang declared." Look at
the money we've paid him. We should sue to get it back."

Director Goldberg was next. "I can't believe that we went along with
Sharon's scheme and that I proposed her to be Brian's Special Assistant
in the plot."

"Do you know how many jokes I've had to put up with since it went
public that we had an Injunction issued to keep a relic from being
transported outside the State of Massachutes?" Bob Singh blurted out.

"I know, it's crazy," Charles Heda roared. "My son keeps asking me if
anyone has turned in the magic wand yet."

Then Goldberg was back. "It's crazy. We must distance the Society from that woman. She'll take us all down."

Oscar Ogland let the palm of his right hand fall flat on the table top. "How are we going to get our money back from that Robertson?"

The Chairman called for order. "Directors listen, our legal counsel has advised against charging Brian with fraud. It would reflect poorly on the Society and make it more difficult to find donors. He said the ED's contract contains a clause which allows us to terminate him immediately should any information in his application prove to be falsified. We don't even have to pay severance."

"That settles it," two Directors said at once. "He goes!"

"Now what about the woman?" Roman Lafrance asked. "We can't just fire her like him. She will sue us. We need a just cause."

"We have a just cause," Goldberg insisted. "The Director of Fund Development has not met her targets in two years. We're entitled to run this organization and we'll give her three months' severance in lieu of a Notice."

The table became quiet. "Are we ready for a vote," the Chairman asked? All heads nodded.

"How say you on the immediate dismissal of Brian Robertson without severance?" All hands raised.

"How say you on the immediate dismissal of Sharon Norris with three months' severance?" All hands raised.

They were both called back into the Boardroom and informed of the decision.

Then the Chairman terminated the issue. "I have called the Security Guard to come up from the Front desk. He will escort you out of the building. You will be notified to come to pick up your personal belongings."

When they had gone he addressed the Directors. "I had a feeling things might go this way tonight. Before our meeting, I took the liberty to have IT freeze their login and passwords."

"A round of applause went around the table and the Directors began to stand.

**

Edwardo Romares had been taken into custody by the FBI in mid-December in the parking lot outside Automatic Bank Corp. He was carrying a briefcase which contained 2,000 counterfeit US \$20 bills. Later testimony revealed he purchased these for ten dollars each and would have distributed them during the following week. No supply of bogus bills was found in the building. Agents did find about four hundred counterfeit \$20 bills in the loaded cartridges that had been prepared for refilling ATM's the following day. None of the firm's employees were knowledgeable of their boss's sideline.

The preliminary arraignment had taken place in mid-January. Philadelphia's District Attorney's Office sought convictions on three charges: buying counterfeit US currency, distributing counterfeit US currency and attempted murder. The defendant's lawyer endeavored to have the attempted murder charge squashed but the DA's Assistant declared they were prepared to support the charge.

Edwardo's was not considered a flight risk. His bail was set at \$500,000. The matter was referred to Philadelphia's US District Court for fixing of a trial date. Several of the provisions in the federal counterfeiting law provides for a fine of up to \$250,000 and a prison sentence of up to twenty years for the counterfeiting of U.S. currency. Offenders typically spend between five and ten years in prison for attempted murder.

The trial before US District Court Judge Joseph Cohn was set to begin on June 1st. Romares lawyer Wilson Swayze met with his client during the week preceding the hearing. "I want to discuss our strategy in court."

"Great!" the Columbian exclaimed. "I'm all ears for any strategy that will help me get out of this."

"I expect the State to commence with the counterfeiting charges," Swayze explained. "I think the attempted murder charge was something the DA tacked on to impress the Judiciary unless you tell me different."

"Oh yeah, it was tacked on," Romares boomed. "I never attempted to murder anyone."

"What about somebody named O'Sullivan in Boston?

"There was no murder in it. O'Sullivan was dragging his heels. He was holding up my plans in that territory. I asked a couple of the boys to give him a nudge."

"Exactly what I thought" Swayze declared. "So I spent last week preparing a defense against the bogus money charges and have come up with two lines of argument."

"Tell me about them!"

"First I intended to allege it was all part of a joke that would not result in defrauding anyone and was to be a onetime affair. The proof is the small amount of counterfeit you had in your possession at the time of arrest.

"Yeah, I like that," his client beamed. "Now tell me the other one."

"My second line of defense is that you are innocent of counterfeiting because the currency in your possession was such a poor imitation that it would likely not fool an ordinary person into believing it was authentic. The law does not require bogus bills to be so similar to authentic bills that only an expert can tell the difference. I have recruited three people who will sit in the courtroom gallery. They will be our ordinary people, incognito. If the judge allows me to call one of them, they have agreed to testify under oath that they can tell at a glance the money is bogus."

"Sounds like a plan Councilor."

When the trial began, the defense was caught off guard. The District Attorney called the two Columbians, Juan Carlos, and Andres Felipe. They wore prison garb and handcuffs. One after another the DA called them to the stand and asked,

"Do you see the man who paid you to kill Arthur O'Sullivan in the Courtroom?"

Both times Swayze objected. He claimed the witnesses were being led. The Judge upheld the objection. On cross-examination, Wilson called Juan Carlos,

"Without identifying anyone, would you tell the Court what someone said to you in Atlantic City in relation to Mr. Arthur O'Sullivan?"

"We were two together, me and Andres. The stranger paid us five thousand dollars each to convince Arthur O'Sullivan that he had to move his machines. He gave us his summertime address and his address in Boston. He also told us he drove a Jaguar and gave us the plate number."

Swayze came back on the testimony, "What type of machines did he want to be moved?"

"We don't know," the Columbian confessed. "He just said machines."

The DA brought in the composite sketches prepared at the time of the arrest of the two Columbians. There was a close resemblance between these and Romares.

The State didn't have much more luck with the counterfeit. The Judge allowed Swayze to pick someone at random from the gallery and let them examine a bill that had been found on Romares. The man identified what he believed were two defects in the piece of currency.

"Your honor, if I was to receive this bill in my change and put it in my pocket I probably wouldn't notice it was bogus; however, later on, if I was to count my money to see how much I had on me, I'd spot this one right off the bat."

Counsel for the defense asked the Judge if he would like him to choose another ordinary citizen from the gallery. The Justice said it wouldn't be necessary. At the end of the third day, he asked both the DA and the Defense to present any other summary arguments they might have. When this was done he informed the Court that he would deliver his judgment at 10 am Friday morning.

On judgment day all rose as Judge Joseph Cohn entered and then sat down. The previous day he had read through his notes twice and prepared bullet points. He looked up minimum requirements for both charges and fit his bullet points to them. Last evening he had taken a walk around the block to think about where he was at in his decision making. This morning he was ready. Both the District Attorney and Counsel for the Defense were standing. He began to speak,

"Attempted murder and counterfeiting of American currency are serious offenses. As such, both the law and the jurisprudence has built up a body of guidelines to deal with them. The State's role as Prosecutor is to try to prove as many of these recommendations as possible. On the other hand, the Defense must concentrate on proving that these guidelines don't exist by raising a reasonable doubt in my mind."

"I have examined all the arguments put forward by each side as well as the case law I was requested to consider. I don't believe the District Attorney has fully discharged his duty. The Police portraits were enough to convince me that there was a connection between the two inmates and the accused; however, at no time was I convinced that murder was to be the end result. Instead of raising a doubt about this connection, the Defense tried to switch the argument to the target's son."

"On the counterfeit indictment once again the District Attorney failed to establish a solid link between the accused and a credible source for the bogus bills and how long the accused has been involved with counterfeiting. The Defense tried to insult my intelligence by suggesting it was a joke when Police testimony revealed counterfeit bills of the same quality were found in pre-loaded cartridges that were to be used the following day. In addition, that little charade with the ordinary citizen from the gallery, who by the way is not present here in Court this morning, didn't fool me for a minute."

"Gentlemen, the law, and the practice give the presiding Judge the option to completely reject the charges or to reduce them to something more in line with what has been proved. I, therefore, declare that I find Mr. Edwardo Romares guilty of conspiracy to assault and with the possession of counterfeit US currency and conspiracy to distribute the same. On both charges, I sentence the defendant to eighteen months in jail and a fine of $100,000. The accused will now be taken into custody and transferred to the nearest federal penitentiary having the capacity to receive him."

**

Ella, Carney, and Dakota skied together eight times during the winter. In all, there were four Sundays, three Saturdays and one Saturday and Sunday overnight. At Easter Mrs. O'Sullivan told her son to bring Ella to their compound at Nantasket Beach. Ella hesitated at first, but then accepted when her father announced he was meeting old friends in New York that weekend. Dakota made sure she met with all the aunts and girl cousins.

On June 15th at 10 am Ella's cell phone vibrated on her drawing board and she answered, "Hello, Ella speaking!"

"Hi, it's Carney. Is this a good time for you?"

"I've done two hours straight. I can take a break. What's up?"

"Do you remember me telling you just before Christmas we were starting a 50-foot sloop?"

"Yes, I remember that. What's happened?

"We ended up with more time available than I'd scheduled for it because of a canceled order. As a result, we lowered it into the water about half an hour ago."

"That's great, but you didn't phone just to tell me that, did you?" She giggled.

"No, I have a proposition for you."

"Oh, he has a proposition for me. What do I wear, heels or sandals?"

"How about deck shoes?"

"I have a pair of canvas platforms."

"Well the canvas part would be okay, but you should skip the platform and go for something flat, like a runner."

"What sort of proposition are we talking about?"

"I'm planning to take the new sloop out for a shakedown cruise over the Fourth of July long weekend and I was going to invite you to be my deckhand."

"I was planning to go to Martha's that weekend."

"I know, I thought we could sail to Martha's and back. You know, kill two birds with one stone."

"I don't know Carney, I've never been out very far in a small boat before. Would we be able to see land all the time?"

"Absolutely, I thought we'd hug the coast and go through the Cape Cod Canal."

"The ocean and the wind can't be predicted. From June until mid-September, the prevailing winds in Massachusetts Bay are from the southwest. If the winds are from the southwest, it would take about twelve hours to get there because we'd be sailing into the wind. It would be a lot faster on the way back as the wind would be behind us."

"So if we left Monday morning from Martha's we'd probably be back in Boston by supper time," the voice on the other end of the line prompted.

"Probably, but there are a few things I'd have to figure out."

"A few things like what?"

"Well, there are the tides."

"What about the tides?"

"We wouldn't want to fight the current in the Cape Canal, and we also don't want to hit it going full force the other way or we'll have a hell of a time steering. Also, there's Woods Hole. We should start going through during slack tide or just as the ebb begins."

"Now it's starting to sound scary!" She squeaked.

"As long as the travel time is well planned, you won't even be aware of what I just mentioned."

"Carney, I'm a visual person. I understand things better when I can see them. You put everything together on paper with times, route and comments then we'll meet up and discuss it. I'll give you my answer after I've digested everything. Will Dakota be coming?" She added.

"No, we'll be alone. She's going to Nantasket for the weekend. But just to put your mind at ease, it will be the same as the last time we were there."

"How was it the last time we were there?"

"I'll take the guest room."

"Call me when you have everything on paper. I must get back to work."

The sail south went smoothly, on the first day of the long weekend. They were tacking against the wind; however, Ella pulled her weight and at no time did Carney feel stressed. Like most kids in New England, she had taken sailing lessons in a dinghy during her teens. All he had to do was motion for her to understand. Several times she took the wheel while he trimmed the sails. They sailed down the Canal on a perfect tide and then picked up speed out in Buzzards Bay. The craft arrived on the west side of Woods Hole around twelve thirty in the afternoon.

Woods Hole is located at the southwest tip of the town of Falmouth. The term "Woods Hole" refers to a passage for ships between Vineyard Sound and Buzzards Bay known for its extremely strong current, approaching four knots. The strait separates Cape Cod from the Elizabeth Islands. It is one of four straits allowing maritime passage between Buzzards Bay and the Vineyard Sound.

By the time they came through the Hole it was after 1 pm. Ella had memorized the sailing plan Carney had given her. She turned to him and spoke, "Now all we have to do is get over to Edgartown."

"That was a lot easier than I thought it would be," he replied. "This boat is a beauty. I'd almost like to keep it for myself."

"Are you hungry?"

"I wouldn't mind a coffee and a couple of those cookies if there are any more left."

"Aye, aye Captain!"

In less than an hour they could see Edgartown Golf Club and then the lighthouse appeared. One more, narrow gap between Martha's Vineyard and Chappaquiddick Islands remained for them to navigate. There were a lot of boats in the passage that afternoon. Ella took the wheel while he brought down the mainsail. They ran under jib coming down the Middle Ground and into Katama Bay.

At last, she cried out with joy, "There, there it is. See the cube house!"

He saluted her and replied, "Well done sailor. There are polyfoam fenders in the cabin under the kitchen seat. Would you please bring them on deck and drop them over the port side once they are tied to the stanchions. I don't want to get any scratches on the hull coming up against your dock."

"Maybe it would be better to anchor and take the rowboat in," she suggested.

"There's a lot of money tied up in this sloop. I'd feel better having it tied up to something secure when we go ashore."

When she came back on deck he said, "Would you take the wheel, please. I'm going to cut the jib." When the last sail was down, he handed her a long pole with a hook on the end. "I'm going to bring us in ever so softly. I need you to handle this pole and hook onto the dock as soon as you are able.

When the sloop was secured they picked up their bags and began to walk the well-made path towards the house.

"Do you feel that?" She asked.

"I know, it feels like the earth is moving under our feet, but it will pass in a few minutes.

On Sunday evening Ella and Carney were doing the dishes together after supper. She was washing and he was drying.

"Do you remember what we joked about when you were here before?" Ella asked, with a quiver in her voice.

"Sort of," he replied. "I think I said I'd find out when the next premarital course was scheduled to take place."

"Did you?" she asked putting the second glass on the draining board.

He sputtered and mumbled, "Not yet!"

"Well I'd still like you to look into it," she said seriously.

"Ella Bowdine!"

"You called," she replied with a bewitching look in her eyes

"Are you proposing to me?"

"You still have to buy me a ring," she smirked

"Oh I'll get you a ring, but after the course. You don't know what you're getting into yet. Your dad told me that if a Catholic becomes a Freemason, they get excommunicated by the Catholic Church."

"I know all that Carney. I spent four years at a Catholic girl's school. Besides I put Freemasonry on the back burner during my first marriage, I think I can do it again," she added setting a plate in the drying rack.

"I'll call Our Lady of Lourdes in Jamaica Plain this week and register us both. That's where Dakota and I attend services."

She flung her arms around his neck and confessed, "I'm so glad to have that out in the open."

"Me too," he laughed and added, "This calls for a toast!"

"I don't have anything to drink here."

"Not to worry, there's a bottle of Champagne on the boat that will be used for her christening. It won't take me more than 5 minutes to run over and pick it up."

"My bike is attached to a post under the house. I'll get you the key."

"Not before this," he exclaimed closing his lips over hers."

***